SHOUTIN' INTO THE FOG

GROWING UP ON MAINE'S RAGGED EDGE

Shoutin' Into the Fog

Growing up on Maine's Ragged Edge

By Thomas Hanna

ISLANDPORT PRESS

ISLANDPORT PRESS • FRENCHBORO • NEW GLOUCESTER

Islandport Press
P.O. Box 10
Yarmouth, Maine 04096

Auburn Hall, Suite 203
60 Pineland Drive
New Gloucester, Maine 04260

www.islandportpress.com

ISBN: 0-9763231-8-4
Library of Congress Control Number: 2006927147

First Islandport Press Edition Published August 2006

Book design by Michelle A. Lunt/Islandport Press
Book cover design by Karen Hoots/Mad Hooter Design
Front cover photographs courtesy of Cora M. Owen and
Thomas L. Hanna

Also from Islandport Press

Windswept
by Mary Ellen Chase

Stealing History
by William Andrews

down the road a piece: A Storyteller's Guide to Maine
by John McDonald

A Moose and a Lobster Walk into a Bar
by John McDonald

Mary Peters
by Mary Ellen Chase

Silas Crockett
by Mary Ellen Chase

Nine Mile Bridge
by Helen Hamlin

Titus Tidewater
by Suzy Verrier

When I'm With You
by Elizabeth Elder and Leslie Mansmann

In Maine
by John N. Cole

The Cows Are Out! Two Decades on a Maine Dairy Farm
by Trudy Chambers Price

These and other Maine books are available at:
www.islandportpress.com.

DEDICATION

This book is dedicated with deep affection to the other seven little Hannas, siblings all, and especially to the memory of brother Clayton and my eighty-pound Mama.

Though we are of differing opinions, we are family.

ACKNOWLEDGMENTS

I am a man among women—and a man or two—and I am truly in debt to each and every one. Without their collective support, *Shoutin' Into the Fog* might never have become reality. There are so many to acknowledge individually, but—man or woman—if you've ever read my work and responded positively, or sat with me in a writing group and listened while I read: Thanks!

To Anne Perry, who suggested I read Frank McCourt's *Angela's Ashes*. That book, along with Russell Baker's *Growing Up* and Rick Bragg's *All Over But the Shoutin'*, guided my early writings. Anne read my early chapters and offered encouragement when I needed it most.

To Billie Todd, who graciously published some of my early stories in the *The Georgetown Tide*.

To Jane Lamb's River Road Writers Group. Jane and Robin Hansen helped me to stay with my voice when I was about to lose it. Joyce Pye pointed me to Dean Lunt and Amy Canfield at Islandport Press. They allowed that with editorial help, *Shoutin'* would become a published Maine memoir. And Amy has made it so.

And my appreciation to members of my current writing group, Janis Bolster, Cat McConnell and Meadow Rue Merrill. Some of you were the first to read the almost completed *Shoutin'*.

To my sister, Cora, who provided photographs and helped fill in some of the blanks in my memory of our family's history.

Once again, you all have shown that women are special.

Also, thanks to Eugene Reynolds for the use of his photographs, and to my son, Lyndon, for his computer expertise.

AUTHOR'S NOTE

T hough I have a keen memory and can vividly recall many childhood events, I couldn't have written *Shoutin'* without assistance
from friends, relatives and assorted documents.

First, there were numerous conversations with my sister Cora.
Together, we arrived at dates, times and places—and sometimes
details—for specific events. Next, there was brother Irving, alter-
nately my playmate and antagonist. He substantiated much of what
I've written about our early days together. I've re-created some of
the dialogue, but the gist of every single conversation is factual.

Lloyd Pinkham, my old Sunday School teacher, who was just
my mother's age, clarified the early history of the bungalow. While I
was writing the book, I sat with him in his living room many times
and talked of the old days. I miss those chats.

In 1982, Martha Oakes, a Colby College student, came to
Georgetown and conducted a study—*Preserving an Inheritance*—about
the one-time Hiram "Hite" Rowe holdings at Five Islands. Her work
contains a wealth of Rowe family history that is also Five Islands history. At other times, I visited the Patten Library or surfed the
Internet to check the accuracy of my memories.

The end results were packed into *Shoutin'*.

Thomas Hanna
Bath, Maine
June 2006

TABLE OF CONTENTS

PROLOGUE

When we were teenagers in the 1940s, my second cousin Johnny MacGillivary and I used to row across Sheepscot Bay from Five Islands to Cozy Harbor in Southport because the girls on the east side of the bay seemed prettier and friendlier. Usually, crossing the mile of open water hardly raised a sweat.

After one sociable evening with some east shore girls, we made our way back to our rowboat only to find that a dense summer fog had settled over Cozy Harbor all the way up to the landing. Heavy mist swirled around the floodlights and sifted down onto our heads. From down the bay we heard the moan of foghorns—the deep-throated groan at Seguin Island Light on the Five Islands side and the more sorrowful wail at Cuckolds Light on the Southport side.

Our parents expected us home by ten, and so we had just twenty minutes to make curfew. Johnny rowed and I listened for the sound of the foghorns as we set out on the longest one-mile row of our young lives.

Once we cleared the harbor and headed across the open bay, the fog-shrouded darkness closed in and blanketed our boat. One time I heard Seguin to our left, the next dead ahead and then to our right. I thought, but dared not say it out loud, "We are lost on Sheepscot Bay!"

Johnny began to yell repeatedly, "Hello, Five Islands!"
Silence.
Then, I chipped in, "Hello, Southport!"
More silence.

Finally, together, "Hello, anybody!"

In that impenetrable darkness, there answered only the sound of the foghorns, surf striking an invisible shore and the *thump-thump* of oars against oarlocks.

Johnny pulled in the oars and rested his tired arms. He wanted to sit there until the fog lifted a little. I'd have none of that. I took over and rowed toward the surf sound.

After what seemed like hours of frantic course changes and pauses to listen for Seguin and to chorus "Five Islands, where are you?"—without an answer—a dark shadow rose out of the fog. We had made the northern tip of the largest of the five islands at the harbor entrance. From there, we eased past ghostly lobster boats to Five Islands landing.

As we secured the boat, I was still chilled by the thought of our isolation out there on the bay. It's a dreadful feeling when you're shouting into the fog, and no one hears. Or, maybe they hear, but they don't answer. Fishermen will tell you that kind of thinking can grab ahold of you, if you let it. But that's when you just have to dip in your oars and make it on your own.

My life in Five Islands was a struggle, oftentimes unaided (or at least, I thought so), through a suffocating fog of privation. The stilted bungalow on Schoolhouse Road where I was raised, centerpiece for this hardscrabble tale, still sits among the alders and mosquitoes. A recent visit to its mostly empty rooms stirred memories that I'd kept locked away for decades. I turned the doorknob and let the remembrances come tumbling out.

Thomas Hanna
Bath, Maine
June 2006

INTRODUCTION

Before we get started, let me tell you a bit about Georgetown, Maine—chiefly the village of Five Islands, my hometown.

Georgetown, located in Sagadahoc County, is an island just six road miles south of Bath, on Route 127, tucked in between Arrowsic Island and the Kennebec River to the west and Sheepscot Bay to the east. First settled by colonists in the 1600s, it was once called Parker Island after its owner. In the early days, only a few isolated plantations dotted the island. The eight-mile-long island, which resembles a long, thin lobster claw, is made up of four widely separated villages: Robinhood in the north, Bay Point in the south, Georgetown Center in the middle, and to the east, on the shore of Sheepscot Bay, Five Islands. When I was growing up it was a village of some two hundred souls, many of whom were related to me in one way or another. The population is about the same today. Most of the development that has occured on Georgetown since I was a boy in the 1920s has been on the north end of the island.

The villages of Robinhood and Five Islands began to prosper in the late eighteenth century, when a couple of fish dealers came up from Gloucester, Massachusetts. Benjamin Riggs headed to what is now Robinhood. Ebenezer Rowe, a Revolutionary War veteran and my triple-great-grandfather on my mother's side, went to Five Islands. They set about buying codfish from fishermen. Riggs had the larger operation with his own fleet of fishing boats, a store and a curing crew that kench-cured the cod (salted them and laid them on flakes to dry in the sun). The fish was shipped south by water. Soon Rowe began selling his fish to Riggs. It stayed that way until the

Courtesy of Thomas Hanna

The Thomas J. Hanna (my great-grandfather) homestead at the top of Chase's Hill in the 1800s.

1840s, when the Rowes started curing their own fish and shipping them to Portland, Boston, and other points south. The descendants of Ebenezer Rowe, especially his grandson Hiram G. "Hite" Rowe, would play a significant role in the development of Five Islands—owning both businesses and property. More on that in a moment.

Today, the cod is long gone. The fishermen who live on Five Islands today are lobstermen and shrimpers—a different breed (but that's another story). Five Islands remains a small place and is still home to the working class—as well as a significant number of summer cottages—although today's residents enjoy luxuries I never dreamed of while growing up. Everyone has a well and septic system, so there are no more outhouses. Homes are comfortably heated. Residents drive their late-model cars on well-paved roads. They're connected to the bigger world through television and computers. And that's just to name a few changes.

But back to the nineteenth century.

My father's folks, the Hannas, were honest, hardworking seagoing men, but they didn't leave their mark on the Five Islands landscape

the way the Rowes did. My great-grandfather Thomas Hanna came to
Five Islands in the 1850s with brothers Charles and Rufus. He shipped
out to sea as a Grand Banks fisherman. When Thomas's son, George,
my grampa, came of age, he followed in his father's hip boots. Later,
Grampa George Hanna would skipper his own coaster sloop, engaging
in trade up and down the coast, until he piled her up on the rocks off
Biddeford Pool in what he called "a squally, hubbly sea."

The Hanna family's seafaring tradition came to a halt with my
father, born in 1893. The fishing industry was in serious decline when
he came of age to work, and his undersized frame—he was barely
five feet tall—was not well equipped for handlining cod or wrestling
about weighted lobster traps anyway. Working for summer people and
door-to-door selling were more to his liking and kinder to his body, if

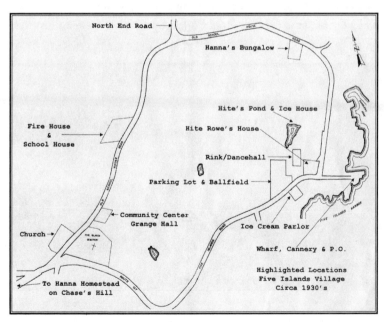

Illustration by Lyndon Hanna

A map showing significant Five Islands landmarks.

not his pocketbook. Except for an overseas tour of duty in World War I, my father never lived anywhere but Five Islands.

If you lived on Five Islands when I was growing up and you weren't a fisherman of some sort or employed by summer people, then you most likely worked at Bath Iron Works, the big shipbuilder.

Now, let me take you on a tour of my hometown.

You'll know we're almost to the village when we reach a fork in the road not far from the official end of Route 127—Schoolhouse Road to the left, Five Islands Road to the right. We'll hang right and climb the hill. At the top of the hill where Jody Stevens once farmed, we round the curve and head down Bowling Alley Hill, past a cluster of houses on either side (please note that some of the hedges you see were sold to the residents by my father in the 1930s). The candlepin alley that my father once managed in his bachelor days is now gone, as is the old Otter Cliff Lodge, which stood against that ledge to your left.

Courtesy of Gene Reynolds

A view of Five Islands harbor looking toward Malden Island (around 1930). The house at the center was once owned by Joseph Rowe. The ice cream parlor can be seen at lower right.

Courtesy of Gene Reynolds

The ice cream parlor at Five Islands. It was once owned by Hite Rowe. It served as a major hangout while I was growing up in Five Islands during the 1930s and early 1940s.

Here the road levels somewhat as we head toward the harbor—we're now in Rowe country. The family once owned a significant portion of the land and the houses in this area. And this is where Hiram "Hite" Rowe, my great-grandfather, made his mark. Hite's grandfather, Ebenezer, and Ebenezer's son, Joseph, were fish dealers and successful businessmen, but Hite was even more than that—he was an undeniable nineteenth-century entrepreneur.

The vacant lot to your right is where his ice cream parlor stood in the early years of the last century. A popular place in its time, it was razed when the town eventually acquired the property. Across the road, beyond the parking lot (which was once the village baseball field), lies Hite's Pond. The pond is still here, but the icehouse where he stowed a summer's supply of ice has long since been destroyed (it is now a tennis court), as has his roller skating rink, which was located next to the parking lot. The rink also served as a village dance hall. Among other things, it was where townspeople once held

The store and wharf complex that was the centerpiece of activity in Five Islands Village, is seen here as it looked in the 1950s. Malden Island is the island in the distance.

blackface minstrel shows. My father and my maternal grandfather performed in those shows before World War I.

To the right down at the water's edge is Hite's century-old wharf. It now features a fish market and snack bar, but still overlooks Five Islands harbor and juts out into Sheepscot Bay. The snack bar was once Hite's oilskin factory and one-time blueberry cannery. There used to be more: a ferry slip for the Boston steamers, which Hite helped bring to Georgetown; a general store, which opened in 1871 as H. G. Rowe & Co. and was called P. B. Savage's when I was a kid; and a post office. Right up until my time, fishermen would set up codfish flakes and dry their salt cod in the open area behind the post office.

If you look out across the water, you will see five small islands ringing the harbor. Those islands—Mink to the farthest south, then Hen, and next Malden and to the north, Big and Little Crow—gave the village its name. Of the five, only Hen and Malden are regularly inhabited, mostly in the summer. Big Crow has a house or two hidden in its trees.

As we continue along on land, the two-story gray house where Five Islands Road meets Schoolhouse Road is where Hite lived until he died in 1910. Of all the one-time Rowe holdings, it is the only one still in the Rowe family—my Aunt Helen, my mother's half sister, owns it. When Hite's father died in 1861, his properties were divvied up between his ten children. Hite bought up all the land from his nine siblings, but over the years his fortunes declined. When he died, what he had left went to my Grandpa Rowe and Grandpa's sister, Edith. When the fishing industry went bust and fishermen were unable to pay Grandpa what they owed him, he went bust, too. He was left only with his house. The Rowes were no longer Five Islands' leading family.

Back on Schoolhouse Road, about a quarter of a mile or so up from the wharf, over there on your left, perched on the ledge, is the old Hanna bungalow where I was raised. If it is spring, you will notice how swampy the ground is because of Hite's Pond. About a quarter-mile beyond that, North End Road forks to the right and runs past the Hanna house where my father was raised. A white, clapboarded, two-story frame house with a kitchen, dining room, parlor, and three bedrooms upstairs, it was a far cry from the bungalow where I grew up. The walls were papered with real wallpaper and the furniture, while not extravagant, was solid. Grandma Hanna had attached a sign to the front gable, WHISPERING PINES.

Continuing along Schoolhouse Road, you will see the village firehouse on your right. In my day, that building was the one-room village schoolhouse. I attended school there from kindergarten through eighth grade.

Just before we get back onto Route 127, we'll pass the recreation center on your left; in my day it was a Grange Hall and rental library. We held our eighth-grade graduation exercises there. Over here on the right, you'll see the Five Islands Baptist Church, the only one I know of that sports a lighthouse on a mural behind the pulpit. Across from the church is a local cemetery. Ebenezer Rowe, my grandfather Hanna, my father, and other relatives are buried there. And finally, here at the intersection of Schoolhouse Road and Route 127, we have finished the trip "around" the mile or so square.

And that is the village of Five Islands, a rocky and forested village on Sheepscot Bay, quite beautiful really, at any time of year.

And for most of my first twenty years it was the center—both good and bad—of my world.

1

THE BUNGALOW

If they ever hand out medals to survivors of the Great Depression, my brothers and sisters and I should move straight to the head of the line. Oh, there'd be others in line, complaining about their hard times, and certainly many, many people struggled along the coast in those days. But unless they'd lived a year at the Hanna bungalow, they hadn't really known poor. At least that is the way I saw it.

The Depression itself was miserable enough for the Hanna family; our bungalow only made it worse. By my recollection, it was the most ramshackle home on Georgetown Island—perhaps even the coast of Maine, for that matter.

Our little hip-roofed house was located on Schoolhouse Road about a quarter-mile or so from the wharf at Five Islands village. From its very beginnings, even before the Depression set in, it was an ass-backward kind of house. Take the doors. They'd been back-side-to ever since my father first set them in place. The door at the back of the house became our front door, because the door my father had planned to be the front door (located on the side) had a wicked first step—six feet straight down to solid ground. My mother blamed my father for that six-foot drop-off, but it was really Uncle Melvin Harford's fault.

In the dry part of the summer of 1924, Uncle Melvin sold my father a half-acre of prime swampland that he had staked out along Schoolhouse Road for the noble sum of fifteen dollars, close to the total amount of money my father had at the time. This wasn't your ordinary four-cornered lot; it had a kind of dogleg to it. Not a smart buy, Uncle Melvin said at the time, when you could have the whole rectangle for another five bucks. That section was too wet from water running down Bars Hill, my father had said. Uncle Melvin failed to mention the whole thing would get even wetter come spring.

The following soggy spring when my father came to clear away the alders, he was forced to give up a huge chunk of Uncle Melvin's "dry-in-the-summer" lot to the spring runoff from Hite's Pond. The brook—and the peepers and mosquitoes that came with it—forced him flat up against a high ledge at the back of the lot. He anchored one corner of the bungalow to the ledge and propped up the rest of the building on cedar posts, leaving him with the six-foot-high front step.

The bungalow was cold. Even with the underpinning banked in fir boughs, the chamber mugs sometimes froze over on winter nights. Come morning, you could see your breath at the breakfast table and frost stayed on the outer walls halfway to noontime. And it was no wonder. Our walls were so thin, a neighbor said, you could throw a tomcat through them and never harm a hair. He might've exaggerated, somewhat. It was more likely only a kitten.

"We live in an icehouse," my mother often complained. And she was right. The Boynton family, summer residents of Malden Island where my father was caretaker from 1922 to 1933, told him they wanted to tear down their icehouse on Ledgemere Road. My father took one look at all that weather-beaten lumber and saw in it enough board feet to frame up and close in a fine house. He made them an offer: He'd tear down the building and cart away the lumber if they'd

Courtesy of Cora M. Owen

Cora, me and Irving on the ledges outside of a neighbor's (Harold Rowe) house in the early 1930s.

give it to him. And that's where the Hanna bungalow that was an ice-house got its start.

With the lumber to build his dream bungalow piled onto the ledges above the swamp on his very own lot, my father took on the air of a man whose trawl net dragged on fertile bottom ground. Early on, however, he ran into his first big problem. Icehouses don't come with bungalow-type windows and doors. To drum up the needed cash for the extra materials, he reduced the size of his dream home from seven rooms to five and hung out a LUMBER FOR SALE sign on Schoolhouse Road. Icehouse lumber had little cash value in those days, though. Crosby's Lumber in Arrowsic agreed to let my father have windows and doors in exchange for a small mortgage on the completed bungalow, gambling that the whole thing would one day be worth the price of the materials that were in it.

A few summers after my father bought the lot, the underpinning and wall studs had been boarded over and wrapped all around in tar-paper, and the hip roof was well under way. Then he ran into more money troubles: nothing left over for shingles. This time he counted on some overdue divine assistance and finished his roofing-in, confident there'd soon be more than enough shingle money to go around.

His help came from a far different source. The very next day he stumbled onto a friendly craps game on the wharf behind the fish market. He loved to roll the dice, and he usually won. He wasn't a high-stakes roller, just a dollar here and a dollar there. My mother, a sporadically staunch Baptist, could never understand why any man would stake even a dollar of his hard-earned money on a roll of what she called "the Devil's Dominoes."

But he wasn't thinking of my mother when he sat in on the game—and he won handily. The big loser, a part-time lobsterman, put up his small motorboat and a few traps against all my father had won. My father covered his bet. The ex-lobsterman rolled snake eyes.

My father promptly sold his new boat and traps to another fisherman and walked away with a pocketful of shingle money. My mother complained about tainted money in her new home, but he turned a deaf ear and set about shingling. Tainted shingles would keep out the rain, quite handily, thank you. She did convince him that he ought to be careful about who he thanked for the tainted money. And he did promise he'd never again sit in on any game that rewarded a natural seven or an eleven. In later years, she used the lobster boat story as an object lesson to show us kids the error of the lobsterman's gambling ways.

It was 1929, and my father's high-and-dry bungalow was complete, except for the pathway out to Schoolhouse Road. Along that boggy way, he laid down a weewary plank that sometimes teetered into the wet if you didn't step on it just right. He used the leftover lumber scraps to build a two-seater outhouse and for a platform—no steps—beside the back door for my mother's mops, brooms and washtubs.

Then he looked at his handiwork and said it was good. Had he known then that his procreative abilities would exceed his expectations—his twenty-four-by-twenty-six-foot bungalow would eventually put up eight children and a tomcat—he might have made other plans, like a simple, two-gable peaked roof suitable for storing little ones in the overhead.

If my mother, Lula Mae Rowe, hadn't been so tiny, the bungalow may have never been built. Lula Mae, called Lulu, was four feet eleven in Cuban heels, a height that didn't escape the eye of Thomas Jefferson Hanna, an even five-footer in army boots just home from World War I.

Courtesy of Thomas Hanna

Lulu (Rowe) Hanna, my mother, as a child (around 1910).

Perhaps he thought if he had a woman who would look up to his thinning hairline instead of down at his bald spot, he'd seem like a bigger man. Then maybe the taller men would quit saying things to him like, "I could eat beans off the top of your head."

Or, maybe at twenty-eight he'd finally realized that women under five feet were in short supply this side of the Kennebec River. Whatever his reason, after he first glommed onto Lulu at a Saturday night dance in her grandfather's dance hall, he had eyes for no one else.

He had been drafted into the army two years earlier, when Lulu was a mere girl. But now she was a young lady of fifteen, a

Courtesy of Cora M. Owen

My family in the late 1920s. (Clockwise from top): My father, me, Cora, Irving and Ma.

My father, Thomas, at full attention in 1928.

My grandmother Lulu (Savage) Rowe. She died giving birth to my mother in 1906.

perky redhead who could dance. And perhaps most importantly, she was just his size. The first waltz became a whole evening of dances, followed by sundaes at the ice cream parlor just across the road, followed by more Saturday evening dances and more sundaes.

My father was the oldest of four children born into a Five Islands family with deep roots in the community. Daddy's sister Ruth lived nearby, his other sister Florence had died in 1918 during a flu epidemic, and his brother Clinton was mostly an itinerant barber. Their father, George, like his ancestors, made his living from the sea—first as a fisherman sailing to distant grounds such as the Grand Banks, and then as a skipper. The family didn't have much, but they did all right, for the most part.

Lulu also grew up in the village, no more than a mile from Thomas. Her family, the Rowes, also had strong ties in Five Islands, and for much of the nineteenth century were the leading family of the village. Lulu was the daughter of a store clerk, Lermond, and his wife, Lulu (Savage), who died giving birth to my mother. When my father started to court my mother, Lermond didn't take kindly to a man of twenty-eight cozying up to his barely teenage daughter. He forbade it, actually. But they continued to see each other on the sly, sometimes at the Grange, sometimes at the church, sometimes behind the church, and finally, on the sofa in Thomas's mother's parlor.

Here I am walking around Five Islands in about 1929 (at about three years old).

Just days after her eighteenth birthday on March 10, 1924, Lermond announced that Lulu and Thomas would be wed on March

Courtesy of Cora M. Owen

My mother, Lulu (Rowe) Hanna, in the 1930s.

23. Thomas' mother, Cora, surely would never have willingly turned her beloved eldest son over to another woman for any reason short of a matter of honor. She'd been leery of handing him over to John J. Pershing himself.

Nothing was said publicly about their rush to the altar. In Georgetown, there was an unwritten code for the unwed: A romp in the puckerbrush, or on a sofa, was just fine as long as the man did the right thing by the expectant one. Many islanders took full advantage of the code. Hasty marriages were so common that a self-appointed historian with time on his hands and a bent for math was said to keep a marriage calendar. On it he recorded every couple's wedding date in town and the birth date of their first child, along with a few notations of his own. When he penciled in December 1 for my sister Cora's birth, he must have marked it, "Too close to call."

The newlyweds, without a doorstep to call their own, moved into Lulu's Aunt Edith's (her father's sister) summer cottage and set about keeping house and raising a family, with my father dreaming all the while of his own bungalow somewhere down the line.

We stayed at Edith's cottage through Cora's birth in 1924, mine in 1926, and Irving's in 1928. My father was feeding us on his caretaker's salary. Malden Island was a summer enclave located just off the shores of Five Islands, but a world away. My father worked as the caretaker for all of the homes (around 12). He was busiest, of course, in the summer when he rowed the summer residents' steamer trucks, big blocks of ice and other supplies back and forth to the island and was called upon for repairs and other chores. During the off-season he maintained the residents' boats and checked on damage after each storm, but he also found the time to supplement his income with some part-time carpentry work.

I was three when we five Hannas finally moved into the bungalow in 1929. All five of us lived in one large room. Bright-orange sheathing paper covered the wall studs and ceiling joists. More paper partitioned off a corner of the bungalow where my father and mother slept. The children shared the open space with the kitchen and the living room.

Mary was born a year later in 1930. We still didn't have our front steps. We did have a screen door, nailed shut to keep little Mary from taking a six-foot headfirst tumble. On stifling summer evenings the front door was opened to let in the Sheepscot Bay breezes, but mostly we got outhouse fragrances. Irving and I loved to sit by the door on those evenings to listen to the peeper chorus, and watch the fat gray spiders climb down their webs under the eaves to wait for the swarms of mosquitoes that rose up from the swamp and whined around our door. The mosquitoes were quite adept at finding the pencil holes Irving had poked through the screen. We had the welts to prove it.

Our one-room home arrangement lasted until the day I noticed how Cora was built different from me. When I asked my father how come she had a couple of parts missing, he allowed it was about time the girls had a room of their own.

Right away he sat down at the kitchen table and went to work on the five-room floor plan he'd had to settle for. On the south side, there would be two thirteen-by-twelve rooms, the kitchen and the living room. Then he laid out three bedrooms on the north side facing Schoolhouse Road: a twelve-by-ten master bedroom and two twelve-by-eights. We children would get the small rooms; Irving and I in the middle and the two girls on the end.

The orange sheathing paper came down as he framed out the rooms. It hadn't been much use anyway, mainly because my father hadn't taken into account that children have sharp elbows suitable for poking holes.

Strips of one-inch board nailed together made the studding. The National Biscuit Company provided the wallboard. They shipped their cookies and crackers to P. B. Savage's General Store, where my Grandpa Rowe worked (and which, under a different name, was started by his ancestors and which he had once owned himself), in heavy, corrugated, brown cardboard cartons. Percy Savage was happy to part with the empties.

My father carted the cardboard home and our National Biscuit rooms took shape. He tacked the cardboard to the studs and sealed the seams with gummed paper. Somehow he came by an old door, painted white, for his bedroom. My mother hung heavy curtains made of cretonne in the doorways of our rooms. The door and the flowery drapes brightened the house, but the cardboard walls were drab, even to my young eyes. Not even the frayed divan or the faded carpet (castoffs from a Malden Island cottage), the picture of my mother's late mother on one wall, or my mother's rocking chair could add much to it. But it was just for the time being, my father promised—until he could afford something more solid.

The cardboard was still in place the day he died.

2

SCHOOL DAYS

I awoke one September morning in 1930 to find that Cora had escaped our cardboard cocoon. She had gone off to school, which must be a very special place, I thought. Why else would she be dressed as if she were going to Sunday School, wearing a frilly dress and a bow in her hair big enough to pass for a hat? I wanted to go, too. My mother said I was too young; next September would be my turn. I thought that was kind of unfair. After all, I was four and already could tie my own shoes.

When Cora brought home her first reader and I saw those colorful pictures and pages of meaningless words, I wanted even more to go to school so I could learn to read, too. I asked Cora to teach me, but she was always too busy. She did show me how to make some of the letters, though, and I'd listen while she singsonged her way through a page for my father:

Mother-sat-by-the-cradle.
Baby-was-in-the-cradle.
Mother-sang,
Bye-bye-baby-bye,
Shut-your-little-eye.

By the time she'd learned it, I'd already memorized a good half-dozen of the words on my own.

I took notice of spelling, as well. When my mother and her friend Vesta Rowe—Vesta's husband Orville was somehow related to my mother, but then most everyone in Five Islands was at least a distant relative of everyone else—got together for a gab session, Vesta always spelled words she didn't think young ears should hear. "It's hotter than H-E-double-L out there," or, "He's such a D-A-M-N fool." I just had to learn to spell so I'd know what she was trying so hard to keep from me.

Next year was a long way off and I had to find something to keep myself occupied until I could get to school. I checked around the bungalow and discovered a brother. He'd been there all along, but up to now he'd been a whiny baby in smelly diapers and hardly worth my time. Now, going on three and potty-trained, he was turning out to be a fine brother, just the right age to do anything I ordered.

I gathered up our leftover Christmas cars and trucks that still had all their wheels in place and, with Irving in tow, climbed the ledge behind the house. I'd spotted a sizable hollow in the ledge, filled to the top with a special kind of gray dirt. Not like your hard clay out front, it was perfect for building roads. I borrowed Cora's sand pail and shovel and set Irving to work digging the gray gravel for Hanna's Highway. By the time cold weather set in and construction was shut down for the winter, we had dug a good-sized pit and our highway was well on its way.

I'd planned to have Irving in my crew again in the spring, but he had spent the winter laid low by bronchitis. He'd always been a sickly child and would continue to be through his teen years. My mother babied him because of that. She wouldn't allow him to sit out on the cold ledges. He'd get a cold in his kidneys, she said. I wasn't sure if there were such a thing as bronchitis of the kidneys, but my mother must have thought so; she kept him on her disabled list until summer. Meantime, I looked around for more workers. Mary was too small, and Cora didn't want to get her hands dirty. Within five minutes she'd have been telling me what to do, anyway. I was ready to quit building for a while. After all, what's a boss worth if he doesn't have anyone to boss?

So, when my father asked me if I'd like to spend the morning with him on Malden Island while he opened the cottages, I dropped my highway construction altogether. Malden Island was special in the spring. It was the largest of the five islands that ringed the harbor. The dozen or so clustered cottages shared a common cookhouse where the summer residents came to eat, called by a clanging ship's bell beside the dining room door. I went to Malden with him two or three mornings a week until Memorial Day, when the summer people began to arrive and my father became too busy to keep an eye on me.

That's when my mother took over. It was time to do some serious planning for school. With two younger ones still at home, my mother wanted me in school with my big sister as much as I did. First she called on the town nurse to check me over to see if I was fit to start. Then she broke out the Sears Roebuck catalog and showed me what a spiffy first-grader would wear. "We'll get you a nice pair of knickers and some golf stockings." Knickers! Lord, how I hated the word. They should have been called bloomers. They were secured at the knees and bloomed out over argyle socks. On any active boy worth his keep, knickers would bag at the ankles before noontime. But it was either that or short pants; I didn't make a fuss.

I turned five on August 30, 1931, and started school just after Labor Day. Mrs. Lena McMahan, my teacher, had told my mother that for the first six weeks I'd be something called a sub-primary. If I didn't cry, fall asleep in class, or mess in my seat during that time, I could stay on as a first-grader. If I failed, I'd have to come home to my

Courtesy of Gene Reynolds

The old Five Islands schoolhouse that I attended from kindergarten through eighth grade. It is now the village firehouse. The boys entered through the door on the left; the girls through the door on the right. We played many baseball games right in front of this schoolhouse.

mother for another year. More than anything, I wanted to be a first-grader so I wouldn't be too far behind Cora, already in the second.

My first day, Cora walked me the half-mile to the schoolhouse. A square, one-story building, its gray clapboards draped with woodbine, it had two front doors and a belfry at the peak for the recess bell. I'd peeked through the school's windows once or twice before, but I'd never been invited inside, until today.

Cora and I parted company at the door—boys to the left, girls to the right.

Inside that single room, the air was heavy with the pungent odor of a freshly oiled floor. That linseed-oil smell on a shiny floor would be part of my first days of school for the next seven years.

Laid out before me in neat rows were thirty or so desks. Most of the older children had already claimed last year's seats. Eddie Carr, Russ Harford and I, sub-primaries all, stood around looking dumb. I spent my time checking out the room. On the far wall was a clock with letters on it instead of numbers, and a kerosene lamp. I hoped the teacher wouldn't often keep school until after dark.

Mrs. McMahan gave us young ones seats up front. When we were settled in, she held roll call to be sure everyone was accounted for, then she got out her Bible and read "The Lord is my shepherd . . ." I was afraid she might call on someone to pray and I didn't know a whole lot about prayer. I could have said a few lines of "Now-I-lay-me," but that wouldn't have gone over big at the start of a school day.

Next, she wound up her phonograph and put on a record. For our morning exercises, she said. I watched to see what the older kids did, then joined in. We must have been a sight standing there by our desks, twenty-five pairs of arms flailing the air while a tinny-voiced man sang:

IF A-BODY-MEET A-BODY-COMIN'—THROUGH THE-RY-EE
UP AND-OUT AND-OVER AND-DOWN AND-UP AND-DOWN-AGAIN.

Before classes began, Mrs. McMahan explained a few things for the benefit of the first-graders. The long settee up front next to her desk was the recitation seat. We'd sit there only when our class was reciting for the teacher. She explained about the outhouse at the back of the room: girl's door on the left, boy's door on the right. She also explained about raising your hand for permission to visit the outhouse—one finger or two. She didn't explain why it was she needed to know what kind of visit we had in mind. Either way, you couldn't very well go in your seat.

I didn't waste any time raising my hand for a one-finger visit, just to check out the place. It was a one-seater, a lot cleaner than ours at home and with real toilet paper, not leftover Sears Roebuck catalog. A wall separated the boys from the girls. Someone had carved a

19

hole in the wall between the two, but someone else had come along and plugged it up. Who'd want to watch a girl in the toilet, anyway?

I didn't learn much that first day, even if you count the recitation seat and the one-finger visit. I did get my first primer, though. I couldn't read it all, but I could still say some of Cora's words. Finally, at school-day's end, knickers sagging, I trudged back down Schoolhouse Road, tired but proud.

My great-uncle, Bridge Southard, was visiting my mother. He was married to my great-aunt Edith, whose summer cottage we had lived in before the bungalow. He loved to entertain us kids with jokes and songs from his minstrel show days.

I ain't never done nothin' for nobody, no time.
I ain't never got nothin' from nobody, no time.
And until I get somethin' from somebody sometime,
I ain't gonna do nothin' for nobody, no time.

Today he seemed more excited than my mother about my first school day. He sat me on his lap. "Well, what did you learn at school today?"

I couldn't admit I'd spent a whole day in school without learning anything important. "I can spell hen," I said.

"Good," he said, "let's hear it."

"H-E-double-L," I blurted, and knew, even before Uncle Bridge started laughing, that I must have missed it by a letter or two. Uncle Bridge would never forget my first day in school. He let everyone in Five Islands know just how smart his grand-nephew was.

I looked around for Irving, figuring I might start up the highway project again. He wasn't home.

"He's gone to Malden Island with your father."

Me, Mary and Cora out behind Aunt Edith's cottage, in the early 1930s.

To Malden Island? With Dad? I didn't like that, not one little bit. The Malden Island trip was mine. No little brother was going to cut me out of it. Hadn't I been the one to go wooding with Dad, and brought home a half-cord of wood on the handsled? And hadn't we gone flounder-fishing together, in the gut between the islands? I didn't say anything out loud, but my mother could tell I was upset. He was just taking Irving while I was in school, she said. She was probably right, but Saturday was still mine. And that's just what I told my father when he came home after work. He agreed; Saturday was mine. "But you'll have to share Malden Island with your brother."

I didn't really want to share Malden Island with anyone. I grumbled about it all evening, and was still grumbling to myself on the way to school the next morning. It wasn't until Mrs. McMahan had called us first-graders to the recitation seat and held up that first card with a word on it, that I let Malden Island go.

"Children, this word is MOTHER. Now, what does this word say?"
"MOTHER!" we all yelled together.

The same went for CRADLE and SANG. The others were fast, but this time I was a good half a word ahead of them. This reading business wasn't so tough, after all. And it got easier. By week's end, I'd learned practically a whole page from my primer.

I went to Malden Island on Saturday but it didn't seem the big deal it had been a week ago. I had something Irving didn't have; I could read. Before another week's end, I learned that I had something else Irving didn't have: friends. While I was at recess with a whole schoolyard full of them, he was in the yard or on Malden Island, all by himself.

Recess soon became one of my favorite times at school. When the weather was good, we played games in a schoolyard that had been twice its size before the town road commissioner discovered gravel under the sod and had carved out a shallow pit that gutted the whole north end of the grounds. There was barely enough space left over to play and it got really crowded when we played baseball. Actually, it wasn't baseball. Mrs. McMahan couldn't allow baseballs batted around the schoolyard when the girls were playing hopscotch just behind second base. She took our baseball and gave us a tennis ball; less chance for injury, she said.

Only Herbie Campbell, the strongest boy in school, and some of the older boys could drive the tennis ball into the pit—"over the banking," we called it—on the fly. So we made a special ground rule: Over the Banking on the Fly is Out. That way, Herbie couldn't hit a home run every time at bat. Then, Herbie took to hitting the ball into the pine trees in left field, and we had to delay the game while someone climbed the tree to knock the ball down and in the bargain got his hands so pitchy they'd stick to his school papers. Then Mrs. McMahan would make the sticky boy wash in the basin beside the water tank, filled by the older boys with water from a neighbor's well.

Our dinky schoolyard forced a shortening of the ball-field— somewhat. Home plate was at the edge of the trees on the south end; first base was the telephone pole twenty feet away on the far side of Schoolhouse Road. Even when the girls played, there sometimes weren't enough players to cover both the bases and the outfield. Herbie said we ought to have "Borings is Out," meaning the fielder could bore the tennis ball into the runner. If he hit the runner before the runner touched first base, the runner was out. It worked fine until Herbie wound up his great baseball arm and drilled one of the girls square in the middle from close range. She dropped like a wet dishrag, right in the middle of Schoolhouse Road. She got up right away and went to the sidelines, but not before Mrs. McMahan came out and scratched "Borings" from the rulebook.

I was too little to play ball, they said. So, I watched from the sidelines or played hopscotch. Sometimes I'd climb up and join the kids on Bare Rock, the biggest boulder I'd ever seen. The gravel diggers had uncovered it and left it sitting there on the side of the pit, a good six feet high and covered with moss, which made me wonder why it was ever called Bare Rock in the first place. A leftover from the Ice Age, Mrs. McMahan said. Sometimes we'd climb up and spend a whole recess just sitting on the rock's mossy surface. Boys on the top half, girls on the lower half (so the boys couldn't peek up under their dresses). When I was lucky enough to gain the very top spot, it was like sitting on top of the world.

The pit collected rainwater and made a shallow pond where the pollywogs came every spring. After school, and sometimes during our recesses, Russ Harford, Eddie Carr and I would go pollywogging. We'd dam up a corner of the pond and corral the little wrigglers. At day's end, we'd take away the dam and let them back into the pond.

The schoolroom was a pleasant place well into the fall, but in the dead of winter it was probably the coldest building in the village—next to the bungalow, that is. The only heat in the whole room came from the stove up front, a funny-looking, long, low affair that could swallow four or five cordwood sticks at a gulp. On below-zero mornings a roaring fire was needed, and that's where Mansfield Moore, a fifth-grader, came in. Every morning in fall and winter, he came to school early and built the fire. And no one could build a hotter fire than Mansfield. He put his very heart and soul into it. The sides of that old stove glowing a cherry red brought a grin of pure delight to his face. When a couple of parents mentioned melted gum rubbers to Mrs. McMahan, she commented to Mansfield that he might be overdoing it just a tad on the heat.

Even with Mansfield's Class A fire, half the heat went up the stovepipe and warmed the ceiling before it went out the chimney at the back of the room. Meanwhile, down below everyone beyond the first row of seats froze.

Not all the children showed up on the coldest days because their parents were afraid their faces would get frostbit on the walk to school. My mother seemed more concerned about our education than our frostbitten faces; she'd wrap scarves around our heads and shoo us out no matter how cold. If we were lucky, Mrs. McMahan's husband would let us ride in the back of his Model T pickup when he drove Mrs. McMahan to school. Mrs. McMahan usually arranged a few chairs around the stove so that we who had been turned out into the cold by our mothers could bring our books down front—our faces were burned and our backsides were chilled.

By Christmas vacation, I was a full-blown reader and couldn't get enough of it. Cora was a reader, too, and took me to the Five Islands Library at the Grange Hall. Even on the coldest days, Aunt Belle Stevens—she wasn't really our aunt, but everyone called her that—would come down, sit beside a smelly kerosene stove and check out the few musty books to us kids for two cents a week. I could usually find a children's book or two. Once you got past the odors, the reading was fine.

And then there were the books my mother had brought from her home when she married: *Dotty Dimple* for the little ones, *The Campfire Girls*, *The Motion Picture Girls* and *Tom Swift* for the older ones. From the beginning, I thought Dotty was too childish for me. I couldn't wait to tackle Tom Swift. The book that impressed me most was one on Greek mythology, but I wouldn't get to know Perseus or Medusa or the others on a first-name basis until I was older.

3

CAP'N GEORGE AND
GRANDMA HANNA

Cora and I made it through the year and moved on to the next grade. When spring of 1932 rolled 'round to Malden Island time, I was ready to join my Dad on our adventures. But all that changed one April morning when Cap'n George, my Grampa Hanna, came down Schoolhouse Road with a better deal.

Since before my earliest memory, Grampa'd been walking past the bungalow on Schoolhouse Road nearly every day. From early spring to late fall, he'd pass on his way to the boat landing in the morning and then home again in the afternoon.

This day I spotted him just as he got to the foot of Bars Hill. He wore a paint-stained suit coat with patches at the elbows, a navy-blue yachting cap and a pair of cut-down knee boots. This morning he didn't pass; he came inside and I had my first close-up look at him. He wasn't much taller than my father, but he was lean and wiry-tough. Nearing seventy, he had a friendly face: apple cheeks, twinkling eyes, and a full, white mustache stained a brownish yellow by the corncob pipe that stuck out of the corner of his mouth.

Grampa was not a man to waste conversation. He'd barely gotten through the door when he let us know the reason for his visit:

He wanted to take me with him to spend the morning aboard *Sky Pilot*, a Friendship sloop.

Ever since he had wrecked his own sloop, Grampa had worked as a kind of skipper for the Malden Island Boyntons, the same family who gave my father the wood from their icehouse, and mostly reverends to boot. He'd been hired as a crewman, but what they really wanted was his seamanship to get their boat out of tight spots. Grampa loved the *Sky Pilot*, and he cared for her as though she were his own. The *Sky Pilot* was forty-five-feet long with a beam of thirteen feet, one of the largest Friendship sloops ever built. It was built in 1909 as the *Ralph A.* and later purchased by the Boynton family and rechristened *Sky Pilot*. Members of the seasonal Malden Island community considered it the queen of Five Islands harbor, and during the summer they kept it busy with fishing and picnic excursions.

It was a grand sloop and I held my breath while my father mulled it over, fearful he'd say no. When he finally gave his permission, I squeezed into my jacket and was out the door ahead of Grampa. Together, we walked down to the town float. How proud I was to be alongside this man with a captain's hat, complete with a gold anchor at the peak.

Courtesy of Thomas Hanna

Grampa George Hanna aboard the Sky Pilot.

Courtesy of Gene Reynolds

Malden Island and its summer cottages as seen from the dock at Five Islands. The beautiful sloop is the Sky Pilot.

His rowboat had leaked during the night and there was water under our feet. Grampa took a wooden scoop from under the seat and showed me how to bail. While he cast off the painter and unshipped the oars, I bailed. I was still bailing as we tied up alongside the *Sky Pilot*.

Before he started work, we toured the boat: the engine room, the berthing and the galley. He named and explained the sails and showed me the helm and the compass and how he steered the ship. I stood at the helm, grasped the wheel, checked the compass and pretended I was the captain sailing the ship past the islands and into the Sheepscot. When Grampa saw how I was taking to the *Sky Pilot*, he went below and brought out his good captain's hat. I guess he kept that one on board for when he went sailing with the Boyntons. He placed it on my head. It was too big. Only my ears kept it from falling down over my eyes.

"Okay, take her out to sea," he shouted. Then he pretended to unmoor and put out to sea under sail while I manned the helm. When he decided we were clear of the harbor, he said, "I'll take the helm. Why don't you go below and get us a cracker. There's a can of hard-tack in the cupboard."

The hard-baked bread—pilot crackers, some called it—was kept on board for seasickness, Grampa said. I couldn't imagine anyone getting sick just from going to sea, and if they did, I couldn't imagine these dry and tasteless crackers being anything a sick person would want to eat. I took one for me and gave one to Grampa.

After we'd eaten our crackers, Grampa secured the helm, laced me into a life preserver and began painting the deck area forward. I was left to amuse myself. "Just don't go near the rail," Grampa warned. "If you're going to be on deck, stay where I can see you."

He paused in his painting long enough to give me a small piece of line and showed me how to tie a square knot and a bowline. The square knot was easy, but it was lunchtime, time for me to leave, and I still didn't have the bowline down pat.

It had been a fun morning. I decided right then and there that I wanted to take more trips to the *Sky Pilot*, maybe go to sea on her one day. To do that I'd have to stay real close to Grampa.

That afternoon when he trudged up old Schoolhouse Road on his way home, I dashed out to greet him. "Grampa, I want to kiss you," I yelled.

He stopped and waited, a grin as big as McMahan Island spreading across his face. He bent over so I could plant one on his grizzled cheek. He reached into his pocket. "Let's see if Grampa can find a copper for you," he said, his eyes a-twinkle. Amongst the lint and grains of tobacco were two pennies. He handed me one. I thanked him and waited for him to invite me out to the *Sky Pilot* the next day. Instead, he moved on up the road.

Here is Grampa Hanna, in his late sixties, still going strong in the 1930s.

After Grampa left, I ran the quarter-mile down to Percy's store to spend the penny that was burning a hole in my palm. I made the mistake of telling Cora about my penny, and what it took to get it. She told Irving. The next evening, when Grampa came 'round the bend in Schoolhouse Road, there were three of us on the ledge behind the house. Three voices sang out, "Grampa, we want to kiss you!"

This time he handed out three coppers. And this time, there were three eager faces pressed against the glassed-in candy showcase, trying to decide whether to get two pieces of licorice or one nougat or maybe a few jelly beans, with Percy all the while glowering at us through the glass.

Our little "Kiss Grampa" game became almost a nightly occurrence for the rest of the summer. By then, Mary, barely two, had made it a foursome. We loved Grampa and probably would have kissed him anyway, but the anticipation of those coppers would keep us running out to meet him.

Grampa took to visiting our house more often that summer, and when he did, he usually came alone. He was a quiet man. He said very little to us children, but we didn't mind; we were just happy to see him. He'd sit on our Morris chair and hold one of the little ones on his lap with the rest of us hovering around him. Sitting on his lap was a treat until he lit up his old corncob pipe. Its charred bowl spewed an acrid cloud that wreathed our heads and brought tears to our eyes. Still, we stayed close.

Grampa may have been gentle with us, but, according to my father, he was a man to be reckoned with when riled. The summer before I was born, the Boyntons wanted Grampa to take the *Sky Pilot* to Marblehead, Massachusetts, for a month or more. Grampa hired his nephew as a deckhand. After only a week, he found his young helper packing his suitcase.

"I've been fired," he told Grampa. "I'm going home."

Grampa hunted down the responsible Boynton and delivered an ultimatum. "If you don't need that young man, you don't need me either. I'll be packin' my bags."

A hurried consultation among the Boyntons followed. They allowed his nephew to stay on for the summer.

Shortly after my first trip to the *Sky Pilot*, Grampa came down the road one early morning accompanied by a short, chubby woman with bobbed gray hair.

"Oh no, not her," I heard my mother groan.

"Her" was my father's mother, my Grandma Cora. We rarely ever saw her. I raced out and planted a special morning kiss on Grampa, hoping for another day on the sloop. I turned to Grandma, expecting she'd want a kiss, too, but she turned her head and ignored me altogether. I concentrated on Grampa, waiting for that invitation, but he was already moving down the road.

I walked Grandma into the house. She breezed past my mother in the kitchen, like she wasn't even there, and went into the living room where my father was getting ready to leave for Malden Island. I stayed in the kitchen with my mother, but, from where I sat, I could hear Grandma talking, something about cups and saucers. My mother heard her, too. She barged into the living room.

"If you're looking to get some of my good china, the ones with the yellow flowers and black rim that Leslie Beebe gave me, you can just forget it," my mother told Grandma. Miss Beebe owned one of the cottages on Malden Island.

Grandma looked annoyed, and favored my mother with her icy stare. "All I want is a couple of place settings, for me and George."

My mother stood her ground. "They're part of a set, and I won't break them up."

"You got service for eight there," Grandma persisted. "Six'll take care of your whole family."

"And what am I supposed to do when Alice Cromwell comes to supper," my mother fired back, "feed her out of a trough?" Alice, my mother's cousin, was a Sunday School teacher and a proper sort.

By now, Grandma was near to tears. "Tommy's poor old mother, who don't have a whole lot herself, is begrudged a few cups and plates."

My mother turned to my father. He gave his shoe tops his undivided attention and said nothing.

Without his backing, my mother weakened. "If that's the way you feel about it, then take the whole set."

"I'll just do that," Grandma said defiantly. Then she turned to my father. "Tommy, would you lug these dishes up the hill for me?"

I wanted him to speak up and tell Grandma to leave my mother's dishes alone, but he just looked helplessly at my mother. "Yes, Ma," he said with a sheepish look that was still there when he left for work.

Courtesy of Cora M. Owen

The four Hanna kids in the early 1930s—(clockwise from top) Cora, me, Mary and Irving. You can just see the corner of the bungalow over my shoulder.

That evening, while my mother looked on in silence, my father packed the dishes into boxes and wheelbarrowed the whole lot up North End Road. I asked myself why my mother should have to give up her dishes to Grandma. It would be years before I could finally answer that.

A few days after the dishes had gone north, my father took Irving and me aside just out of my mother's

earshot. "I want you boys to go up to your grandmother's for a visit."
He was certain she'd want to see us.

I wasn't as sure. Hadn't she turned her cheek just the other day
when I wanted to kiss her? When I said as much, his request became
an order and we trudged up North End Road. I hoped Grandma
would offer her cheek today. She didn't. When she opened the door
her first words were, "You boys can't come in; I'm just washing my
floors. You'll have to play out in the yard until I'm through."

Then, without a word, she closed the door in our faces.

Playing in Grandma's yard wasn't fun; there was nothing to
play with. The only things out there were a big old pine tree and a
woodshed. Before we could decide what to do, Grandma opened the
door and said, "Stay out of the woodshed." Now we were down to
the pine tree. A pine tree was no fun unless you could climb it, and
someone had cut all the lower branches. That left us with just the
pinecones. The ground was covered with them. We tossed a few at a
gray squirrel sitting on a branch just out of range. When he skittered
off to a higher branch, we threw the cones at each other.

Sometime during the morning, while we waited for Grandma's
floors to dry, we took off our sneakers and went barefoot. We didn't
wear socks in the summertime and the smell inside our shoes was
getting so bad, not even I could stand it. And no wonder. Those
sneakers hadn't seen clean water since early summer when we
waded in Hite's Pond looking for bullfrogs. At night, my mother usually set our sneakers out on the back step to keep them from stink-
ing up the house. We put our sneakers on Grandma's step, thinking
she'd probably appreciate our leaving the smell outside, too.

We were still barefoot when Grandma called us in for lunch. A
peanut butter and jelly sandwich and a cup of tea in a Miss Beebe
cup for each of us was on the kitchen table. Grandma took one look

at us and screamed, "You won't be eating at my table with pine pitch all over your hands and feet!"

She sat us down beside the door and set a basin of water and soap on the floor beside our chairs. While we washed, Grandma scolded. "You boys shouldn't be runnin' around barefoot, anyway. You might get bit by a lizard."

Mrs. McMahan had told me about lizards, salamanders and chameleons. Chameleons changed color when you picked them up, but none of them would bite.

I told that to Grandma.

"They most certainly do," she came back. "When I was a girl, the woman next door went walking barefoot in the woods. She was crossing over this rotted log when a lizard crawled out and bit her on the foot. Three days later, she turned all green like a bottle and died."

If it had been a chameleon, I could understand the changing color part, but I was leery about the dying. Even so, I couldn't put that poor dead bottle-green woman out of my mind.

With pitch-free hands and feet, Irving and I sat down to eat. The bread was dry and the tea was weak. I was hungry and didn't care. The last morsel was barely eaten when Grandma suggested that just maybe we were wanted at home. On our way home I commented to Irving that visiting Grandma wasn't much fun. Irving agreed. Besides, Cora had always been Grandma's favorite. In the spring or fall, when the Boyntons weren't around, Grampa and Grandma took Cora to eat supper with them in the ship's galley. And, whenever Grampa Hanna was at sea on the *Sky Pilot*, Grandma'd invite Cora to stay overnight with her; she was afraid to stay alone in the dark, she said.

Before the china incident, we children had almost never seen Grandma at the bungalow. My mother said she only came when she knew my father would be there. Now that she was the proud owner of a set of yellow flowered china with a black rim, she seemed to want to show her gratitude by visiting the bungalow more often, a favor my mother openly wished she'd never seen a need for.

Grandma was old, I thought. Well past seventy, my mother said, older than Grampa. She believed that children should be seen and not heard, and she was fond of reminding us of that. "Don't speak unless you're spoken to" was another of her admonitions. I figured if everyone lived by that rule, it would be hard to get a conversation started.

Now and again, Grandma would hobble downhill to take supper at the bungalow. When we were seated, she'd tut-tut in her squeaky, little-girl voice, "Now children, let your food stop your mouths."

Grandma wanted my father's undivided attention, and she couldn't very well get it with his wife and houseful of kids around. She commanded that he come to her home—alone—every Sunday to take dinner with her. Until the day she died, he still hadn't learned how to tell her no. Bright and early on Sunday, he'd heat a basin of water, shave, and wash his armpits. Then, he'd slip into his old brown suit with frayed cuffs and a shiny seat and head up North End Road.

After my first visit to the *Sky Pilot*, Grampa took me several more times. Sometimes, he let me handle one oar on the row out to the ship. Eventually, I would learn to row, both oars, backward and forward. He tried to teach me how to scull, but I failed miserably and nearly ran his boat onto the rocks in the bargain. I never did go to sea with Grampa. The Boyntons wouldn't allow it.

4

A MODEL A FOR AN
AILING MAN

That same spring, in 1932, we were making do on my father's
caretaker's pay when the government sent him a check for five
hundred dollars. He said it was half of the bonus they owed him for
serving in World War I. With close to half a year's pay in his pocket,
he paid the grocery bill, and he closed out his mortgage with
Crosby's Lumber, who'd been hinting that they'd take their windows
back even if they had to take the whole house to do it.

He was left with a little more than a hundred dollars in his
pocket. My mother favored using some of that to move the bungalow to level ground so we'd have a proper front door for receiving
company. A guy in town had said he could move it with house jacks
for fifty dollars.

My father had other plans.

Late one afternoon a shiny black Model A Ford sedan pulled
into our yard and came to a stop. Our neighbor, Harold Rowe,
brother to Vesta's husband Orville, was behind the wheel and my
father was next to him. Harold headed home and my father came
inside. He couldn't wait to break the news. "What do you think of
my new car?" He was as proud as a boy with a new bicycle.

My mother was stunned. "I hope you didn't spend the rest of your bonus money on that contraption." She'd been counting on new curtains and wallpaper, at the very least.

"I paid the dealer what I had," he said sheepishly. "I'll pay the rest a few dollars a month."

She was leery of the easy payment plan and wanted to know just how he planned to get a few extra dollars a month. She'd given him the opening he was looking for. He'd get back into selling, like he had done before they were married. When she reminded him that he hadn't done all that well with that the first time around, he was ready for her. "That's because I was on foot. If I use the car, I can cover the whole twelve miles to Arrowsic and Woolwich, too."

My mother wanted to know what he thought he could sell in Arrowsic, or Woolwich, what with the Depression and all.

"Same things I did around here, only I'd have a lot more people to sell to." He warmed at the thought of it. "I still have the shoe sample case. And I could get in touch with the Zanol people and the fire extinguisher company. They'd be glad to have me back." Zanol sold all sorts of herbs and other household products.

She sensed that nothing was likely to sway him now, but gave it one last shot. "You don't know how to drive!"

Harold would teach him, he said; then he'd get a license.

Harold taught him. Together, they cruised the gravelly roads of Georgetown. When Harold wasn't available and my father had a few spare minutes, he'd start up the car and spend a half-hour or so backing and filling in our cramped front yard. I usually watched from the ledge above the house. He was coming mighty close to peeper territory where he could get stuck.

One morning, after a heavy rain, the soil was mush. His rear wheels sank into the muck up to their hubcaps. He shoved the car into reverse and revved the engine. The wheels spun. Gobs of slick clay flew up against the house. He was mired.

He opened the door, jumped out and hit the boggy ground cussing—"cross-eyed, moss-backed, knock-kneed, cripple-toed, double-jointed . . . " In all of Sagadahoc County, no one cussed like my father. He always intoned those syllables in the same measured litany, like a nun saying her beads. It must have taken a great deal of practice for him to string the words together so that anyone within earshot would know that Tom Hanna was spittin' mad. I wanted to laugh whenever I heard him cuss, but I knew better.

That cussing was a balm to his shattered composure. He rummaged around in the space under the bungalow and came out with a straw-filled cot mattress. He slid it up to the rear wheels, got back inside and revved the engine. He rocked the car back and forth—reverse, forward, reverse, forward—until the rear tires were atop the mattress. The tires grabbed hold. The car shot backward at full speed and rammed the house with a jolt fit to knock the posts out from under. He got out of the car, this time without so much as a "knock-kneed," and he went 'round to the back and checked the damage; a large dent on the back of the car near the rear window. The house had a loose shingle or two at the corner, but it was still anchored to the ledge. He spent the rest of the morning inside the car, banging out the dent. From then on, he stuck to the roads, which at times were little better than the swamp, until he learned to handle the Ford well enough to earn his driver's license.

As spring blossomed into summer and the rutted roads became hard-packed and dust-blown lanes, he'd come home from Malden Island every afternoon at four and slip into his threadbare suit. Then he and the Model A took to the road with his catalogs and sample cases. He was more at ease in that suit and tie than in working khakis and ankle-high brogans. He was a good salesman. In a more prosperous time in another place, he might have become a successful sales rep.

By midsummer, business had picked up and he was able to put something toward his grocery bill. I'd go with him to the store, because whenever he paid a little on his bill, Percy would give him a little bag of candy to take along home. And I'd get to pick it out. Once in a while, my father would even pick up a half-pint of vanilla ice cream for my mother. Sometimes, he'd take home a bag of cookies from Percy's National Biscuit Company showcase.

With business good, my father ventured all the way to Woolwich. The goods he ordered were freighted to the bungalow on the back of the mail truck. There was great excitement at the bungalow whenever the Zanol packing crate was deposited on our back step. After it had been opened, and the excelsior tossed out, I'd help him sort the herbs, spices, and sauces and put each customer's order in a paper bag with their name on it. Sometimes, he'd take me in the Model A with him to help deliver. Those were exciting times.

A car in the family meant that we all could travel. At first, it was just Georgetown roads. The Model A took us to places on the island I'd never seen before, spots for all-day family outings. My favorite place was Little River, a narrow beach beside a shallow tidal stream near the Indian Point section of Georgetown. At low tide, we could wade in the knee-deep water and catch flounder on the sandy bottom with our bare feet. Sometimes, we'd bring along a bathroom plunger—a scarce item in a town full of outhouses—and dredge up a mess of white sand clams for a good chowder.

It was at Little River on a warm Sunday at the start of a picnic lunch that I first came face-to-face with an ominous thunderhead on our sunny summer horizon: the caretaker of the Indian Point summer colony. Summer Complaints, as my father called them, had bought all the shore property at Indian Point, built their cottages, and then closed

Cora, Mary, Irving and I sitting on the running boards of the Model A in 1933.

Little River to the locals. To reach Little River, we had to pass over a stretch of the private Indian Point Road. The caretaker had strung a chain across the only access road and hung a PRIVATE PROPERTY—NO TRESPASSING sign on it. Any Five Islander worth his keep claimed squatter's rights where town beaches were concerned. When the caretaker wasn't around, they ignored the sign and went on in.

At the barricade, we pulled up. My father got out and lowered the chain. He was prepared to move on, when a man stepped out onto the road ahead and flagged us down.

"You can't come through here," the caretaker said. "This is private property."

Without a word, my father put the car into reverse and backed down the road. The caretaker, satisfied that the Indian Point turf had been nobly defended against the encroaching peasants, moved away. Just down the road, my father pulled up on the shoulder and parked.

Cautioning us to hold our tongues, he led us back to the barrier. We slipped under, unnoticed, and spent a pleasant afternoon at Little River.

I built a strong contempt for those Summer Complaints who could so callously deprive a local boy of a day at the beach. Even after I was full-grown, whenever a stranger told me, "I live at Indian Point," I was tempted to treat him as though he carried some highly contagious disease. Although the summer residents paid my father a salary and came to help my family out more than a few times, they were a constant reminder to me that they were the "haves" and we were the "have-nots," and it seemed to me they worked hard at making sure we knew that. The children, especially those from Malden Island, rarely if ever would even think of fraternizing with us local kids.

Grandma Hanna had never ridden in a car, not even in one of the town's few Model Ts. When she first laid eyes on the Model A, she informed her Tommy in no uncertain terms that she wanted her share of rides. That's when my mother came down hard with her size-two (narrow) heels. She let my father know that Grandma was not going to horn in on our family fun. Grandma never would have ridden in the car with my mother, anyway. She wanted her son all to herself. And she cooked up some sneaky ways to go about it.

On sunny summer days, she'd hobble down the hill from her home and spend an afternoon with her sister, Lettie. When my father approached Aunt Lettie's on his way home from Malden Island, Grandma would waylay him and ask him for a ride home. She loved to sit in the rear seat and wave good-bye to her sister, who didn't have a Model A to ride in. My mother sometimes watched as they passed the bungalow. Grandma had the good sense not to wave to her.

My father made occasional trips to Bath in the Model A. I'd never been off the island and was beginning to wonder if I ever would. Finally, late that summer of 1932, just days before my sixth birthday, I came right out and said I hoped I'd get to see a big city just once before I graduated eighth grade. He took the hint. Even so, I almost missed it. We awakened to rainy weather that morning and my father hated to drive gravelly roads in the rain. When he saw me gawking at the lowery skies, he made me a deal: If I could find enough blue in the sky to make a Dutchman a pair of pants, we'd go, just he and I. It was close to noon, after several exaggerated estimates—I was thinking small Dutchman, he was thinking big— he agreed that the tailor was indeed ready to make the Dutchman his pantaloons.

Once the car crossed the low, wooden bridge between Georgetown Island and Arrowsic, we chugged along the rutty, gravel road toward Bath for what seemed like hours. Then, my father called out, "We're almost there. The Carlton Bridge is just over those trees."

We were on a low, flat stretch of road beside a river, the Sasanoa. To our left, soaring above the trees, I could see the twin green towers of the drawbridge that crossed the Kennebec River. We rumbled over a second low-level rickety wooden bridge that spanned the Sasanoa, and crossed into Woolwich. At the Carlton Bridge toll-booth, we paid our nickel and drove onto what I thought must be the longest bridge in the whole world. Halfway across we passed under the towers and, as I looked up, they seemed to reach the sky.

At the far end, the bridge sloped into Bath. We rode straight down Front Street and made a circuit around downtown. I was fascinated by all those buildings, not bungalows or Cape-style, but three-storied buildings, some brick, some wood, joined together all the way down both sides of the street. On the first floors of many of them were shops and stores with awning-capped entrances. There were hotels, a theater, a couple of bars, a J.J. Newberry and an F.W. Woolworth.

We pulled up to the curb just down the street from Newberry's and climbed out. My father took my hand. As we waited to cross the street, I got my first close-up look at a trolley car. Steel on steel, it rattled and squealed past us on tracks that went right up the middle of Front Street, its bell clanging, and electricity sparking from its overhead wire. It squeaked to a stop in front of Newberry's and was still boarding passengers when we arrived. I insisted on watching until that magnificent machine closed its doors and groaned around the corner and down Center Street.

Inside Newberry's still more wonders awaited me. The air was heavy with the scent of new clothes, chocolate, and fresh-roasted peanuts. Just inside the door, next to the peanut machine, a glass showcase housed a variety of candies that put Percy's store to shame. A young woman stood behind it scooping candy into small bags for waiting customers.

My father bought me a nickel bag of roasted peanuts. "While we're here, we ought to get you something for your birthday," he said. "What would you like?"

"A tricycle," I said, not expecting even a maybe. Tricycles were what boys my age rode in those days.

"That will have to wait for another year or two," he said. "Let's look around and see what they have."

We passed down aisles of linens, ladies' lingerie, blouses and denims. Near the back, on a counter filled with small toys, I spied a wind-up army tank. My cousin owned one just like it. It had rubber treads, and when you wound it up, it would creep along and climb over things.

"I want this," I said. I'd wait until Christmas for my tricycle.

He paid the clerk and we made our way back to the car and headed for Five Islands. Usually, when I went in the car, it was with the whole family. Today had been different—special—with just my father and me alone together. I spent the trip home trying unsuccessfully to make my tank climb up the steep back of the front seat. Once home, I pushed the tricycle to the back of my mind and occupied myself with winding up the tank and knocking Irving's cars off Hanna's Highway.

The Model A would come in handy in the months ahead. Since the early summer my father's health had been going downhill. The demands of his Malden Island caretaking job—tugging at ice blocks, lifting steamer trunks and wrestling with heavy freight—were getting to be too much. Now, at age thirty-nine, he was suffering severe stomach pains, and he belched up his food.

After he had closed all the island cottages that fall, he drove to the Togus veterans hospital in Augusta for a full day of testing. The doctors told him he had an ulcer, and that there wasn't much they could do to speed the healing. Eat bland foods, drink milk, no coffee or tea, and no heavy lifting, they said.

"How will you handle your Malden Island job next spring, with all that hefting?" my mother asked him.

"I'll talk to Mr. Cranshaw about getting help with the heavy stuff."

"Precious little good that'll do," my mother said.

Cranshaw—I never heard my father mention his first name—was his boss on Malden Island. He was an executive with some manufacturing company in Massachusetts, and my father said he was the richest man on Malden Island, a millionaire. A million dollars didn't mean much to me, but to him it must have seemed like half the money in the world.

My father disliked him. "That man is as mean as turkey-turd beer," he told my mother. "He's always putting me down. He says my house looks like a nigger's shack."

He'd probably never seen what Cranshaw crudely referred to, but he understood "shack," and Cranshaw's words hurt him. Then Cranshaw took to snidely addressing his letters to "Thomas Hanna, Esq." My father looked up "Esq." in the dictionary and saw it was short for Esquire, a title of respect for landed gentry.

Cranshaw flatly refused to find someone else to do the heavy lifting. He told my father he could stay on through the fall and winter, but if he hadn't healed by spring, Malden Island would find a new caretaker.

Burned up, my father laid plans to strike a blow against Cranshaw and the other Malden Island snobs. "They're Republicans, every one," he railed to my mother. "You couldn't find a Democrat in a trainload of those people. And the trouble starts with the top Republican in the White House. Hoover's the one who pampers the Cranshaws and makes it harder for us poor folks to provide for our families."

That's when he decided that the Democratic Party was his only hope for a better life, and Franklin Delano Roosevelt with his New Deal was the man to do it. He'd fix the Cranshaws of the world. On that day, my father became a Roosevelt Democrat. In the process, he riled a goodly number of folks in a town, like the state in those days, that was overwhelmingly Republican.

Their attitude didn't faze him, though. He and the Model A spent the next two months preaching the New Deal gospel according to Franklin to every home on his route, and a few places in between. He managed to rankle both neighbors and relatives.

"My uncle says that Roosevelt wants to hand the country over to the freeloaders," he once told my mother. "Does he think that every poor man is a freeloader? All we want is a chance."

On another occasion, he said of the same Republican uncle, "That man is so conservative, he probably don't even use Cloverine Salve, because it says on the can, 'Apply Liberally.'"

When Roosevelt won the 1932 election handily, my father truly believed that with his lone Democratic vote, he'd struck a blow against the Cranshaws of the world.

5

A Merry Christmas

With Roosevelt's election victory behind us, and my father's door-to-door sales supplementing his caretaker's income, I had high hopes that the Christmas of 1932 would be merrier than the last. Ever since I could remember, my father had warned us that Santa Claus didn't have many toys to give out in such hard times, but

Inside P. B. Savage's store. My Grandpa Rowe (far left) once owned this store. Even though he lost it because of financial reasons, he continued to work there. Later in life he was able to reacquire part of it. Here, around 1940, are (l to r): Grandpa, (probably) Edie Pinkham Carey, Vern Gray and Percy Savage.

I had my doubts about Santa. He usually left a lot of toys—and much better ones—at my friends' houses, making me think that he had left some of our toys elsewhere by mistake. I figured my mother ought to write Santa a letter and get it straightened out. I was still hoping to get a tricycle from him, although there was always a chance I'd find it under the church Christmas tree instead.

Every fall along about November, my Grandpa Rowe wrote letters to the summer people and asked them to donate money for a Christmas Fund, which he used to buy presents for all the needy children in Five Islands. I didn't believe there was anyone in town more in need of a trike than I, and I couldn't think of anyone more deserving. Didn't I have the Sunday School attendance stars to show for it, and a consecration certificate to boot? And didn't I know by heart the story of how seventy-five years ago, the people in the village had taken apart the old church at Robinhood, brought it to Five Islands piece by piece, and built this beautiful building next to the cemetery?

With Grandpa Rowe buying all those church gifts, I didn't think a little hint from me would do any harm. During those early days I knew him a lot better than I knew Grampa Hanna. I saw a lot more of him. He was the Five Islands postmaster, and the post office was inside Savage's store. When he wasn't doing postal business, he worked out front with Percy. Sometimes, when Percy was attending to his plumbing business, Grandpa Rowe ordered supplies and stocked Percy's shelves for him. I can still see him standing behind the counter, wrapped in his gray grocer's smock, a ruddy-faced man with prematurely white hair. A stale cigar butt dangled full-time from the corner of his mouth and waggled whenever he talked.

Born in 1880, he was close to twenty years younger than my Grampa Hanna, and his outgoing manner stood in sharp contrast to Grampa Hanna's quiet ways. He enjoyed a good joke, and when he told one he laughed just as hard as when we told ours. In addition to my mother, Grandpa Rowe had another daughter, Helen, with his second wife, Geneva, who had raised my mother. Helen was thirteen years younger than my mother. Grandpa was a good sort, even though many in town avoided him when they'd see him coming. Many of the poor Five Islanders owed money on their accounts at the store, and they didn't want to face him.

Grandpa Rowe made regular Sunday visits to the bungalow while Geneva took supper with her sister. He never stayed for a meal; he just came to see his grandchildren.

Christmas was drawing nigh and my trike prospects were still dim. I figured it was time to bend Grandpa's ear about that three-wheeler. One Sunday afternoon I waited for him to show up. Like always, he took the shortcut through the woods, past Hite's Pond, over the neighbor's stone wall, and across the ledges to our front door (which was still in the back).

He was barely seated on the divan when I climbed into his lap and took his gold watch from his vest pocket. When he asked me what time it was, I piped right up and told him it was almost time for Santa to come and bring me my trike, which I had a great need for. My mother had already told him I had an even greater need for warm clothes, but all he said to me was that a trike was a pretty tall order. Then he changed the subject, like he wanted to take my mind off Christmas.

"Knock, knock," he said.

"Who's there?" I came right back.

"Sadie."

"Sadie who?"

"Just Sadie word and I'll be there."

I hit him with one of my own. "Knock, knock, Grandpa."

"Who's there?"

"Chester."

"Chester who?"

"Chester song at twilight."

We all shared a hearty laugh, as though either of the jokes rated it.

Grandpa was just hitting his stride. "Got a riddle for you, Tommy. Now pay close attention. A man went to a prison to visit a prisoner. When someone asked who the prisoner was, he replied, 'Brothers and sisters have I none, but that man's father is my father's son.' Who was the prisoner?"

I struggled so hard with that one for the rest of his visit that I forgot to mention the Christmas trike again before he left. Grandpa wouldn't tell me the answer. I'd have to figure it out for myself, he said. He never did tell me, and by the time I finally figured out that the man was visiting his son, I don't recall whether I bothered to tell him I'd gotten it.

In late November, my hopes for a decent Christmas brightened. A package the size of an orange crate came in the mail from the Boynton family. Christmas presents, I was told. When I wondered out loud why the Boyntons had our Christmas presents, my father explained that sometimes Santa gave our gifts to them to send to us. I thought it strange Santa would leave our presents with Summer Complaints, but I didn't really care how they came as long as they arrived by Christmas. The Boyntons collected used toys, clothing, and books from the other Malden Island families and sent them to the Hannas. My mother put the box away until later. "This is not for prying eyes," she warned. "And I don't want to catch anyone peeking."

The arrival of the gifts seemed to fill my mother with the Christmas spirit. She said it was high time I spoke a piece at the Christmas concert. The director gave me a short poem about Baby Jesus in the manger and I was supposed to memorize it before Christmas. My mother worked with me every evening until I had it down pat.

As the holiday eve approached, Cora, Irving and I took to standing by the chimney and hollering up at Santa. He never really said much to us on those occasions. He usually let us know he was up there, though. He'd make a funny little "Ho-ho" noise in a voice that sounded a lot like my mother's.

A week before Christmas, my father took me into the woods. We picked out a Christmas tree and he set it up in the living room. My mother broke out the box of colored balls and the few pieces of tinsel and garland she had brought with her from her childhood home. Cora, Irving and I sat at the kitchen table cutting up strips of paper, coloring them with red and green crayons, and pasting them together to make a chain that we draped over the tree. It was a beautiful tree. I loved the cheery twinkle of the balls as they caught the flickering lamplight.

On the afternoon of Christmas Eve, my mother scrubbed our necks and ears, combed our hair and shined our shoes. We ate an early supper and, just after dark, we piled into the Model A for the short haul to church. Just before we left, I went to the chimney corner and called up, "Hey Santa Claus, are you up there?"

As usual, all he said was, "Ho-ho."

This time, I persisted. "Santa, I need a trike."

Santa again said "Ho-ho."

My father took my arm and scooted me out the door.

The church was brightly lit with kerosene lamps in sconces on the walls and a goodly crowd was filing in. Christmas Eve brought out many new faces. Some were parents whose children usually came without them, but they came now to hear their little ones speak their pieces. They'd be back again come Easter Sunday. We children were herded down to the front near the stage beneath the pulpit. To our right, in the corner, stood the tree, a tall spruce that scraped the ceiling.

I couldn't keep my eyes off it. Among its tinseled branches, I could see dozens of packets in Christmas wrappings. On the floor around the base were more. I didn't see a tricycle.

I fidgeted in my seat until the concert got under way. After some praying and carol singing, we kids said our pieces. When it came my turn, I dashed up onto the stage to the exact spot the director had marked, looked out into the crowd and spoke in my loudest voice:

Long ago in Bethlehem,

In a manger filled with hay,

The baby Jesus Christ was born.

I started to leave the stage, but the director motioned me back and held up one finger. There was one more line. I hurried back to the spot.

On that first Christmas day.

Then I dashed back to my seat while the grown-ups chuckled and my parents beamed. Nobody clapped; it wasn't permitted in the house of the Lord.

After the final prayers, Grandpa handed out the presents. There was no tricycle for me, only socks, a union suit, and a sweater. Cora got a Flying Arrow sled. Disappointed, I tucked my presents under my arm, climbed into the Model A and rode home.

My mother got us undressed and ready for bed. She said I could sleep in my new union suit. I'd need it, she said, because tonight would be one of those below-zero nights. She spread our coats over our blankets for good measure. After the "Now I lay me down to sleep" prayers, I stood by the chimney and made one last plea to Santa. This time, he didn't even answer. I crawled back into bed, pulled my coat over my head, and fell asleep thinking about that trike.

On Christmas morning, we children awoke before dawn. The house was frigid, the stoves full of yesterday's ashes. I gave my father his Christmas wake-up call. "Can we get up now?" I sang out from under the covers.

"Not until I build the fires," came the reply.

There was nothing to do but wait until he rolled out. I got up to use the chamber mug. The floor was like ice and I was glad I'd slept with my socks on. I peeked through the curtain that hung in the doorway between our bedroom and the living room, but in the darkness I couldn't see anything. "It's no fair peeking," my mother had said, so I climbed back under the covers and listened as my father shook down the grates in the kitchen, then lit a lamp in the living room and built a roaring fire in the potbellied stove. Around the edge of the curtain I could barely see a limb of the tree. I turned my head away. I wouldn't peek.

"You can come out now," my father yelled. I was the first one out. Right away I spotted the tricycle. The tag attached to the handlebars said FOR TOMMY. I recognized that trike. It had belonged to one of my cousins and I'd ridden it at his house. Did I care? No; it was every bit as good as new to me.

I ignored the rest of the gifts under the tree and hopped onto the trike. My father lifted me off it and set it aside. "You can play with that later, after we've seen all the presents."

He sat us down and handed out our presents one by one. He reached far under the tree, came out with a toy steam shovel and handed it to me. It had a long crane with a bucket on the end. You could lower it to pick up a load of dirt and then crank it back up. It would be just the thing to load dirt into Irving's new dump truck when we built more roads behind the house. I noticed that the bright yellow paint was chipped in a few places. We'd have to write and tell Santa to be a little more careful with my toys in the future.

There were other gifts for all of us and a stocking for each of us hung by the chimney. I was too busy with my shovel and tricycle to notice what anyone else got, and as soon as everything had been opened, I climbed back onto my trike.

"Keep that thing out of the kitchen," my father warned. "Your mother will be cooking Christmas dinner." He had gotten a small chicken and my mother was peeling squash and potatoes. This was turning out to be a fine Christmas.

We all sat down to a roast chicken dinner with all the fixings. My father had brought his appetite to the table and managed to eat a little of everything, except the stuffing. Afterward, he stayed out of the baking soda and remarked to my mother that his ulcer must be getting better; he should be ready for Malden Island come spring.

By bedtime, when I put away my trike, I guessed this had been about the best Christmas anyone could have.

I forgave Grandpa Rowe for not putting a three-wheeler under the church tree and took to hanging out at the store. Whenever my mother needed a loaf of bread or a quart of milk, I'd volunteer. Then I'd stick around for a spell and visit with Grandpa. The store itself was a wondrous place to a wide-eyed six-and-a-half-year-old. Mostly I remember shelves stacked high with canned goods and bins filled with dried beans and peas, flour and sugar.

Next to the candy showcase, my favorite spot was the ice cream cooler. Grandpa mostly ordered Wiseman Farms ice cream in bulk and sold it by the pint, the quart, in double-scoop five-cent cones, and, sometimes, in sandwiches. It came in the standard flavors of the day: vanilla, strawberry and chocolate, and the best French vanilla in the state. Each canister was stored in the cooler and, until Central Maine Power finally came to town, was packed in dry ice to prevent melting. In summer, whenever I had a nickel to spare, I bypassed the candy counter and went for a Wiseman's.

Handy to the cooler was Percy's National Biscuit Company cookie display rack. It stood in the middle of the floor, a dozen or more kinds of cookies, each in its own cardboard box with a hinged glass cover. I preferred the molasses cookies with MARY ANN stamped across the top, and my all-time favorite, Fig Newtons. Cookies were sold by the pound, and my father usually bought a few of these and a few of those, enough to make a decent-sized bagful.

Percy kept kerosene and molasses in a room beside the post office. The kerosene was stored in a fifty-five-gallon drum and pumped out by hand into customers' gallon cans. The molasses that made great cookies and sweetened my oatmeal came in a barrel and was hand-pumped into quart milk bottles. Grandpa Rowe always said it took two men and a boy to draw off a quart of molasses around New Year's time. One winter morning he asked me to help him pump and that's when I learned the truth in the old saying, "slower than cold molasses running uphill in the wintertime."

In winter, Grampa arranged orange crates around the wood-burning potbellied stove to accommodate the seasonal workers until spring. The men would sit and smoke and now and again one of them would get out his knife, reach up and cut himself a chaw from a salt cod hanging off a stanchion.

When the men grew bored, they'd hold gas-passing contests. The champ's had the sweeter tone. "Just a little bread and honey'll do it every time," he'd say.

That old store holds almost as many memories—sights and smells—as the bungalow.

6

Saturdays are Special

During the winter months, we Hannas usually entertained ourselves as a family at home. When we had a battery for our radio, we tuned in to *Amos and Andy*. When my father wasn't reading, storytelling or singing to us, we children played cards—Fish, Old Maid, Authors—around the kitchen table. Sometimes Cora would break out her hymnal and lead us in a rousing exaltation to the Almighty. But of all the fun evenings during the early 1930s, my father's entertainment on a Saturday was the best.

Children always slept late on Saturday, but my father was up at dawn, laying a fire in the kitchen stove. My mother joined him and started breakfast. Then my father would build a roaring fire in the potbellied living room stove and place four chairs around it. While the house warmed, I lay in bed and watched my steamy breath escape. Maybe it helped to make the beautiful leafy pattern that frosted my bedroom window.

When he finally called us out, Cora, Irving, Mary, and I would scramble for choice seats by the fire. I always grabbed the warmest spot, in the chimney corner next to the stovepipe. The losers had their backs to the living room wall where the pale red sunlight could barely penetrate the frosted windowpanes. Like around the stove at school, their backsides froze while their faces roasted.

Irving was my chief competition for the stovepipe seat. One morning he and I arrived at that choice chair at the same instant. During the inevitable scuffle, I lost my balance and fell against the red-hot stovepipe. The crinkled pipe joint left ugly red sergeant stripes on my right shoulder for months after. But I'd never again lose my seat to Irving. I'd point to my stripes to let him know that this was the sergeant's chair.

Even though the house was banked with fir boughs, the floor underfoot was so cold that we stood in our chairs to catch the rising warmth. We stood there until my mother yelled from the kitchen, "Rolled oats are ready." Oatmeal with molasses was my favorite breakfast. While we ate, my mother prepared the beans that had soaked overnight for baking in a huge earthen pot.

My father set a galvanized washtub on top of the stove and half-filled it with our Saturday night bath water that he hauled from Clarence Mack's well across the road. Then he broke out his handsled and axe and headed for the woods on the far side of Schoolhouse Road behind Clarence's house to cut firewood. He had permission to do so as long as he cut only the dead and dying trees.

In the course of a Maine winter, the two stoves in the drafty bungalow ate up cords of wood. My father stored the wood under the house in the closed-in area, which wasn't more than a crawl space for your average man. To my father it was a woodshed with headroom to spare, where he cut, sawed and split every stick of it. Sometimes he'd take me into the woods with him to help pull the sled. Then I'd stack the wood after he'd cut it. And I'd carry arm-loads into the kitchen to fill the woodbox.

Later in the day, my mother baked biscuits. When it came to baking, she could make the old Glenwood B talk, even though the oven had only a balky temperature gauge on the oven door. The black needle that pointed out the temperature was almost never right. Still, she knew exactly when the oven reached the temperature that she needed. She'd open the oven door, stick her hand inside and pronounce it ready.

That evening after a hearty meal of baked beans and biscuits, my mother cleared away dishes. Then she and my father set the tub of water in the center of the kitchen floor close to the stove. When the temperature of the water was just right, the bath was ready. One by one, oldest first, we entered the kitchen and sat in the tub while my mother scrubbed all exposed flesh above the high-water mark. Underwater surfaces, except for the feet, were our responsibility. I was second behind Cora so I got to loll in almost-clean water.

When we were dry and comfortable in our union suits (complete with a backdoor flap), we gathered around the kitchen table. By the flickering light of a kerosene lamp, his eyesight failing even then, my father read to us. He read almost every evening in those days, but Saturdays were special because we got to stay up later. His words carried us away to wondrous places of fantasy and adventure.

Early on, I especially liked the animal tales by Thornton Burgess. His short stories were a daily feature of *The Boston Post*. At the kitchen table, I followed the adventures of Peter Cottontail or Reddy Fox. Later, I walked the beach of a remote island beside a shipwrecked *Robinson Crusoe* as he first found the footprints of his man Friday. We all had a laugh over the *Blunders of a Bashful Man*, and I got a warm glow inside when my father read about the *Five Little Peppers and How They Grew*.

My father strummed on both mandolin and guitar, although he didn't play either that well. He had a battered guitar that was almost impossible to keep in tune, but tuning didn't much matter to us anyway. He only strummed the chords, and we were more interested in the words he sang.

Oh where have you been, Billy Boy, Billy Boy?
Oh, where have you been, Charmin' Billy?
I have been to seek a wife,
She's the joy of my life.
She's a young thing
And cannot leave her mother.

How old is she, Billy Boy, Billy Boy?
How old is she, Charmin' Billy?
Three times six and four times seven,
Twenty-eight and eleven,
She's a young thing
And cannot leave her mother.

And on it went with an endless number of verses describing Billy's wife, from her height and her beauty to the size of her feet.

Occasionally, he gave us an old standby from his minstrel days:

I know a thing or two.
Yes, you bet your life I do.
My name is Ebenezer Joshuay Brown.

While my father was entertaining, my mother usually stayed in the background. Sometimes she'd sit in the corner and rock Mary, all the while singing to her:

Come, little leaves,
Said the wind one day.
Come to the meadows
With me and play.
Put on your dresses

Of red and gold;
For summer is past,
And the days grow cold.

She was no Jeanette MacDonald, but she could carry a tune. And when Mama wasn't singing or rocking, she'd sometimes add to the evening's entertainment with a little nonsense of her own. She'd chip in with something like:

Once a big molicepan saw a bittle lum
Sittin' on the sturbcone, chewing a gud of gum.
Aye, said the molicepan, will you simme gum?
Not on your tintype, said the bittle lum.

She'd laugh, and that would make me laugh.

On some evenings my father would wear his storytelling face. He had always been a yarn spinner and we little ones were the perfect listeners. We never questioned—out loud, anyway—when he may have gussied up a few facts for the sake of a good story. Sometimes, though, his stories turned out to be pure fabrications with a touch of humor thrown in at the end. We'd never know until the punch line, and then he'd tease us about being fooled.

Take the ghost story about the feller in Arrowsic who did in his wife and disposed of her, properly weighted, in McFarland's Pond.

Shortly after he began hearing an eerie voice in the night, saying, "It floats. It floats."

After several checks of the pond's surface, he worked up the courage to ask the voice, "What floats?"

And the voice said, "I-I-I-vor-e-e-e soap."

It didn't take much to make a kid laugh in those days.

Although my father had spent time in the trenches and on the battlefields of France, and had the medals to prove it, he didn't like to talk about the war. One Saturday evening, as we sat at the table, I asked him for a war story.

"And show us your medals," Cora begged.

We must have hit him at a time when he wanted to reminisce. He rummaged through a drawer and came back with three ribboned, bronze medals. We had seen them before, but I never tired of touching them and hearing him tell of those faraway battlefields. One by one he held them up. "This one's for St. Mihiel. This one's Belleau Wood. And this one," he held it up for a few seconds, "is for the Argonne Forest."

I wanted to hear about the Argonne.

He set the medal on the table beside the others, took out his can of Velvet pipe tobacco and his Zig-Zag papers, dumped a few grains of tobacco into the guttered paper, and rolled himself a cigarette. He stuck the end into the lamp chimney and puffed until blue smoke wreathed his head. Only then did he begin, holding the smoking butt between nicotine-yellowed fingers.

"The Argonne is where I got separated from my company and almost got shot—by the Americans."

Had I been older, I doubt I would have been so quick to believe the getting shot part, but this was a story I wanted to hear.

He adjusted the smoky lamp while we sat in silence. His company had been ordered to bivouac for a couple of days just outside the woods. He pitched his tent in a hollow. It rained during the night, a cold, wet rain. He awoke drenched and freezing, without a dry change of clothes. Some of the boys had built a small fire. He sat beside it and dried off. Too late; he had already taken a bad chill, and it got worse. The next night, his unit was ordered to decamp and move up. By then, he was burning with fever. It was dark and cold.

He could hardly walk. Finally, he slowed down and dropped out. In the darkness, he fell, unconscious, and his outfit moved on without him. When he awoke he was so fevered he was out of his head. He wasn't sure which way he should go. He only knew that he had to get medical help. He started walking, not knowing whether he was going toward American or German lines, but he was too sick to care. He saw a light in the distance and headed for it. It turned out to be American.

"And who wanted to shoot you?" Irving asked.

"The captain in charge of the unit said I had run away from my unit on the battlefield and would be shot as a deserter. And they would have, too, if I hadn't been so sick. They sent me to a field hospital. Doctors said I had pneumonia."

"What did they ever do about you being a deserter?"

"Nothing. I stayed in the hospital until I got better, then they sent me back to my own unit."

One Saturday night, he took down his gas mask from the overhead. I'd tried it on once but it was so full of dust I couldn't breathe. I asked him if he'd ever had to use it.

He nodded. "Especially around St. Mihiel."

"Were you ever gassed?" Irving wanted to know.

He paused again, and I thought he was going to let it go at that, but he went on. "It was at night. My platoon was in the middle of this big field, looking for a place to take cover. The German lines were on the other side of that field. We came across this barn and sneaked in."

Three excited faces watched and waited for him to continue.

"There we were, all huddled together in the pitch black. Our sergeant whispered for us to keep it down and show no lights. But one damn fool private didn't get the word. He struck a match to light his cigarette. Seconds later, we heard firing and two shells exploded just outside the barn. 'Gas attack,' the sergeant yelled. I struggled to get my mask out, but it caught on my backpack. By the time I had mine on, I'd already got a little of the gas in my eyes and some in my lung. It burned like the devil."

Irving picked up the gas mask. "You must have been some kind of war hero."

I doubt he would have said so, even if it were true, but he smiled and shook his head.

"Just another doughboy," he said.

I was disappointed. I wanted us to have at least one hero, if only a small one. I became obsessed with the idea of a heroic Hanna.

"Didn't anyone in our family ever do anything special?" I asked hopefully, one Saturday evening after story time.

My father replied with dead seriousness. "Cousin Forrest was shot at by the FBI."

Shot at by the FBI! I had to know more.

"It was during the Prohibition."

He stopped, enlightened us a little on that subject, then started anew.

"During Prohibition, rumrunners brought in whisky by boat from Canada and landed it at Herm Spinney's wharf at Bay Point. Then it was trucked to Boston and other cities. Forrest drove one of those trucks. One night the FBI set a trap along the road to Bath and waited for Forrest to come by. When he wouldn't stop they fired on him, but he just kept going and got clean away."

Cora and Irving were disappointed that there wasn't more, but I was thrilled. Cousin Forrest was shot at by the FBI! Nobody else in all of Sagadahoc County could make that claim. Surely Forrest was somebody special. I couldn't wait to spread the word. I thought about it long after I had gone to bed. *Shot at by the FBI!*

The next day, I boasted to anyone who'd listen, "My father's cousin Forrest was shot at by the FBI."

I couldn't drum up much support for Forrest, though. I guess people didn't see his rumrunning in the same heroic light as I did. In fact, some thought it was too bad the FBI had missed. I finally conceded that I'd have to look elsewhere for my family hero. And, when I grew older and came to know Forrest better, I tended to side with the "too bad the FBI had missed" crowd.

Those evenings around the kitchen table would be the happiest times my childhood would ever know. And, come to find out, we did have a Hanna hero. Marcus Hanna, Grampa Hanna's first cousin from down New Harbor way, won the Medal of Honor during the Civil War. Later, as a lighthouse keeper, he won the lifesaving medal when he rescued two drowning seamen from a foundering ship at Two Lights in Cape Elizabeth.

7

BROKEN TRIKES, LOST WATCHES AND MISSING CATS

By the spring of 1933, my father's bland diet had done little to improve his ulcer. He still spewed up his meals on a regular basis. He met with Cranshaw and again pleaded for a helper to heft the heavier freight. Cranshaw said they couldn't afford another hand and, without so much as a how-do-you-do, fired my father and hired Lloyd Pinkham to replace him. Lloyd wasn't a whole lot bigger than my father, but he was thirteen years younger.

Without the full-time, salaried job on Malden Island, my father concentrated on selling, which by itself could not support his family. In addition to selling, he was able to pick up some part-time work or odd jobs—substitute school bus driver, carpenter's helper, working at the Ledgemere boathouse during boating season. And still later he helped build a log cabin for Walter Reid—father of nearby Reid State Park—on Seguinland Road, across from his stately home overlooking Harmon's Harbor. That's the way my father's job situation went through 1936—a little here and a little there.

Meanwhile, his original faith in Roosevelt was finally justified. In May of 1933, the Federal Emergency Relief Administration was born. After some bureaucratic paper-shuffling, the first shipment of government surplus food arrived in Georgetown. My father came home from the store one day, bubbling with excitement. They had just brought in a whole truckload of food for needy families. Even as he spoke, he said, the selectmen were at the Grange Hall passing it out. My mother had no idea what "government surplus" was. My father wasn't so sure either, but he'd heard that it was food that Roosevelt had bought up from farmers and was giving to the needy.

My father ran down the list of needy families in town. He couldn't come up with a Georgetown family more needy than his own. There were a couple of other families nearby that had as little as we did, but their families were smaller. He hopped into the Model A and hurried on over to the Grange to be sure he got there before the surplus was all gone. In less than an hour he was back with the first from what would become a periodic giveaway. He backed the car up to the house and unloaded bags of rice, dried beans, flour, boxes of prunes and raisins, and a rasher of bacon. Even so, the early pickings were lean compared to what they became once the program got rolling. Later we'd see eggs by the case, canned meat, cheese, tub butter, and more.

My father wasn't totally happy, though. He'd run across Uncle Ellie in line behind him. He was right there for his handout. And after the way he'd been mouthing off about Roosevelt.

Right smack in the middle of our struggles came the news that a new baby might be coming to the bungalow. I first got wind of it when a neighbor woman from up the hill came by to show my mother her month-old daughter. My mother offered the neighbor a cup of tea. While she drank it, my mother took the little girl into her arms and cooed at her. "My Lord, ain't you some cunnin', ain't you some cunnin'," which she'd say to just about any baby.

After the neighbor lady and her baby left, my mother said we might have a new baby around the bungalow before long. What would I say to that? I told her it might be all right if we could find room for it. Then I asked her how you got babies anyway.

"They come from a seed," she said. That made sense. Every summer my mother planted seeds in an old tire out in the yard. Then, a bed of pansies and nasturtiums would appear.

I waited but I didn't see any sign of the baby. Then my mother got sick and Dr. Barrows came by to see her. She stayed in bed for a few days after. She told me the seed had died. I could understand that, too. One year her pansies didn't come up. My mother seemed sad at first. But when my great-aunt Ruth comforted her, she reminded Mama that four kids was a nice-size family. And Mama agreed.

My father's struggle to make a living and his poor health began taking its toll on him. He became irritable and did spiteful things. He'd kick the furniture or knock over a bucket of wash water that got in his way. Once, while he was fixing a flat tire, he couldn't force the tire over the rim. He smashed out the windshield on the Model A with a tire iron, all the while cutting loose with his cross-eyed, moss-backed, knock-kneed, cripple-toed, and a double-jointed for good measure.

At first, his fits didn't trouble us children much, because they weren't aimed at us. Then one morning he came out of his bedroom and tripped over my tricycle. I kept it inside when the weather was damp. I'd left it standing in the middle of the kitchen floor. He picked himself up and grabbed the tricycle. Doing his "cross-eyed" thing, he opened the kitchen door and flung it onto the ledges behind the house. I ran out to check the damage. The mangled front wheel wouldn't turn. I ran back inside and screamed at him through angry tears. "You've ruined my trike! Now you gotta fix it."

He had already jammed his hat onto his head and was on his way out the door. "I don't have to do anything I don't want to."

As he left the yard, I screamed after his retreating back. "I hate you!" I hoped he'd turn around and come back to fix my trike, but he didn't.

After a time my father returned. Through the window, I saw him examining the bent wheel. He worked on it for a while until the wheel wobbled around without jamming. I knew it would never be the same. Then he came inside and hung up his hat without a word to me.

Later he came into the kitchen where I was sitting. He held his pocket watch in his hand. It was a Westclox with a fob on it so you could pull it out of your pocket. He called it his Dollar Watch.

He held it out to me. "How'd you like to have a watch for your watch pocket?"

I couldn't believe it. My own personal watch! And I had just learned to tell time, too. It fit perfectly in my pocket. I must have taken it out a dozen times in the first hour to check it against my father's alarm clock. In the excitement of the moment, I'd almost forgotten the trike.

When I showed my prize to Irving, he wanted it. My father explained that it was mine. Irving promptly went into a dry-cry tantrum. My father ignored him for a while, but Irving was determined. After a while, I could see my father weakening. Finally, he said to me, "Let him wear it for a little while. He'll give it back."

Once he got it, I knew he wouldn't give it back. I told my father so.

"Now, don't be selfish, Tommy. A little sharing won't do you any harm. And it's only for a little while."

Reluctantly, I handed it over. "You can keep it for just one hour, starting right now. And I'm keeping track of the time, too."

I couldn't stand to watch him strut around with my watch in his pocket. I went up the hill to find Johnny MacGillivary, all the while stewing. When the hour was up, I returned to reclaim it. Irving didn't have it. He'd lost it, playing in the swamp, he told me.

I didn't believe him. "You know where it is and you'd better have it back here in five minutes, or I'm going to tell Daddy."

Five minutes later he was still insisting he'd lost it. I told my father. He helped us search the area where Irving had been playing. We turned up nothing. When my father quit, I insisted that he make Irving stay in the swamp until he found my watch. He didn't see how that would do any good.

Nothing more was said about the trike or the watch. My father tried again several times to repair the wheel, but it had a permanent wobble and was never much fun to ride after that. I scoured the swamp for the watch almost every day until snow flew; I didn't find it. Both the trike and the watch would become early scarring chapters in the story of life at the bungalow. I never again mentioned either one. I guess I needed a father more than I needed a trike or a watch.

Not even pets fared well at the bungalow. Pets were a nuisance, my father said. With the vet bills and all, they cost too much to keep. We might have stayed petless, if my mother hadn't liked cats. She inherited a near full-grown, chuckle-jowled tom from someone in the neighborhood. She called him Mickey Mouse because of his mouse-gray coat. What I really wanted was a dog, but if the best we could come up with was a cat, I'd settle for that for the time being.

Mickey slept under the house, but every morning at first light my father would let him in. One cold morning, Mickey took a great leap and landed on all fours in my bed, right between Irving and me. We let him snuggle between us. We covered him with our blanket. Mickey's leap that day became a daily ritual, even in summer.

I loved Mickey, but he didn't hang around long. Mickey had a weakness, one that would shorten his life considerably: females. Whenever a neighborhood lady cat was receiving, he'd be there, ready to take on any and all other suitors for the honor of getting next to her. He'd come in some mornings after a night on the village, bloody and torn. We'd have to handle him gently—we even let him sleep on the kitchen floor for a while—until he healed. Then he'd go right back at it again.

One morning he staggered in, more dead than alive. One ear had been torn half off. One eye was shut tight. Probably torn out, my father said. Great patches of fur were missing from his hide. He needed a vet, something we couldn't afford.

My father took him away and came back without him. I don't think he ever told us where Mickey had gone. I surmised he was at the bottom of the Sheepscot along with all the other cats who couldn't afford a doctor.

I missed Mickey so much that when someone in the village offered me a free kitten, I jumped at the chance. I got my mother's okay, and then chose a black tom with a white face and a ring of black around one eye. He looked like Charlie McCarthy with his monocle, so that's what I named him.

Charlie was a good cat, but from the start I could tell he'd never be Mickey's replacement. He didn't take kindly to being tucked in bed and covered over. He preferred to sleep under the kitchen stove.

I lost interest in Charlie, and it's a good thing I did; he wasn't long for the bungalow either. Charlie's weakness was shellfish. Oftentimes lobstermen gave my father messes of crabs and short lobsters. After they'd been cooked, he'd bury the shells from the illegal lobsters so the game warden couldn't find them. The crab shells he threw onto our private dump behind the outhouse. Charlie had a nose for those shells. When he found them, he'd make a meal of them; then he'd toss them up, along with a quantity of his blood. By the time he'd discovered the lobster shells and begun to dig them up, his insides were so torn up, he couldn't even take milk from a saucer.

I don't remember when or how Charlie left us. One day I just noticed he had gone. If anything was said to me about his absence, I don't remember. He had probably joined Mickey.

8

MY MOTHER GETS
A LITTLE HELP

The entire time we had lived in the bungalow, my father had lugged wash water bucket by bucket from Clarence Mack's well just across Schoolhouse Road to fill my mother's laundry tubs. My mother's Aunt May in Bath somehow got wind of her washing woes and offered to pay to have a well dug close to the house.

The frost was scarcely out of the ground that spring of 1933 when Clemmy McMahan, the town's first-rate dowser, came by to check on the best place to start digging. He cut a crotched limb from a bush in the swamp—an alder, I think. He grabbed one side of the crotch in each hand. Pointing the other end away from himself, he moved around our yard. Right in front of the bungalow the limb tilted downward until the bark on the crotch twisted off the wood under his hands.

"Here's your water," he said. Clemmy was a man of few words.

My mother wasn't sold on Clemmy's dowsing ability. As swampy as our land was, she thought it would have been hard for him to find a spot where water wouldn't turn up. Clemmy was right, though. Water poured into the well until it was deep enough to be way over my father's head. I couldn't be sure, but it seemed that the water level in the swamp had gone down somewhat.

Aunt May was my mother's protector, really, and had been ever since my mother's mother, May's half sister, died. May wasn't done yet. She bought a hand pump and some iron pipe for my father, and he set it in our kitchen next to the old cast-iron dry sink and piped the water in. Now, we had to send a water sample off to Augusta to see if it was fit to drink.

While we waited for word on that, Aunt May took another notion: with all that water inside the house, my mother needed a washing machine. She freighted a hand-operated model with a hand wringer down to Five Islands. It had a wooden tub and a wooden agitator that favored an upside-down milking stool. When the handle was cranked back and forth, the agitator rotated. There was a bung-hole at the base, with a stopper in it, for draining.

Immediately, my mother pumped up and heated a tubful of water and washed a load of clothes. The loaded machine took all my mother's strength to operate. She had to brace her foot against the side of the tub to give her eighty-pound frame the leverage to pull the handle. Pushing was easier.

When she judged the clothes clean enough to rinse, she set the washtub—our bathtub—on two kitchen chairs, filled it with water and passed the clothes from the washer through the wringer into the rinse water. Next she drained the tub, a bucketful at a time, and tossed it out the kitchen door. Finally, she passed the rinsed clothes back through the wringer into the washtub. Now, they were ready for hanging on her clothesline that ran from the back door to the outhouse. Her outdoor dryer worked fine in summer, but winter was a whole other matter. Within minutes on cold days the clothes would be as stiff as scarecrows, and they'd stay that way until she took them off the line, stacked them up like cordwood, and brought them inside. She stood my father's pants and my union suits, stiff and tall, in the corner behind the stove until the heat collapsed them into a soggy heap.

Washday became a weekly event. Every Monday morning Mama would set up the washer in the middle of the kitchen floor and do the laundry. That machine fascinated me. During summer vacation I'd hang around and watch her crank out her wash by the tubful. She let me crank the wringer, after warning me over and over again to be careful not to get my finger jammed between the rollers. She showed me how to hit the roller release in case the clothes got caught.

One morning in the midst of a wash, Vesta yelled from her house behind ours for my mother to come over. Probably she had a choice piece of gossip that just wouldn't keep. While Mama was gone, I fooled around with the wringer, idly cranking it and wondering all the while just how painful a jammed finger could be. If only I had a finger or two to slip in there, I'd know for sure.

Irving had been watching me crank. He was curious, too. I suggested he put his two fingers right in there. He was more than willing to go along with the experiment, but it was cut short when Irving let out a scream that could be heard all the way over to Vesta's. I hit the release clamp and Irving yanked his hand free, but he was still yelling bloody murder about his jammed fingers when my mother rushed through the kitchen door. I was hoping Irving wouldn't squeal, but he poured out the whole sad tale while I edged toward the door, ready to go and hide away in the swamp. My mother noticed that sneaky move and ordered me to stay right where I was.

She made a big fuss over Irving, who was probably laying it on a little thicker than necessary. Though, by this time his fingers had taken on a slightly bluish cast. She soaked them in cold water for a full ten minutes to keep down the swelling, with me scared out of my britches and not moving a muscle the whole time.

Then she turned to me, grabbed my hand and shoved my fingers into the wringer, at the same time scolding me for pulling such a tomfool stunt. Lucky for me, the rollers had been released or the pain might have been unbearable. However, I dutifully ouched and ow'd until she stopped cranking and pulled my fingers free, saying something about letting that be a lesson to me. By the next morning Irving's blue fingers had returned to a more healthy pink. Lucky for me, he wasn't old enough yet to hold a grudge.

It turned out our well water contained harmful bacteria and we could use it only for wash water. There was no way to purify it, the state said. My father was forced to continue using Clarence Mack's well across the street.

9

THE SALESMAN AND THE STUDEBAKER

By 1934, my father could no longer afford to make payments on the Model A. He drove it to the dealer in Bath and came home with a cheaper car, a 1928 Studebaker.

I can still recall the day he drove it into our front yard, all black and shiny. He had barely come to a stop—motor still running—before I opened the door, climbed in, plopped myself down on the black seat, and began to coax for a ride.

I coaxed some more until we were headed down Schoolhouse Road. My schoolmate Russ Harford was in his yard. He pretended not to see me wave, but I was sure he had. And that provided partial satisfaction for the way he'd pedaled his Christmas tricycle over to my house so I could be properly impressed.

Our Studebaker became even more special when the new plates for it arrived; the Registrar of Motor Vehicles had given it license plate number CS 1. Our neighbor, Orville, came by to check it over and promptly dubbed it "Comfortable Studebaker No. 1," and that's how I remembered it.

In those depressed times, most people in Five Islands considered any kind of car a luxury. More than a few jaundiced eyes were cast in CS 1's direction. Jokes were passed around about Hanna's

Courtesy of Cora M. Owen

My father, ready to sell in the 1930s.

sporty car. My father ignored them. He considered CS 1 a necessity. With her he planned to make up for his lost Malden Island caretaker wages in year-round door-to-door sales. He still had all his sales materials, and most of his customers knew and trusted him. To his line of goods, he added a variety of nursery products—shrubs and the like—for his spring and summer sales. The dreamer in him said this new venture was sure to succeed.

Almost daily he dressed up in his only suit—the threadbare, brown silky one—and black felt hat, tossed his sample case and catalogs onto the backseat, and settled all five feet of himself onto a cushion in the front seat of old CS 1. Then he putt-putted down the dusty road, his eyes barely over the rim of the steering wheel. His full-time drumming did increase sales enough so that he eked out a living.

The dirt roads he traveled to reach his far-flung customers in Georgetown, Arrowsic, and Woolwich were rutted and rock-strewn, a lethal combination for tread-bare tires and over-patched inner tubes. CS 1 hiked up on a jack, with my father patching a tube, was a common sight in our driveway.

From a mail-order catalog, he had come up with a gadget that used the engine's compression to inflate the tube. I couldn't wait to see his wondrous pump at work. The first time he used it, I hung around to watch. He'd have none of it.

"Get out of here," he said. "If this thing blows up . . ."

I pulled back to a proper out-of-here distance and watched as he screwed the cylinder into a spark-plug socket, connected its hose to the inner tube and started the car. While the engine did its work, he fiddled with the tire, paying little mind to the ballooning tube.

The tube was filling too fast, I thought. An ominous bubble was forming on one side. I edged toward the car, eager to help. "Hey, Dad," I said, "the tube."

He looked up and repeated his warning. "I told you to keep . . ." He didn't get a chance to finish. Just as he turned to check the tube for himself, it exploded into shredded fragments, and he sat down on the ground hard.

He cut loose with a good "cross-eyed, moss-backed, knock-kneed, cripple-toed, double-jointed" rant. The cussing helped. He picked himself up, found a second tube, patched it, and inflated it without incident. I kept well clear, so he couldn't find a way to blame me for the explosion.

Unfortunately, that wouldn't be the end of it for my father. Woody Gray had come down the road just as the tube blew up. He'd

seen my father sitting there doing his cussin' thing. If there was one
person in Five Islands you wouldn't want to catch you in an embarrassing position, it was Woody. He was a great imitator and had a
knack for retelling such incidents over at the general store—complete with exaggerated motions, of course. He had my Daddy's
cussin' down pat, even to the smallest intoned inflection. My father
got wind of Woody's gussied-up story—he didn't chuckle.

CS 1 was our new leisure wagon, and that was just fine with
me. It was more of a fun car than the Model A. On warm, sunny
days, my father removed the side curtains and lowered the fold-
down top. Then, with our parents up front and Cora, Irving, Mary
and me hanging out the back, we cruised the dusty back roads of
Georgetown, with an occasional trip to Bath, where we'd park on
Front Street and watch the people go by.

Grandma Hanna wanted even more rides in our sporty
Studebaker than she had the Model A. On warm summer days, she
took to hobbling down to the bungalow. After a brief visit, she'd ask
my father to drive her home.

One day she huffed into our front yard to find my father tinker-
ing with the Studebaker's transmission. After "just a taste" of my
mother's baked beans and brown bread, she announced to my father,
"I'm ready to go home now, Tom."

"The only gear that works on this car right now is reverse," my
father told her. "I just can't take you home today, Ma."

Grandma couldn't understand why it should take more than
one gear just to get from the bottom of the hill to the top. "Now,
Tom," she pleaded in her most persuasive voice, "you know I can't
walk back up that steep hill." She cited her bunions and her arthritis.
"You'll just have to take me home."

"All right," my father groaned. "Tommy, I'll need you to come
along and help me steer."

We backed out of the driveway with me riding shotgun. Grandma, her bobbed, gray hair crowned by a spring straw hat, and looking as high and mighty as Queen Mary herself, sat enthroned on the black-leather rear seat.

I rode with my head out the door, looking back toward the direction we were going. My father watched the rearview mirror. "Ditch," I'd say, and he'd get us back into the middle of the road.

We backed on to North End Road just as we saw Henry Moore come walking down. Henry had been blessed—or cursed, depending on your point of view—with a wry Down East sense of humor. When he spotted us backing toward him, he stepped off the road and into the ditch. When we came abreast, he flashed a lopsided grin and said to my father, "Hey, Tommy Hanna, you comin' or goin'?" My father gripped the steering wheel in stony silence and concentrated mightily on the mirror. Grandma muttered something about "that cussed fool," then lapsed into silence, her dignity intact.

When Grandma was safely home, we backed our way downhill without further incident. Fortunately, we didn't run into Henry. CS 1 would run forward again, but only after my father found the junk-yard parts to reassemble the transmission. It would serve us well in the months ahead.

10

FIVE ISLANDS ABLAZE

Some folks allowed that the spring of 1934 was the hottest and driest in fifty years. It had gotten so warm inside the bungalow that my father had opened the front door a whole month early. The bright sun and balmy southerly breezes parched the land and made a tinderbox of our heavily wooded island. The threat of a forest fire turned critical, but if the islanders noticed, they seemed unconcerned. Few carried more than a distant, time-softened memory of the last great forest fire in 1912. So, they went about the business of battling the lingering Depression and took scant notice of the scorched earth, other than to occasionally check the water level in their wells.

A crew of surveyors from the National Geodetic Survey arrived on Georgetown Island in late May. The surveyors backpacked their gear to an isolated ridge near the east shore of Robinhood Cove, where they cut down and trimmed out a stand of birch trees for a tower. With a platform on top, they could see over the surrounding trees.

They worked the week, finished the survey and left the site on Friday afternoon. On Monday morning they returned to clean up the site. Their first task: pile up and burn the slash. If similar conditions existed today, the Forestry Service would issue a warning and prohibit such burning, but this was 1934, so they burned. Late that afternoon, they were seen leaving town, their gear packed on their truck.

On Tuesday morning a Georgetown Center resident reported smoke rising above the trees at the survey site. Selectman Earl Hagan recruited a few men and they gathered at Town Hall, where the fire-fighting equipment was stored. Their equipment consisted of axes, shovels and Indian pumps—small tanks that could be filled with water, strapped to the back and carried to the fire scene and then pumped out by hand. The firefighters filled their tanks and hiked in to the site. Fortunately, there was little wind and the fire hadn't yet reached a nearby dense growth of evergreens. They hosed down the area, put out the fire and left. My mother, who was deathly fearful of fire, fretted all afternoon until Vesta, the neighborhood informant, came over and assured her that the fire was out.

Wednesday was Memorial Day and there was no school. My father was on a selling trip to Arrowsic and Woolwich. The morning dawned warm, clear and calm, but by midmorning, a brisk southerly breeze had sprung up. Shortly after noontime Vesta came over to tell my mother that she had just gotten off the phone with Earl Hagan's wife, Marjorie. "The fire has started up again," she said. "They've called in the Bath fire department. It looks really bad."

I saw panic in my mother's eyes. We walked to the top of Bowling Alley Hill. From here, we looked to the west where dense smoke roiled above the treetops. It couldn't have been more than a mile and a half from where we stood, but to my eight-year-old eyes, it seemed far away. Surely that fire could never come all the way to Five Islands.

My mother spent several nervous hours waiting for my father to return from work in the late afternoon. He had stopped at the store and brought news. The fire had burned all the way to the

McMahan farm, he told her, but the wind had died down and it was under control. The McMahan farm was a mile or more northwest of Five Islands village—a safe distance from us, my father thought, especially with a southerly wind.

"Is anybody watching to see that it don't spring up again?" my mother worried.

The Bath firefighters had gone home, but a company of the Civilian Conservation Corps was mopping up. The CCC was a Roosevelt make-work organization for young men hit hard by the Depression. They lived like soldiers—they even wore uniforms—and built roads and bridges across the state.

My mother tucked us into bed early, but her fear had rubbed off on me, so I spent a fretful night imagining the fire raged just outside our door. The next morning at seven, she roused me from a fitful sleep, fed us children our breakfast, and sent us off to school.

The air held an acrid tinge of wood smoke, the only remaining trace of the dense smoke clouds that had filled yesterday's sky. After an uneventful morning at school and a light lunch at home, we settled back in for our afternoon session.

By the time afternoon recess rolled around, the wind had swung around to the northwest. A pall of hazy blue smoke hung over the schoolyard. Some of us boys crossed the road and climbed Dave's Hill. From a perch high in a tall fir, we could see a mile or more to the north, where hungry flames devoured trees and threw up swirling clouds of smoke.

The raging forest fire was making hard for Five Islands.

After recess a worried Mrs. McMahan hurried us into the classroom. "Children, there will be no more school today. I want you all to go straight home, don't dally."

She didn't explain the urgency, but most of us already knew why.

My father was drawing buckets of water from the well to wet down the house when I arrived. My mother, deeply afraid, divided her time between peering nervously out the windows and preparing a sparse supper.

Around 6:30 my father rushed in: "Get the children together. We have to leave now!"

Alarmed by his stern tone, I ran outside and was overwhelmed by the magnitude of the conflagration: to the north, trees exploded into flames, live embers rained down, and a dense blanket of roiling black smoke darkened the sky.

With only the clothes on our backs, we piled into the car and cleared the village, our headlights piercing the smoky gloom. I didn't look back.

"I'm afraid the house won't make it," my father warned. My mother just stared straight ahead.

The Town Hall, a few miles down the road in Georgetown Center, had been opened as a shelter. My father dropped us off and returned to the village. Several families were already there, but the hall, with only hard chairs and a few crude tables, was ill equipped to accommodate us. I sat by the window, staring fearfully toward Five Islands, where I imagined I could see flames towering above the trees and my home. The bungalow wasn't much, but it was all we had.

From time to time a neighbor from Five Islands came in with news. Some of the villagers without cars had literally run for their lives; others gathered at the town wharf waiting to be evacuated by water. A fire engine from Bath was set up at Hite's Pond in the heart of the village and was pumping water onto the most threatened homes. The National Guard formed a bucket brigade with a group of volunteers from Bowdoin College. Despite these efforts, the reports were depressing.

"Ellie Pinkham's house is gone."

"William Marr's is gone."

When Mary and Irving grew tired and fussy, my mother made them a bed on the floor out of an enormous American flag borrowed from the storage room. Later, relief came—Red Cross, I think—and brought cots and blankets. With them came news that the wind had shifted around to the west, sparing the center of the village. My mother put me into a cot and tucked me in. I soon dropped into an exhausted sleep.

The next morning my father came to take us home. Our bungalow had been spared, but we were unprepared for the devastation in our end of the village—solitary chimneys rose starkly from smoldering ruins. To the north, only a cluster of blackened skeletons remained of what only the previous day had been a stand of graceful evergreens. In all, three year-round homes and ten cottages had been reduced to ashes, but the blaze had been stopped at the edge of Sheepscot Bay, just north of the general store.

The Red Cross rebuilt homes for Uncle Ellie Pinkham and William Marr. I heard a neighbor remark that it was a shame our bungalow hadn't gone up along with the others, so the Red Cross could build us a new one. When I saw the nice new home they were building for William Marr, I sort of wished it had, too.

By the following summer a few new cottages dotted the devastated ridge overlooking Sheepscot Bay. More would be built in the coming months. The village recovered quickly, but the healing of the surrounding woods and our emotions took much longer. Years passed before I could listen to the wail of a siren or see the glow of fire against a night sky without a tide of panic rising within me.

Shortly after the fire, the Five Islands men—my father included—gathered to talk about getting enough equipment together so that they'd be prepared if another fire sprang up. At that meeting the Five Islands Fire Fighters was formed. My father was proud to sign up as a charter member.

Their first piece of firefighting equipment was a gas-powered portable pump. When there was a fire, it was rolled onto the back of a pickup truck and brought to the scene. Sometimes, the men could do no more than save the cellar. Their back pumps came in handy for preventing the fire's spread. Later they would buy a 1928 REO— hand-cranked—with a water tank on behind. Both were stored in a one-room building beside the church—Charlie Mack's old Hockomock Spruce Gum Shop, actually. Charlie and his gum had long since passed on by then.

11

QUARANTINED

I returned to school in September of 1934, a proud eight-year-old fourth-grader. We had put the fire behind us, but something even worse lurked just down the calendar.

In October, one of the schoolchildren coughed in the schoolyard during recess. It wasn't an ordinary kind of cough. It was more of a hoot. Mrs. McMahan heard it and wouldn't let him back inside. She said it sounded like whooping cough and sent him home with a note to see the town health officer.

Whooping cough it was. One by one, our school friends gave out with that distinctive *whoop-whoop* and were sent home to stay for the "catching period," as my mother called it. The incubation period carried a quarantine with it; you couldn't leave your yard for six weeks.

November replaced October, and still the four of us Hanna kids couldn't come up with a whoop to call our own. My mother was breathing easier, which was a mistake. You shouldn't ever breathe easier at the bungalow. A cold snap hit us and the water in our pipe froze, making the pump useless until spring. My father was forced to draw our wash and bath water from the ice-covered well with a well pole, one bucket at a time.

It was Irving who actually carried the whooping cough into our house. He was playing on the kitchen floor one day when he gave

out with that short, sharp sound. That one whoop was the extent of
his bout with the whooping cough. Not so for the rest of us. In quick
succession, I came down with it, then Cora, and finally Mary.

It took twelve weeks for the disease to run its course—six weeks
coming and six weeks going was what they said. For about a week, it
was nothing more than a dry cough and a runny nose; then it began in
earnest. First the whooping, then the vomiting, and, occasionally, the
suffocating attack our mother warned us about. "Sometimes you'll
catch your breath, then you won't be able to get it again," she said.

The remark might not have made a whole lot of sense to an out-
sider, and wasn't clear to me, either, until that first breathtaking
attack. "But don't panic," she added. "Stay calm and you'll be all right."

I kept her advice in mind until the night Mary, only four, gave
us all a big scare. We had just finished supper. That's when the most
violent coughing spasms seemed to come on, and we'd fight to hold
down our meal. Mary began a series of violent whoops, tossed up
her supper, then quit breathing. My mother panicked, but my father
grabbed Mary up into his arms and began to blow on her face. When
she didn't respond, he tried bouncing her into the air, also to no
avail. Her face was turning blue. He opened the kitchen door, carried her out into the near-zero weather, and plunged her face into
the snow. Sudden contact with the frigid air and the cold snow must
have shocked her. She began to breathe again. I took in the whole
scene and was left shaken and fearful that it might happen to me.

And it did. Blame it on the cod liver oil.

Both my father and my mother swore by the power of cod liver
oil to prevent and sometimes even cure disease. Because of my
father's poor health, I supposed that his mother had gone easy on the
cod liver oil.

"It'll keep you from getting hydrophobia," my mother always said
when we were forced to take any icky medication. I had no idea what

hydrophobia was, but I knew it must be a terrible disease if it took something as awful as cod liver oil to cure it. My father was no stranger to exotic diseases, either. With him, it was the epizootic. Whenever he came down with one of his sneezing fits, probably from the dust under his bed, he'd say he was coming down with the epizootic. As far as I know, nobody in Five Islands ever came down with the epizootic. Makes sense, since an epizootic is an epidemic among animals.

After supper every whooping-cough evening, my father gave us each a spoonful of cod liver oil. His wintertime cure-all would save us from the cough, he said. I hated the oily yellow liquid that stank of fish. One night I clamped my jaw and refused to take it. My father, not one to take no for an answer, pinched my nose, then forced my mouth open and dumped in a spoonful. Once out of his grasp, I gave one big whoop and ran for the slop bucket to throw it up, along with half my meal. On the second whoop, I involuntarily sucked in a great volume of air and it caught. I couldn't expel it. I felt suffocated, then I panicked. I danced crazily around the kitchen, desperately struggling for air and hoping someone would help.

My father had little sympathy. "You're doing that on purpose," he shouted at me, "just so you can get away with spittin' out the cod liver oil."

This time my mother came to my rescue. She gently sat me down in a chair, all the while talking to me, soothing and calming. Gradually, the paroxysms subsided. I lay back against the chair. As I began to breathe more freely, I understood my mother's meaning about catching my breath and not being able to get it back. The air had caught in my lungs, I couldn't let it out or take in more. There'd be other spasms, but I'd handle them, sometimes with my mother's help. And I'd survive in spite of that cod liver oil.

In late February the weeks of confinement dwindled to the last few days. The fits of coughing came less frequently and we no longer

Courtesy of Cora M. Owen

Cora, me, Irving and Mary in 1934.

upchucked our food. My struggle was nearly done, but Cora's was just beginning. She developed a severe earache. Earaches were not uncommon in our family in those days, and mother had just the remedy. She'd heat a flatiron on the stovetop, wrap it in a towel and hold it against our ear while she poured vinegar over it. The steam usually stopped the ache. At times, though, the remedy didn't work out as planned. Once, the iron slipped out of the towel and slid across my mouth. My lips were scabbed over for some time after. People looked surprised and somewhat skeptical when I explained that my injury was caused by an earache.

This time vinegar didn't help Cora, either. A lump formed behind her ear, until it bulged from her head. She screamed from the pain of it. Her obvious pain drove my father to ask a nurse in town to look at her. She chastised him for his delay.

"All this time and you've not had her seen to? That child has to see a doctor," she told him. "She has a mastoid infection. She'll need surgery right away or she'll die."

They took Cora to Dr. Kirschner in Bath, who immediately admitted Cora to the hospital, operated and removed the infected mastoid bone. The doctor said she'd have to stay in Bath where he could check the drain he had placed in the incision. Aunt May, always my mother's protector, decided that Cora would stay with her until she was well enough to come home to Five Islands. My father didn't object.

No eight-year-old boy worth his salt would ever admit that he missed his ten-year-old sister, and I suppose I was no different. For the first couple of weeks, at least, I hardly even mentioned her name.

Spring had come, the ice had left Hite's Pond and it was time for frog eggs, tadpoles, pollywogs, and peepers. Irving and I would dip our hands into the frigid water in search of jellied masses of frogs' eggs. We'd put them into a tub of water outside the house and watch them until the tiny black tadpoles emerged; then we'd return the wriggling mass to the pond.

We were up to our elbows in icy water one morning when Eliot Bold, driving a truckload of building materials, rolled to a stop at the edge of the pond. Eliot lived in Bath, but was married to a Five Islands girl. He and the man with him unloaded boards, beams, nails and steel panels and carried them to a ledge on the far side of the pond behind the dance hall. Irving and I wandered over to watch.

"Watcha goin' to build?" Irving wanted to know.

"A movie theater," he said.

"Must be an awful small movie," I said, sizing up the pile of lumber.

He explained that the movie would be inside the dance hall. This was just for the powerhouse. He was building his own generator with an automobile engine.

Imagine that! A movie theater right here in Five Islands—with electricity. I couldn't wait to see my very first motion picture show. I ran all the way home to tell my folks the good news.

My mother was ready with a bucket of cold water.

"Movies are an instrument of the Devil," she declared.

It seemed to me that any fun thing a Five Islands church member did was sinful. Even the Saturday night dances were in trouble. That dance hall, the same one she and my father had danced in, had become a den of iniquity, she told me. "You're not to go near that place when a movie is showing. And that goes for dances, too."

And that was that.

But sometimes I'd stop by and peek through the dance hall door to check Eliot's progress. He built a projection booth above the front entrance. The movie screen was on the stage at the back of the building. The seats were removable folding chairs, spread out along the dance hall floor. Outside, he hung a marquee taken from a demolished theater in Bath.

Eliot opened the Liberty Theater sometime in May. Whenever he fired up his generator, the sound carried all the way to the bungalow. I'd sit on the broom platform just outside the door and wish I could be at the theater with the others. One evening I couldn't stand it anymore. I just had to take a peek. I sneaked down through the swamp, circled around Hite's Pond and crept as close to the dance hall as I dared. I tried to peek in, but I couldn't see through the windows. I put my ear against the wall. I could hear scary noises and talking, but I couldn't make out any words.

I was still straining to hear, when Eliot's generator quit and there was dead silence inside, except for a few boos. It stayed that way until Eliot ran out back and restarted his engine. I probably would have listened some more, but I had to be back in my yard before my mother knew I was missing. Long after I'd gone to bed, I lay awake and tried to imagine just what had made those creepy sounds.

The next day I listened in disappointed silence while the other boys described in frightening detail the gruesome features of Frankenstein—or was it the creature from *The Mummy's Tomb*?

I visited the theater a few more times that summer, but I wouldn't see my first movie for another four years.

It was late spring and Cora was still in Bath. I missed her and wanted her home with us. I began to ask my mother, "When's Cora coming home?" Her reply was always the same. "When the doctor says she can." I asked every day, until my mother announced, "Cora will be home tomorrow."

The next morning, I was up at dawn. I was standing out front by the side of the road when the taxi Aunt May had hired to bring Cora home pulled up. There was a whole lot of hugging and excited chatter as we went back inside; then we joined hands and the four of us kids walked down to the store to let the whole town know that our sister was home.

Meanwhile, the Hannas saw the next concrete sign of help from Roosevelt's New Deal. The president had decided that his surplus food dole was not enough; the food takers needed work, for their self-respect if nothing else. It came through the Work Progress Administration (WPA), another government program that provided jobs and small incomes to the jobless. In some areas, the work meant building schools, hospitals and airports. It came to Georgetown Island in 1934 in the form of road construction.

If ever there were roads that needed fixing, Georgetown had them. From the S-turn near the Arrowsic-Georgetown bridge to Five Islands, old rutted wagon roads still snaked their way across the island. Spring thaws sometimes left our car stranded in the middle of a Georgetown road, mired to the hubcaps. My father took to carrying an old mattress in the back of CS 1. With that, and a few choice cusswords, he could back the Studebaker out of just about any rut Georgetown roads had to offer.

He signed on as Georgetown's first WPA road builder. He was handed a shovel and sent to the other side of town in the back of a dump truck, a bona fide, twelve-dollar-a week, full-time working man. And what a job he and the other full-time road builders did. With shovels and pickaxes, and a little help from a grader and a couple of dynamiters, they straightened, graded, and leveled. Even the S-turn was dynamited away so a new road could pass straight through. They topped the whole new road with a coat of tar. Later, the three rickety, water-level wooden bridges between Five Islands and Arrowsic were replaced by high-level steel ones.

Not everyone in Georgetown was as happy as the shovelers to see the WPA come to town. A joke started going around that all Maine hunting licenses should warn hunters not to shoot anything standing still because it might be a WPA worker.

Another joke claimed that it took two WPA workers to do each job—one to dig the hole and the other to fill it up again. My father said that he hadn't heard of any jokester who'd refused to drive on the new tarred roads. With his new job and a small but steady paycheck, my father was again able to buy and pay for his groceries at Savage's store along with the other customers.

12

SADIE AND CLAYTON

In the summer of 1935 I was almost nine. The nation was six years
into the Great Depression. We had been living at the bungalow for
six years as well, and except for our useless well, nothing had been
done much in the way of home improvements. When the WPA work
ended, my father limped along, taking sporadic carpentry jobs and
struggling to make ends meet.

I went to Vacation Bible School and sailed Irving's toy sloop on
Hite's Pond. Grampa Hanna had given him this very special boat with
a green hull and deep keel. Irving called it his *Sky Pilot*, named in
honor of the sloop Grampa piloted for the Boyntons. When a breeze
filled the white sails, it sometimes skimmed all the way to the far
shore. We four Hanna kids expected our fun to last until Labor Day,
unaware that our parents were about to disrupt those carefree days.

One July evening they sat us down at the kitchen table. "What
would you think of a new baby brother or sister?" my mother asked.

I doubted we could find sleeping space in the bungalow for
even one more little one, and I said so.

Babies were gifts from God, she said, and He'd want us to
make room for the new one.

"But where can you make room for it?" I asked. I worried that
someone might soon be crowding in between Irving and me.

"We'll put a crib in the bedroom with your father and me for the time being."

"When's the baby coming?" Cora wanted to know.

"Dr. Barrows will deliver it sometime in August, but we'll have to start making plans now."

Dr. Barrows had delivered Mary at our bungalow five years earlier. I'd been too young to remember if any plans were made then.

"After the baby arrives, your mother will have to stay in bed for a week or so," my father took over.

A week in bed? Who'd look after us kids? He said he'd asked Sadie, a woman from out Brunswick way, to come and stay with us. She was a widow woman who earned her keep by taking care of other people's children. I didn't know it then, but she wasn't coming all that distance just to take care of us children; she was also a midwife. She was the backup in case Dr. Barrows was delayed. He lived in Boothbay on the far side of the Sheepscot across several miles of open water. If the weather turned nasty, he might be late, and Sadie would have to begin the delivery.

Cora wondered where we'd all sleep with only three bedrooms. My father had the answer. Cora would visit with a cousin in Kittery. He and my mother would take over Cora's room. Mary, Irving and I could have the master bedroom where there were two extra feet of floor space for me to sleep on with a pillow and a blanket, while Mary and Irving slept in the bed.

Everyone, even Sadie, was getting a bed with a mattress except me. It didn't seem fair. When I complained about having to lie on the hard floor, he reminded me that it would only be for two or three weeks at most.

I accepted the arrangement grudgingly and was still pouting on the August morning when Sadie blew in. She was a buxom woman

with graying hair and a take-charge attitude. A suitcase in one hand
and a hymnal in the other, she took over our house.

Her first words to Irving and me were, "I want you boys out
from underfoot."

Then she opened the door and shooed us outside. Fresh air
would do us good, she said. She must have thought that small boys
and the great out of doors belonged together, because for the next
couple of weeks we'd spend most of our days in the skimpy shade of
the backyard maples.

I wanted to take Irving to Hite's Pond to sail his boat. She
wouldn't have it. We stayed right there in the yard where she could
keep an eye on us and sailed Irving's *Sky Pilot* in a washtub under the
trees. She made quite a fuss over that boat. She'd stand in the doorway
and watch us try to blow a little air into its sails. She said we were
lucky, that her little grandson would just love to have a boat like that.

We discovered right away that Sadie's hymnal wasn't just win-
dow dressing; she was a first-rate, born-again Bible-thumper without
peer. She was filled right up to here with that Old-Time Religion.
And she was right at home in the Five Islands Baptist Church.
Whenever services were held—Sunday afternoon, Sunday evening,
Wednesday evening—she attended. On weekdays, around the house,
she sang hymns at the top of her voice. She swept the floors to
"Sweet Hour of Prayer" and cooked to a chorus of "Church in the
Wildwood." She thumped a wooden spoon against the cupboard to
the beat of "Come, Come, Come."

Sadie also fretted about the condition of my soul and bugged
my father about it. "That boy ought to be baptized," she told him one
day. "It'll keep his soul from the fires of Hell."

My father allowed that I was still a tad too young. I was with
him all the way. I wasn't about to be dunked in the chilly waters of

Dave's Cove with the congregation standing on the shore singing "Nearer My God to Thee," even if it would save me from a scorched soul.

Unfortunately for Irving and me, Sadie's concern for my soul never seemed to discourage her from hectoring us—just words at first. Then one morning, as Irving and I sat at our little table under the maple tree, she came out onto the back step and tossed a pan of dishwater all over us.

"I'm goin' to tell my father," Irving screamed at her.

She ignored him and went back inside, chuckling to herself, while we tried to clean up the mess.

My father was hardly into the yard when Irving waylaid him and complained about the dishwater. His face took on an expression that said we were probably somehow to blame for it. We must have gotten in her way. Sadie wouldn't do a thing like that on purpose. Sadie told him exactly what he expected to hear. She'd just tossed out the water. Some of it might have landed on us. He shrugged and that was the end of it.

Sadie had been there less than a week, when I awoke early one morning to excited conversation filtering through the paper-thin walls of Mama's bedroom. "I'll go down to the store and call Dr. Barrows," I heard my father say. Then he must have looked out the window. "Oh my Lord, it's like pea soup out there." A dense fog meant that Dr. Barrows might not arrive for some time.

Although I still didn't understand the need for such urgency, I wanted to be in on the excitement. I jumped up, hurriedly slipped into my clothes and met my father in the kitchen. Sadie was up and had a kettle of water on to boil. My father and I ran to Percy's store. He used the pay phone inside to call for Dr. Barrows.

Grandpa Rowe came out of the post office to see what was going on. My father told him why we were there. "Dr. Barrows is on his way. He says they'll need help locating Five Islands once they are out on the open bay."

"As soon as I bag the mail," Grandpa said, "I'll get my megaphone."

We made our way to the wharf beside the store. The fog was so thick we couldn't see the boats moored in the harbor. When Grandpa joined us, we huddled in the wetness that engulfed us until we heard the throb of a marine engine.

My father cupped his hands around his mouth and called, "Hello, Hello. Five Islands over here." Grandpa joined in and soon the three of us were shouting directions to the invisible Dr. Barrows. From a distance, we heard an answering, "Hello, Five Islands."

Within minutes the boat idled into the landing and Dr. Barrows climbed out carrying his black bag. We hurried him up the road to the house.

I had hoped that I could stick around and find out what this delivery business was all about, but my father sent me and Irving to visit Grandma Hanna for the day.

After we explained to Grandma the reason for our visit, she shooed us outside. She must have been talking to Sadie about the fresh air thing. To her credit, though, she did let us sit at the kitchen table for lunch.

When Grampa Hanna came home from work that afternoon, he said my father wanted us to come home.

"Did the doctor deliver the baby?" I inquired.

"He surely did," Grampa replied. "It was a boy. A big one, too. Over ten pounds."

Ten pounds didn't sound so big to me. We had a cat bigger than that.

We raced home and stormed into the house to see what the doctor had brought in out of the fog. The baby was at the foot of Ma's bed, where Sadie was changing his diaper.

He was a boy all right, all red-faced with his eyes shut tight. He didn't look like a ten-pounder to me. I wanted to hold him, but Sadie said no.

"Boys, meet your new brother, Clayton," my mother said.

That's when I noticed just how thin she looked.

Sadie was an industrious woman from the Idle Mind–Devil's Workshop School. When she wasn't hymning her way through housework or tending the baby, she was casting about for ways to spruce up the bungalow.

"These old walls are awful bare and dingy," she told my father when he came home from work the next afternoon. "They need brightenin' up; they ought to be papered." Sadie was also outspoken.

She was right. The heavy, brown corrugated-cardboard walls had become soiled and worn. My father planned one day to wallpaper them when he had the price of a few rolls.

"Maybe I can do a little something to brighten up the place while I'm here," she said.

That's where my father made a fateful mistake; he didn't ask what kind of "brightenin' up" she had in mind. Sadie took it as a go-ahead.

After my father left for work the following morning, she put Irving and me outside for another day in the fresh air. With my mother and Clayton in the bedroom and Mary too young to cause much fuss, Sadie was free to tackle the project. From our location under the maple tree, we could hear her warm to her task with "Work, for the Night Is Coming," one of her favorite hymns.

My father came home late that afternoon and we went inside with him. When he opened the kitchen door, he stopped in his tracks, his mouth agape. She had kept her word; the kitchen walls certainly were brighter. She had papered them with pictures, some black-and-white, cut from newspapers and magazines, and a few in full color from Lord knows where.

I expected my father would blow up right then and there, but all he said was, "Sadie, whatever possessed you to do a thing like this?"

Sadie was unfazed.

"I did my cousin's house, and she thought it was lovely." She moved toward the living room. "Wait'll you see what I did in here."

She had "done" the living room in early newspaper—walls and ceiling—covered with sports, advertisements, obituaries. My father said nothing; he just jammed his hat back onto his head and went outside. I didn't go with him, but through the open door I thought I heard him mutter a "knock-kneed" or two. After a while he came back inside and no more was said about Sadie's handiwork.

Soon after her decor disaster, it finally came time for Sadie to leave. On the eve of her departure, Irving's *Sky Pilot* disappeared. We searched the house and the yard, but it didn't turn up. We peeked into Sadie's room. Her half-packed suitcase was open on the bed. The sloop was right in there, beside her underdrawers. Irving wanted to take it out, but I thought we ought to leave it there until my father could see it. Then I waited for him to confront Sadie with it.

After he got home from work, we cornered her in her room. He pointed to the boat. "All right, Sadie—how come?"

Her cheeks flushed and her face got sheepish. For a while she just stood there blushing. Then she said, "I don't know how it could have got there. One of the boys must have dropped it in there when they were playing and forgot about it."

She didn't fool me for a second, but my father was teetering. Before he could open his mouth she reached into her suitcase, took out a worn copy of a New Testament, and handed it to me. She said it had belonged to her nephew. She'd been saving it just for me, she claimed.

My father wilted. His scowl faded, and when he spoke his tone had changed. "That's nice of you, Sadie." He turned to me. "Thank Sadie for the gift."

I didn't have a great deal of use for a testament, new or old, but I wouldn't be an ingrate before my father's very eyes. After I'd mumbled my thanks, he said, "You can take that to Sunday School next week. You and Irving can use it together."

Then, he took Irving's sailboat out of her suitcase, but instead of handing it back to Irving, he held it out for Sadie.

"Why don't you take this for your little grandson?"

Sadie must have thanked him a half-dozen times before he left her room. She and my father may have been pleased with the swap, but Irving and I didn't think a beat-up testament was a fair exchange for a sailboat that could sail clear across Hite's Pond all by itself.

The next day one of Sadie's country cousins came and took her away. I never saw her again, or ever wanted to. We were all happy to see her go, though her papering artistry stayed on. My father could never find the means to replace those bits of historical trivia pasted to our living room walls and ceiling. They became a part of the bungalow's long-term decor. I can still recall that a brand spanking new 1935 Ford cost five hundred dollars, and you could see *Mutiny on the Bounty* at a Portland theater for twenty-five cents.

While Sadie was gone, the new baby—Hanna child number five—was not. This would be the last time I'd make such a fuss over the arrival of a new baby in the bungalow. Before the next birthing, I'd learn that the Overseer of the Poor had arranged for the town to pay Dr. Barrows for the delivery and Sadie for her services to our family—the Hanna family was truly "on the town."

Those events signaled the beginning of my father's regular dependence on the town to support his growing family. No self-respecting family in fiercely independent, staunchly Republican Georgetown could be long beholden to the town and still keep its head held high.

13

Reluctant Baptist

C layton's arrival in 1935 marked the first of a number of changes for my family. The bungalow with the new baby, plus the four older children, was more crowded than ever. As my father was forced to accept more and more handouts from the town, he grew quiet and cranky. Our evening sessions around the table became increasingly less frequent, until finally, the reading, singing and storytelling became just a memory.

There was change in my mother, too. When Clayton was about six months old, she decided she had to get out of the house once in a while. I knew she was planning some kind of an outing when she broke out her hair curler one Sunday morning. I was fascinated by the way she set her hair. She'd light the kerosene lamp on the kitchen table, stick a curling iron down inside the chimney, and then wet down her hair while she waited for the iron to heat. Then she'd separate a few hairs just above her forehead and apply the hot curler, leaving behind a twenties-style crimped wave and a few singed hairs in the bargain.

While she crimped, she told me she had plans to attend evening services at the Five Islands church. She'd been so busy getting us children off to Sunday School, she said, that she'd been neglecting her own spiritual needs. Sadie must have talked to her

about her immortal soul, too. My mother decided that taking me
along with her wouldn't do my soul any harm, either. I squawked
because I figured Sunday nights were mostly for praying out loud and
testimony by those hard-core believers who hadn't gotten their fill of
religion in the afternoon. But I felt somewhat better about it when
my mother said there'd be a whole lot of hymn-singing—my favorite
part of the service.

We arrived at the church just as the meeting was about to
begin, and took a seat in front of deacons George Gray and Jimmy
Stevens. I loved to sit near Jimmy because he had a fine bass voice
that could make my seat vibrate. I was glad we had arrived on time;
most of the singing was done early. Except for an open Bible on the
pulpit at center stage, there was nothing much to remind me that
this was the house of God. There wasn't even a picture of The
Almighty with his long white hair and flowing beard. The mural on
the wall behind the pulpit helped somewhat. It showed a lighthouse
on a shore looking out to sea. I imagined it sending its beam across a
dark and angry ocean. It reminded me of the hymn, "Let The Lower
Lights Be Burning."

After a time, the leader of the service called a halt to the
singing and the praying and announced it was time to give testimony.
I hadn't heard that word since Sadie. One by one without prodding,
each faithful Christian stood and said a few words in praise of God.
Some would tell of a recent experience that had strengthened their
faith and changed their lives. Others would detail some past trans-
gression and say how happy they were to be saved.

Testimony time was Deacon Gray's favorite part of the service.
It usually roused his soul-saving zeal to a fever pitch. Aside from giving his own testimony, nothing gave him more satisfaction than to
see the younger ones at the service stand and do likewise. That

The Five Islands Baptist Church.

evening, he must have seen in me the makings of a rank backslider—like my father—a circumstance he planned to rectify at once.

He leaned forward, poked me in the ribs and whispered in my ear, "Get up and say you love the Lord!" My shyness would never permit me to stand and make such a public declaration of faith. Besides, I still wasn't sure I had any faith to declare, and I didn't want to be a hypocrite, someone whose traits were to be detested more than those of a backslider. I ignored him.

A minute later, another poke. "Get up; say it now!" By the third poke, I knew I'd have to do something, or suffer a cracked rib. During the next lull in the testimony, I leaped to my feet and shouted, "I love the Lord!" Then, red-faced, I sat down to a chorus of "Hallelujahs" and a "Praise the Lord" or two.

I spent the rest of the meeting wishing I could crawl under the seat and hoping for an early benediction. My mother saw I wasn't ready for such open expressions of faith; she didn't insist that I go to another evening service until I was somewhat older. If Deacon Gray was bent on rescuing a young soul he thought needed saving, he'd have to do it without any assistance from me.

Prayer was a nightly ritual at the bungalow, however, and Sunday School was still mandatory. Every bedtime my mother listened while Irving and I went through our "Now-I-lay-me-down-to-sleep" prayers, to ensure God's blessing, she said. We hadn't seen a blessing for so long, I doubted I'd recognize one if it landed right in the middle of my dinner plate, which most needed whatever He had to give.

It was the Sunday School teacher, Lloyd Pinkham—a good man and a devout Christian in the finest Baptist tradition—who helped me with my prayer doubts. One Sunday I told Lloyd I was too big for "Now-I-lay-me." He agreed. It was time for grown-up prayers, he told me. I could just use my own words the way grown-ups did, and I didn't even have to say it out loud. That sounded reasonable to me. The "Now-I-lay-me's" weren't getting anything done, so I was ready to try anything. Right there in my pew, I decided to test it out. I sent off a silent plea—please send me a nickel for candy—not expecting to hear back anytime soon.

Irving and I were walking home from Sunday School that afternoon, when Irving spied a small leather change purse lying in the road. Inside was a whole shiny nickel. God surely hadn't wasted any time answering my first grown-up prayer.

"That nickel is mine," I told him.

He didn't see it that way. "I found it—finder's keeper's."

I explained about the grown-up prayer, but he wasn't having any of it. I could see heaven's gift slipping away. "Of course," I reasoned, "the Christian thing to do is share. Half of it is yours."

He knew I might take it from him anyway, so he agreed, and we were soon mulling over the kinds of candies we each could buy for half a nickel.

I had planned to keep the nickel a secret from my mother, but Irving couldn't wait to blab. She saw my newfound power of prayer in a whole other light.

"That nickel belongs to someone in this town," she said. "They probably dropped it. And they may be looking for it right this minute."

"He put it there for me to find," I argued.

"Maybe He put it there to test you, to see how honest you are. So why don't you wait for a few days to see if anybody claims it. If they don't, then it's yours."

I favored Irving's finder's-keeper's position, but I knew she was right. We both agreed to wait. I still had hopes that God wouldn't let anybody claim it.

We hadn't been home long when Cora came in along with her Sunday School teacher, my mother's cousin, Alice Cromwell, who was to take supper with us. Over Scrapple—a canned food that tasted a lot like sausage—scrambled eggs and hot tea, my mother told Alice about the purse with the nickel in it, and how we were trying to find the owner.

Our search ended right there at the table. Alice thought that the purse might be hers. She had lost one just that morning on the way to her neighbor's.

I showed her the purse. She identified it, nickel and all, and thanked us for getting it back to her. She sided with my mother. God had indeed been testing us, she said, and we'd passed with honors.

I was glad Alice had found her purse, but I figured there'd been some kind of mix-up, and I'd been sent the wrong nickel. Even so, I hoped He might persuade Alice to spare a penny reward out of that nickel. Honesty has its own reward, my mother had always said, but I preferred cash. If He did speak to Alice, she didn't hear. Still, the whole thing hadn't been a total loss. I'd learned a valuable lesson about honesty. On the other hand, I still wasn't sure whether my first real prayer had been answered, or if any prayer ever would be answered. Even so, all these years later, I still give it a try now and again.

14

SON OF A SALESMAN

I'd always taken an interest in my father's sales jobs. No matter what other job he had at any particular time—caretaking, WPA work, carpentry—he'd always supplement those wages by selling. Fire extinguishers, condiments, shoes, plants and bushes, he sold them all. When there was no school he'd sometimes take me along with him on his route. He made selling look easy. I wanted to try my hand at it.

I was thumbing through an old magazine someone had given us, when I spotted an eye-catching ad. BOYS, EARN VALUABLE PRIZES, it said. Then, in smaller letters, SELL CLOVERINE SALVE. It went on to say how an ambitious salesboy might even earn a bicycle. "Send today for a free catalog of prizes," I read.

I was hooked.

Cloverine Salve was an ointment with amazing healing powers. Almost every home in Five Islands kept at least one of those little round, flat cans on hand for cuts, burns, and scratches. Some of the older boys in the village had sold it in the past, but nobody that I knew had ever earned any really big prizes. I'd be the Georgetown Island Cloverine salesboy.

I mentioned it to my father and he was delighted. He handed me a sheet of paper and a pencil and I scrawled a short note asking for the catalog. Then I hung around the post office every day at mail time until my Cloverine Salve packet arrived. There was the promised catalog and a personal letter to me from the sales manager.

"Dear Cloverine Salesboy," he began, and explained that the salve cans came in tubes of twelve cans each and sold for twenty-five cents a can. He told me how easy it was to put a can of this miraculous ointment in every household. Boys were winning fabulous prizes every day, he said. Or, I could save the credit for what I'd sold and put it toward a larger gift, maybe even a bicycle.

When I got to the part where he signed it "Sincerely yours," I knew he had been speaking directly to me. A good Cloverine Soldier, I'd march out and conquer Georgetown.

I flipped through the prize catalog where I saw everything from a pencil box for two or three tubes, to the bicycle for a hundred or so tubes. Somewhere in between, there was a baseball glove. I decided that my first order ought to be at least a half-dozen tubes, and I told my father so.

He praised my enthusiasm, but offered a word of caution.

"Maybe you ought to go slow until you find out if you're going to like selling. Why don't you start with two tubes? If they sell, you can order more."

"It'll take forever to get a real good prize that way."

"I'll tell you what," he said. "If you sell the first two tubes right here in Five Islands, I'll take you along with me when I go selling. That way, you can cover the whole town."

He was right, and I knew it. I ordered two tubes. When they came, I hit the road and soon discovered just how hard it would be to sell twenty-four cans of salve in a village of fifty homes. My father took me on the road to Georgetown to finish the last few cans. I wasn't discouraged, though. Selling was in my blood.

I ordered two more tubes. Over the next several weeks I sold them, but the effort took in all of Georgetown and a fringe of Arrowsic. I ordered another tube, hoping to cover Woolwich. Sales were slow, and I was growing impatient. I wanted a reward for my effort right away. I cashed in the credit for the first two tubes and sent for the pencil box. The rest I planned to put toward the glove. The box was a beauty, made of heavy blue cardboard. The top compartment held several pencils and erasers. In a drawer underneath, I found a dividing compass and a protractor. I took it to school every day and kept it on top of my desk where I could inhale that new pencil box smell.

I finally sold the last of the salve, but I knew that the salve wasn't enough. I'd need more than one product. My father was peddling a half-dozen products at a time; I should be able to handle two. I scoured every magazine I could lay my hands on, looking for a favorable sales opportunity.

Finally I saw an invitation for a bright young boy to sell colorful stamps to stick on letters and packages. Convinced that I was that bright young boy, I sat down and dashed off a letter—this time without letting my father know—and told them I was their man. In return, they sent me enough stamps to cover every letter and package in Sagadahoc County for the next year. The stamps they sent weren't all that colorful, and the prizes didn't measure up to Cloverine Salve's. I wanted to return them, but my father said that I should at least give it a try. I hit all my Cloverine customers. They weren't as ready to buy as I had thought they would be. Some did buy my stamps, as a favor, but sales were slow. I soon tired of the stamp business. I told my father that I would retire from it as soon as I had sold all my stamps. I put my money into a can and set it, along with the unsold stamps, on a shelf in the kitchen cupboard beside my Cloverine can. It would stay there until I had sold enough stamps to send for a worthwhile gift.

There had always been a radio in the bungalow. My mother's Aunt May had given her an early model when she was first married. From my earliest memories, it had sat on a small table in the living room. It wasn't much more than a long, low wooden box, stained a dark mahogany with a hinged cover on top, which lifted to reveal several tubes, a couple of tuners and little else. On the front panel there was an on/off toggle switch and two large dials, one for tuning in a station and one to control the volume. There was no speaker. Two earphone jacks, one at each end of the panel, allowed only two listeners to hear a program. I can still recall my parents sitting in front of the set, each with a pair of headphones plugged into the jacks, listening to *Amos and Andy*. Occasionally, my father would put the earphones on my head so I could listen to the voices coming over the airways.

Reception was poor. To bring in the Portland stations, my father put up a twenty-foot pole a good fifty feet from the house and ran a wire from the roof of the house to the pole. A wire running from the roof through the living room window attached to the back of the radio to boost reception. Our radio was supersensitive. If we came too close to the set, it would whistle and squeak and squawk.

We had no electricity. No one in Five Islands did during the early 1930s. All radios in Five Islands were battery-powered. They ran on a six-volt automobile battery that would last only a few weeks. Kraft's Battery Service in Bath made regular trips to pick up the dead batteries and deliver freshly charged ones. The worst fate villagers could imagine was to be caught with a dead battery during a winter storm.

By the time Cora and I were old enough to listen, Uncle Bridge had built us a speaker, an eighteen-inch disc that sat on top of the set and plugged into one of the jacks. It was tinny and scratchy, but the whole family could listen at one time. We loved *Amos and Andy*, and on Sunday evenings, we gathered around for a half-hour with the unforgettable Moylan Sisters, followed by Olivio Santoro, Champion Boy Yodeler, with his Spanish guitar and a triple yodel. He was put on the air by Scrapple. He'd come on the air singing:

Scrapple-odle lay-de ay
Comes from Philadelph-eye-a.
Try it once and you'll agree
It's the food for you and me.

Then, I found *Tom Mix*. Olivio and the Moylans were no match for old Tom. Any boy in Five Islands who couldn't tell you that Tom Mix owned the TM Bar Ranch and was spiritual leader of the Ralston Straight Shooters just wasn't paying attention. He came on the radio in the early evening and fought rustlers, bank robbers and stagecoach bandits. The Straight Shooters always won. At the close of each show Tom Mix spoke directly to me and thousands of other boys, urging us to come forward and be Straight Shooters, too. All we had to do was send in Ralston box tops and twenty-five cents to get a Tom Mix ring with his own personal TM Bar brand on it. I was the first of many village boys to get my ring. When we met we'd flash them to show that we were fellow Straight Shooters. Ralston always seemed to taste better once I had my ring, too.

Tom was followed by *Jack Armstrong, The All-American Boy*, and Wheaties, Breakfast of Champions. They'd open the show with a bunch of guys singing:

Won't you try Wheaties?
They're whole wheat with all of our bran.
Won't you buy Wheaties?
The best breakfast food in the land.

Jack and a girl named Betty traveled with her uncle to exotic places and got caught up in exciting adventures. Jack offered a Dragon's Eye ring that glowed in the dark. The ring was a replica of the one he had somehow gotten from a tribesman in a steaming Philippine jungle. An All-American Boy could have one in exchange for Wheaties box tops and a few coins. Again, I led the All-American charge. The ring was a pale green plastic material with a jade green stone in the shape of an eye set on top. When I took it from a lighted space into a darkened room, it glowed and the eye stared at me. Whenever I went out to meet with the rest of the All-American Boys, the ring went with me. Soon, all us Straight Shooters were All-American Boys, too. And the Dragon's Eye took its place on the finger next to the TM Bar.

One evening, Jack told us that he wanted every All-American Boy to own the Jack Armstrong All-American pedometer, like the one he used to count the miles he walked through the jungles. More box tops, a few more coins, and I had mine. With it hooked to my belt, I clicked off the distances from my home to any point on the Five Islands side of the Georgetown bridge, including Mile Beach, years before it became Reid State Park.

Eventually, Kellogg cereals got into the box-top act. In exchange for Corn Flakes or Rice Krispies tops, they would send me large color prints of military aircraft. I liked the fighters best. Then it was Hood ice cream. A few lids from their Hoodsie Dixie Cups would get you a color picture of a movie star. Hoodsie lids were easier to come by than box tops. I could always find a few lying around outside the ice cream parlor or the store. And when word got around that I was collecting again, the whole village pitched in—even those who wouldn't touch a Hoodsie—until my movie stars outnumbered my aircraft.

Still I wanted more. I'd go anywhere, even risk my life for just one more Hoodsie lid. No challenge was too great. One day at high tide, I spotted two lids floating in the water under the wharf. Two were all I needed for one more picture—Tyrone Power, I think. Through an opening in the wharf, I could get down close to the water. My plan was to grab a beam and stand on a huge timber that floated on the surface. Once I got down in there and sat on the timber, the lids would be mine. My feet hit the timber and it immediately floated out from under me. I was left dangling over the open water with not enough strength to pull myself back up onto the wharf. I did the only thing a non-swimmer poised over water above his head could do; I screamed for help. Cora and two of her girlfriends were outside the store and came running. The three of them grabbed my arms and yanked me to safety. I was grateful to Cora until I found that she had blabbed the whole thing to my mother, and I came home to a tongue-lashing. I never collected another lid after that. My collection was big enough anyway.

Eventually my enthusiasm for collecting tapered off. I still treasured my pictures, but I had lost my TM Bar ring, the Dragon's Eye had faded and quit glowing, and the clicker in my pedometer began to lie to me. It was time for me to find my excitement elsewhere.

15

DADDY WAS A DREAMER, AND DESPERATE

My mama said my daddy was a born dreamer, always coming up with cockeyed notions that wouldn't amount to a Hannah Cook. She had a case.

One evening in 1936, we were sitting around the claw-footed oak table when my father mentioned that he'd soon be coming into some money. The government was going to give all World War I veterans the rest of the bonuses they were owed. Could be as much as five hundred dollars. I wondered what he'd do with all that money. I should have guessed he was already making plans, building another dream. Gilbert Lewis wanted to sell his farm on the Bay Point Road—the far side of Georgetown Island—for six hundred dollars. Daddy might try to buy it.

My Mama was leery right from the start. "How you goin' to run a farm all by yourself in your health? Jody Stevens is strong as an ox, and he still needs a full-time helper."

"The boys are getting bigger. They'll be able to help."

I'd had a taste of farm work, and I hated it. I'd been given the chore of weeding our postage-stamp plot. I didn't even want to think of an acre or two of weeds.

"And how will you plow the land? You don't own a horse like Jody does."

"Gus Collins will plow it with his tractor for a few bucks."

"And what will you do for money, once the bonus is spent?"

"We'll sell vegetables to the summer people. I'll put a stand out by the road."

He had an answer for everything.

We drove by the Lewis place every few days and gawked at the neat yellow farmhouse, the roomy barn out back and the open fields beyond. We didn't have a horse or a cow, but I was dreaming of playing in the hay in the barn loft.

When his check arrived reality head-butted his dreams. The creditors held out their hand for their share of his good fortune. Some even came knocking on his door. After the overdue bills were paid, there were only a few bonus dollars left. No more was said about the farm.

To my father, now nearly a decade after he started building it, the bungalow seemed more cramped and shabbier than ever; the tiny piece of swampland more confining. His dream bungalow remained a stilted, hip-roofed hovel, with no hope for improvement. Gil Lewis's farmhouse would never be any closer to him than the distance from Gil's kitchen door to Bay Point Road. His sales route would show a profit only as long as he had a car to travel it. At the rate his family was growing, keeping his car would soon be beyond his meager means.

Still he dreamed.

One day in the spring of 1936, I came home from school to find a stack of weather-beaten lumber next to the well. To add a second floor to the bungalow, I was told. A neighbor had torn down a barn and told him to cart away as much lumber as he could carry. Another neighbor trucked the materials to our front yard. The dreamer was already at the kitchen table sketching out a plan. A neighbor had a roof like ours; he'd raised it, and it looked great. If the neighbor could do it, my daddy reasoned, so could he. His tools were every bit as good and, in his mind, he was a better carpenter. The neighbor had one thing my father didn't, though: money for windows and shingles. Daddy put aside his plans. Just until he raised enough money for a few windows and some shingles, he told my mother.

The lumber lay there, weathering away. From time to time, he'd break out his plan and show us children where we'd be sleeping. I'd get a room with one window looking out on Schoolhouse Road and another where the morning sun could shine in. He showed me where he'd place the ladder so we could climb up to our beds. I could hardly wait. I even had thoughts of putting the money I earned picking blueberries toward the windows, or a few shingles at the very least.

My second-story bedroom dream was dashed the same as the romp in Gil Lewis's hayloft had been, only more abruptly. This time the dasher was the owner of a tiny summer camp just up the road beyond Bars Hill. He'd been planning for some time to add a bedroom. When he noticed our lumber rotting away, he made an offer: twenty dollars for the whole lot. My father accepted. If he didn't pay something on his grocery bill soon, Percy would cut off his credit.

I stood in the yard and watched as the lumber was carried off, board by board, stud by stud, up Bars Hill. Soon there was a bedroom on the back end of the neighbor's camp.

All I could do was lie on the living room sofa and stare up at Clark Gable on Sadie's *Mutiny on the Bounty* ceiling and wonder what it would have been like to lie in my upstairs bed with the morning sun peeping through the east window and a cool summer breeze ruffling a curtain, while just outside a robin chirped: *Cure him-kill him-give him-physic.*

The last board had barely passed out of sight up Bars Hill when a boat showed up in our yard. I didn't know where it had come from, or who had brought it. I came home one day and there it was, just where the lumber had sat. My father planned to fix it up and try his hand at lobstering. The dreamer in him wouldn't allow him to consider how he would haul traps with the ulcer that still troubled him.

It wasn't much, as boats go: a good twenty feet long, badly weathered, with no engine, no shaft or propeller. Paint was peeling off its planking. Lying there, on its side next to the well, it looked somewhat like a beached whale carcass with its ribs showing through.

My father came by some caulking materials to stuff in the cracks between the planking; then he painted the hull a sickly pea green from an outdated can or two that Percy Savage was about to toss out. He even broke out his pothead-knitting needle and knitted himself a few potheads for the traps he didn't yet have, hoping all the while he could swing a deal for some used ones. And while he was at it, he canvassed the fishing community for an engine. The established lobstermen, it turned out, were using their used traps, thank you, and none had a spare engine or a propeller to give away.

So, there the boat sat until one day someone came by and gave him a few dollars for it. He passed those along to Percy, too.

16

LIFE IS CHEAP

In 1937, the twentieth century cast its light on most of Five Islands—just not on the bungalow. After New Year's, Central Maine Power Company asked all residents of Georgetown who wanted electric power to sign up. Each subscriber agreed to pay a monthly fee over and above the cost of power to defray installation costs. I was hoping my father would sign up, but he let us know right away that we'd use kerosene lamps until he could come up with a decent job. He did brighten the kitchen somewhat. He bought one of those Aladdin lamps. It had a mantle instead of a wick and gave off a white glow.

When most of the residents had signed up, work began on the lines. Power was brought onto the island from Parker's Head in Phippsburg on the west shore of the Kennebec River to West Georgetown on the east shore. Power lines would have to be strung all over the island from Bay Point in the south to Five Islands. The job would last through the summer.

They hired a crew to clear a right-of-way for the power lines. My father was one of the first to sign on. Work began on the Phippsburg side. After the first couple of weeks, my father was assigned to work on the West Georgetown side of the river. Each morning, before daylight, the CMP truck, a large, rack-bodied affair, came 'round and picked up the workmen. The ride to the work site in an open truck bed must have been bitterly cold. Each day when they reached the work site, they piled up the slash and set it ablaze for warmth where they could sit around the fire and warm their feet while they sipped coffee from their Thermoses.

With full-time employment, although temporary, my father was again able to pay cash to put food on the table. All through the spring, the mood around the bungalow was a little more positive. Then, in June, I noticed a bulge in my mother's belly. Number six was on the way. I was almost eleven, but I still didn't know how it got there, and I was afraid to ask. Maybe God just pointed his finger at my mother and said in a booming voice, I'm sending you another gift, and the baby began to grow. If that were so, I wondered why this time, she hadn't asked for a gift of cash instead.

But then there was good news, even though my father hadn't intended it that way. At the supper table one day, my father mentioned that one of his fellow Central Maine Power workers had told him his dog had just given birth to a litter of pups. Too late, he saw the look on my face and realized his mistake.

He knew what I was going to say, even before I opened my mouth—"I want one of those puppies."

It costs money to feed a dog, he said. "Besides, we can't have a dog with all those cats around here."

A while back, someone had foisted a stray female onto my mother. The cat had thanked her by dropping a litter of kittens under her bed.

"Maybe if you got rid of the kittens, we could make room for a dog," she said.

"Just how would I do that?" I said, knowing down deep just what she had in mind.

"There's a crocus sack down cellar. You put some rocks in the bottom for weight, drop in the kittens and tie it up; then you take them to the wharf and dump them overboard."

"And the mother, too, while you're at it," my father said.

I could tell my mother didn't like that part of the plan, but she didn't say anything.

I did as I was told.

The kittens went into the sack with no trouble, but the mother put up a hellacious struggle, and scratched me a couple of times. I carried them, kicking and squirming, to the wharf and tossed them in. To this day, I can still see the bubbles rise to the surface as the sack sinks into the Sheepscot, and I'm reminded how poverty can cheapen life.

When the puppies were weaned, my father brought mine home. He was a big puppy. My father said he was a mongrel that would probably outgrow the bungalow. If I named him, I've forgotten what. I've always thought of him as just The Pup. He took to me right away. He was always at my heels and slept on the floor beside my bed.

Right away I set about housebreaking him, but not before I'd had to clean up a mess or two. As it turned out, though, his messes were the least of Pup's problems. In one of his droppings I spotted worms. When my father heard that, he reminded me he had no money for a vet. If Pup started throwing fits, we'd have to get rid of him, he said.

The housebreaking went well. Pup seemed like a healthy, happy dog. I'd just about decided he was going to be fine. And he might have been, if he'd gotten past the Fourth of July. That morning some-one lit off a big firecracker in our yard. Pup had been lying under

Courtesy of Thomas Hanna

Grandpa Rowe.

134

the maples. The boom must have spooked him. He took off running wildly and blindly around the house and across the yard. Under the maple, he collapsed onto his side and lay there, quivering and foaming at the mouth.

My father had watched the whole thing. He didn't say a word to me. He went straight over to Harold's house. Pup staggered to his feet and was staring at me with glazed eyes. I wanted to help him, but I was afraid in his condition he might bite me. Pup was almost his old self again by the time my father returned, accompanied by Harold, who carried his shotgun.

I knew what was going to happen and I didn't want to hang around to watch. I took off running into the swamp. I ran as far as I could go, almost all the way to Hite's Pond. I clapped my hands over my ears, but I could still hear the shotgun blast. My jaw quivered, but I fought back the tears. This was the way it had to be. A shotgun shell cost less than a good worming at the vet's.

I didn't come home until I was sure Pup was gone. My father was behind the dump patting down the soil of a freshly dug hole. I stared at him, accusingly. He shrugged. It was just something that had to be done.

I knew right then and there that life in the bungalow would never change. Whenever anything good came inside its drab walls, it would soon be snatched away and followed shortly by something totally bad.

Pup had been gone only a short time when I was hit by another loss. Grandpa Rowe quit coming to the bungalow. His Sunday visits had dwindled since Clayton's arrival. I couldn't understand why, and I was hurt by it. But I can see now how he felt. His daughter and her husband, who he hadn't approved of from the start, were bringing still another child into the world and living in dirt-mean poverty because of it. He didn't want to go there and see her heartbreaking squalor, knowing, too, that he couldn't afford to do a whole lot about it.

If my mother was concerned by Grandpa's Sunday absences, she didn't mention it and no explanation was ever given by either Grandpa or my mother. Instead, she took to spending Sunday evenings at his house and she usually brought me along with her. I was happy to go because I missed our time together.

As I had grown older, Grandpa Rowe replaced his usual riddles with brainteasers. On a Sunday evening in front of the radio, to a backdrop of the Jack Benny, Edgar Bergen and Charlie McCarthy, and Fred Allen comedy shows—great entertainment for a young boy—he was likely to provide a problem for me to solve. I've forgotten most of them, but I do remember one in particular. "If a hen and a half lays an egg and a half in a day and a half, how many eggs will six hens lay in six days?"

I had only one question for Grandpa. "What if the half chicken I have isn't the half that lays eggs?"

He laughingly assured me that my half did lay eggs. I struggled to solve it, finally conceding that Grandpa had a knack for posing puzzles that had no solution. He never did offer to give me the answer.

Meanwhile, the talk around Five Islands was about my other grandfather, Grampa Hanna. An accomplished sailor, he could handle anything from a small dory to a schooner and a sloop. In my mind, he was the best around. However, there was some debate around the stove at Savage's as to who was a better sailor—Grampa or his nephew, Everett Cromwell. Grampa and Everett finally agreed that a race between the two was in order. They borrowed two small, one-man boats with a mainsail and jib. Winabouts, I think they called them.

They laid out a course and set the rules. The racers would sail down the gut between the islands, around Hen Island and Malden Island, then back into the harbor. They were to use no oars or paddles.

There was no doubt in the minds of the Hanna family, as well as many of the villagers, that Cap'n George would win hands down. His health wasn't good, though. He was in his mid-seventies and hadn't been quite right since the last year's flood.

In 1936, the cresting Kennebec and the Androscoggin rivers had overflowed their banks, sending cords of pulpwood and rafts of lumber from upriver paper mills and lumberyards downriver into the Sasanoa and into Sheepscot Bay. The locals took to their boats and began their finder's-keeper's salvage operation. Some brought ashore enough lumber to build sheds or additions to their houses.

Grampa went after the pulpwood to fuel his stoves. He had stacked a sizable amount by his woodshed and had plans to harvest more when he was taken ill. He awoke in the night, teeth chattering with a violent chill. By morning, his jaws had locked shut. My father took him to Bath to see a doctor, who had no idea what to do. He tried to force an instrument between Grampa's teeth and managed only to break his jaw. Grandpa underwent surgery to mend the doctor's mistake. I never did learn what they did to cure his lockjaw.

The only visible sign of his ordeal was a hole in his cheek that would remain an open wound for the rest of his life. He wore a patch over the incision to absorb an intermittent discharge. In later years, he grew a beard to cover the unsightly scar.

Still, a little old case of lockjaw couldn't hold Grampa back, and on the morning of the race, spectators gathered on the shore at Five Islands and on Malden Island. He and Everett left the harbor and were neck and neck as they rounded Hen Island and disappeared from the view of the Five Islanders. They were not seen again until they cleared the northern end of Malden and headed back into the harbor. Everett was in the lead! And to my dismay, he held it until the finish. How could Everett possibly outsail Grampa?

Later in the day, I found out how from a spectator who went out in his own boat to watch the entire race. In the lee south of Malden Island, when they were in a dead heat, both boats had been becalmed. They lay dead in the water, hoping to catch the fresh breeze that rippled the surface just yards away. As the boats drifted on the outgoing tide, Everett was seen to slip his hand into the water and paddle until his sail picked up the breeze seconds ahead of Grampa's boat. He forged a slim lead that he never relinquished. There were some who said that Everett would have won, anyway, but I didn't believe it. As for Grampa, he shrugged it off and, as far as I know, never questioned Everett about it.

17

IVA'S CLEAN SHEETS

"Iva's coming today and she's bringing good news for somebody," my mother informed me one summer morning at breakfast. Iva was her first cousin. Iva was also a cousin to my father on the Hanna side of the family. She lived in Bath and had always been concerned about my mother's welfare. She visited us whenever she could persuade her husband, Charlie, to bring her down.

I asked her how she could be so sure.

"I had a present'ment just this morning. And you know my present'ments are always right."

"But even if Iva is coming, how do you know about the good news?" I insisted.

"Well," she said, "I knew somebody was coming when I dropped my dishrag first thing; I just didn't know about the good news part until I had my present'ment."

I had never put much stock in her visions, but she had great faith in presentiments, dropped dishrags and a whole lot of other superstitions. Some were too preposterous for even a small boy to swallow whole hog. "If it rains when the sun is shining, the Devil is beating his wife." I wondered if she believed that one herself. Others were downright scary for me. A whippoorwill's call outside your window in the night meant someone in the house was going to die.

When I went to bed on a summer night, I stuck my head under the pillow so I wouldn't know it was calling. But I could still hear that bird and I'd lie awake for hours, fearful that he might have been calling my name. Sometimes in that dark, I'd reach over to see if Irving was still breathing.

"Death always comes in threes," was another. Whenever someone in the village died, my mother and Vesta would tick off a complete list of the sickly to come up with those most likely to fill the other two slots. Then, just when they'd narrowed it down, someone who'd never been sick a day in his life would drop in his tracks and mess up a whole afternoon's work.

So I was still doubtful about Iva's good news, when Charlie's Ford Beach Wagon pulled up in front and Iva came on in. She and Charlie and her three sons, Norman, Donald and Warren, had come down for an afternoon visit, and to check on my mother.

Iva remarked at how peaked my pregnant mother looked. "Taking care of all these kids must be awful hard on you in your condition, Lu. Why don't you let us take Irving and Tommy to stay with us for a couple of weeks? On Saturday we'll all go to the Soap Box Derby races in Portland. How would you like that?" she asked us.

How could two boys refuse?

I'd seen pictures of those little cars and their young drivers with their funny hats and had hoped that one day I could watch them race.

"Charlie will come down and pick you up next Friday after work." Charlie was one of the lucky ones. He had a full-time job as a tinsmith at Bath Iron Works where they built ships for the U.S. Navy and yachts for people like the Vanderbilts. He owned a house in Bath, with all those marvelous sidewalks, and a car he could afford the payments on.

"I'll have them ready for you at five," my mother said as they were leaving.

After Iva left, my mother had a worried look on her face. "There's a part of my present'ment I didn't tell you," she said. "When I woke up this morning, I felt all tingly. And you know what that means: There'll be a big thunderstorm before the day's over."

My mother had always predicted coming thunderstorms, sometimes a day or two before they arrived. She said that was because a lightning bolt had marked her when she was an infant. I knew the story by heart. She was sleeping in her steel crib in an upstairs bedroom, when a lightning bolt blasted through the upstairs window, shot into her bedroom, and passed directly over her steel crib before it charged downstairs and left the house through the kitchen wall, leaving a gaping hole over the kitchen door. She must have been right about the lightning, at least, because there was still a two-foot-wide plaster patch marking the spot at Grandpa Rowe's house.

My mother spent most of the early afternoon peeking out at the darkening sky. By two-thirty, she was making preparations for the storm. We moved the kitchen chairs, along with Clayton's high chair, into the living room and made a small, tight circle in the middle of the room. At the first lightning and thunderclap, she called us all into the living room. We knew the routine. We each took a seat, hiked up our legs and hooked our feet around the rungs. The trick was to not let our feet touch the floor. Chairs in the middle kept us away from the windows, another no-no. After a few near misses, the storm went south and things returned to normal.

The rest of the week was the longest of my life. I could think of nothing but those little cars racing down a Portland street. Friday afternoon, I heated a pan of water and took it to my old bedroom and washed myself. I secured the drape across the doorway so that Mary or Cora couldn't come bursting in while I was stark naked. I slipped into a clean pair of pants. In the summer, neither Irving nor I wore undershorts under our pants—except when we dressed up for church, because we didn't want to soil our good pants.

My mother had packed our small battered suitcase and issued her last-minute instructions. She had packed our good pants and a pair of undershorts. We were to save them for Sunday. The pants and the shorts were new from the Red Cross field worker who had given them to my father the last time he'd been in to see her about assistance.

We stood at the roadside, suitcase beside us, and waited until Charlie came. We stopped to pick up Gene Stevens, a boy about my age, who lived with Iva's stepmother. He was coming along for the soap-box races and would go home on Saturday evening.

Iva's house was a roomy two-story home on a short dead-end street. I couldn't get over how fresh and clean the place smelled, and the bright, flowered wallpaper on the walls made me happy inside.

Our upstairs bedroom was as bright and airy as the downstairs rooms, with more fresh wallpaper, gleaming linoleum on the floor and fluffy curtains on the open screened window. The double bed was turned down and I could see clean white sheets, not brown flannels that stayed on year-round like those on my bed at home. Next door was a bathroom with an honest-to-God sparkling white bathtub and wash basin that Iva said we could use anytime. The toilet was downstairs in a closet. I'd be a good eight feet from what I left behind.

I was eager to climb into that shiny tub, but tonight I just wanted to sleep in that beautiful bed. I got my chance early. Iva called us in from outdoors just at dusk and suggested we turn in because of the long day ahead of us tomorrow. Her three boys had been tucked in before sunset. Norman was seven, Donald six and Warren five.

Neither Irving nor I owned pajamas. When we went to bed, we merely slipped out of our pants, shoes and socks. But for some unexplainable reason, that night we climbed in wearing our shirts. The shirttails didn't reach past our navels. We were naked from the waist down. When you're just short of eleven, that can be a troublesome thing.

As we were crawling in, Gene came into our room wearing a fancy pair of pajamas and razzed us. I leaped into bed and pulled up the covers, wishing I'd put on those shorts. "Get back into your own room!"

He left chuckling at my embarrassment. I was too tired and too excited to stay riled, though. I stretched out on the mattress, felt the softness under me and wiggled my toes against the soft, clean sheet. A wispy breeze from the open window ruffled the curtain. The whisper of tires on tarred road, as an occasional auto headed south on Route 209, lulled me into a deep, contented sleep.

Iva roused us at six. We dressed, brushed our teeth in the washbasin—with real toothpaste instead of baking soda—and went downstairs. Gene was already at the breakfast table along with Iva's boys. As soon as I sat down, Gene started to say something about my nakedness the night before. I kicked him under the table, and he shut up.

Iva was frying eggs and bacon and making toast. There was a quart of fresh milk on the table and a glass of milk beside our plates.

A whole glass of milk for each of us! I couldn't believe it. We sat impatiently and, when the eggs were on my plate, I began to shovel it in.

"You can't eat until Mama says grace," Norman scolded.

I'd forgotten. We hadn't thanked anyone for the food on our table in a while. Sometimes it was hard to be thankful for the food we got, anyway. Perhaps someone should have been asking Him to provide us with better fare—a little more meat, if you please.

Iva finally sat down and gave thanks; then we dove in. I wolfed mine down and wanted more. Iva must have noticed that I was eyeing that second egg on Irving's plate. He was just playing with it, anyway.

"Tommy, would you like another egg and more toast?"

"Yes, please," I said, holding out my plate.

My mother had always taught us to say please, and I wasn't about to forget it when Iva was offering seconds. When she brought the egg and toast, she poured more milk into my glass. I wanted to stay at Iva's all summer.

After breakfast, Charlie loaded the picnic basket into the beach wagon and we were off. I had never seen what lay beyond Bath and now I was traveling thirty-five miles beyond it to Portland. I kept my head out the window the whole time so I wouldn't miss any of the sights. I was amazed at the number of gas stations and overnight cabins along the way. And I read every single Burma Shave sign—out loud.

We reached Portland. "Baxter Boulevard," Charlie called out. I had never seen so many beautiful homes. They seemed to stretch out for miles, with their green velvet lawns and bright flower gardens. We came off the boulevard and onto Forest Avenue. I had thought that buildings in Bath were huge; here they were mammoth. One super-tall building on a hill had a tower on top. On the side it said Eastland Hotel.

"Hey, that's where the radio station is," I informed everybody.

"WCSH," Charlie finished.

"Boy, that's some kinda building," I said.

Charlie pulled up to the curb along Forest Avenue. We could see the big wooden ramp that sat smack in the middle of the street.

"That ramp was put up just for the races," Charlie explained. "The racers come down over it in pairs and end up way down the street. That's the finish line."

A man with a loudspeaker announced the first two racers, and their cars were brought up to the top of the ramp. A raised board held them in place side by side. When both cars were in place, the board was removed and the cars shot down the ramp, their drivers scrunched down inside.

They raced in heats. The winner of each heat advanced to the next heat until there were only two racers left. I rooted for the North Bath boy to be one of them, but his car didn't make it; he lost out in one of the final heats. One of the final two would be the champion and go on to race in the national championships in Akron, Ohio. I wondered how they got those cars all the way to Ohio.

When the races were done, we ate lunch in the park nearby. Late in the afternoon we packed up. I couldn't remember when I had ever been so happy. I lay down on the blanket and dozed on the way back to Bath.

The next day, with Gene back home, our vacation began in earnest. Norman and his brothers were too young for us to play with for very long, so Irving and I spent our time exploring the neighborhood. Sometimes, we'd walk down to Washington Street and watch the trolley rattle down toward Winnegance. The motorman would wave at us and we'd wave back.

One day we walked all the way up to the feldspar mill where the noisy and dusty crushers ground chunks of rock into powder to be used for dinner plates, Charlie told me. And further up Washington Street, the box factory stack spewed out mountains of sawdust. It must have taken acres of trees to make those piles.

On the way home, Irving and I stopped at a ramshackle house where a bunch of children played in the yard. Peters, they said their name was. There was a boy, about my age, Fred, and every day he had to walk to the poor farm and bring home milk for the family. He asked me to go with him. I told him I'd have to ask Iva first.

When I mentioned the Peters, Iva wasn't too happy. The mother was divorced and the city was giving her assistance. Iva believed, as my mother did, that a good Christian woman just didn't get a divorce. She finally said I could go, but I could tell she didn't want me hanging around with the Peters tribe. I didn't see a great deal of difference between the Peters tribe and mine, except they had no father around. I went with the Peters boy and continued to spend some time with him for the next few days. Iva said no more about it.

During our stay at Iva's, I tried to keep myself clean so I wouldn't dirty her house. I saved my undershorts and wore them to bed every night to protect her sheets. I took two baths in her tub in one week. I worried that she'd say something about using too much water, but she didn't.

The two weeks sped by and I enjoyed every minute of it. I couldn't remember when I'd ever seen that much good food in one place at one time. When we left for home on Friday afternoon, I knew I'd miss the good food, the bed, and the bath.

18

IF A TREE FALLS

I had barely gotten my suitcase through the door at home when Cora came bursting in to tell me of a great surprise, one that took the edge off my disappointment at having to leave Iva's. Beyond our house was land owned by my father's Aunt Lettie and Uncle Melvin, who had sold us our swamp lot. On that land were two very tall and very sturdy maple trees spaced about fifteen feet apart. My father had gone into the nearby woods and cut a small tree, straight and true. He'd trimmed it out and strung it across in a kind of ridgepole between crotches high in the two maples. Using rope left over from his Malden Island days, he hung three swings. Immediately, Cora, Irving and I hit the swings and set out to see who could soar highest.

We'd been at it for a good five or ten minutes, when my classmate Russ Harford came over. "Okay, it's my turn to swing, now."

"You can't have a turn to swing until we say you can," I told him. "They're our swings."

"I can so," he said, "any time I want. This is my grandmother's land, not yours."

When nobody offered him a swing, he went home. Later, he was back. "My father says you better let me swing. Five minutes, or you'll be sorry."

I didn't know what Russ's father had in mind to make me sorry, so I let him use my swing—twenty swings and no more.

After I'd counted twenty, he refused to get off. I grabbed the swing and we tussled. Finally, he said, "I'm going home to get my father. He'll throw you off all the swings."

"Oh yeah?" I said. "Well, my father won't let him, and he can lick your father with one hand tied behind his back."

"Oh yeah?" Russ came right back. "My father can eat beans off the top of your father's head." Russ must have gotten that from his father. Then, he stomped off.

Neither Russ nor his father came back that day, but the following morning, I saw Russ Senior and another man at the swings. He had an ax and a crosscut with him. Without a word to any of us, they chopped down the trees and cut them up into little pieces. We could only stand and watch and wonder how anyone could be so mean.

That afternoon, when the Central Maine Power truck dropped my father off out front, we rushed out to tell him so he would go and give the Harfords a piece of his mind. I could tell he was mad, but he just shook his head. "There's not much I can do. The land does belong to Russ Senior's mother."

I was so riled that I kept after him to do something. I was hoping that he'd at least give Russ Sr. a little of the old "cross-eyed, moss-backed, knock-kneed . . ." so he'd know just how put out my father was about the maples.

After supper, my father went over and talked to Russ Sr. for a while, but to me, he didn't seem angry enough. When he came back after a few minutes, he shook his head. Russ had told him he'd cut the trees for firewood for his mother this winter. "He's lyin', though," he told my mother. "That wood is as green as grass and it won't be dried out by winter."

The pile of maple stayed where Russ had left it, and never saw the inside of a stove. I was disappointed that my father wouldn't do something to get even, and I told him so. My mother reminded me that getting even wasn't the Christian thing to do. That's when I decided maybe a Christian attitude could be a very unhandy thing, if it got in the way of a little honest payback.

I was still stewing over the swings when I spotted Ida Hinckley on the ledges outside our back door. Ida, Vesta's mother, lived on the far side of the swamp behind our house, and a worn footpath led straight from her house to our ledges. She was just standing there holding a garden trowel and talking into thin air, as if to an invisible friend. Her graying red hair hung in ropy strands under the brim of a floppy black hat. Her big-breasted body was crammed into a raggedy, black lace dress. She had on a pair of white gloves that reached halfway to her elbows, and, as usual, an odd pair of stockings—one black, one white. My father used to tell me that Ida had another pair just like that at home. He said if Ida had been as poor as he was, she'd have been called daft, but because she owned stock in the telephone company and went to South America in the wintertime, she was deemed eccentric instead. One of our neighbors called her just a plain old rig.

"I think she's looking for you," my mother said to me. "She was here yesterday morning. You'd better go out and see what she wants."

"She's been looking for someone to do odd jobs," my father said. "Some of it's man's work, but she won't hire a man to do it. It's not very steady work, either, an hour here, an hour there. It might be enough for you to buy yourself some clothes, though."

I joined Ida on the ledges. She didn't say anything for a few seconds. She just sized me up through a pair of wire-rimmed glasses she wore on the very tip of her nose. She clutched at the trowel and I could see a couple of fingers peeking through holes in her glove.

Finally, she said, "Don't suppose you'd want to do some work for me in my garden this summer." She spoke with a doleful Down East twang. "Pay's twenty-five cents an hour."

She went on to explain that there might be other harder chores now and then. Nothing I couldn't handle, she supposed.

I wasn't sold on the idea of gardening, but I knew, in light of my experience at Iva's, that I did need underwear and socks. I said I'd do it.

She nodded. "You be there bright and early in the morning."

I didn't know what bright and early meant to Ida, but I decided that eight A.M. was a reasonable hour to start work. I made my way through the swamp to Ida's small white cottage with a screened-in porch. It overlooked Schoolhouse Road and commanded a pretty fair view of the Sheepscot. Her small lawn was dotted with flowerbeds and shrubs.

She was waiting with the gardening tools laid out. She set me to work spading up a new plot and announced that she was going to drive down to the Stevens farm to get a bucket of manure.

Ida had a brand spanking new car, a Chevy. She kept it in a garage just below her house alongside Schoolhouse Road. Even a short trip with Ida behind the wheel held the makings for a disaster. In a few short months she'd dinged the car in a half-dozen places. Once, she'd slammed it into the hitching post in front of the general store. Only a stone pillar had kept her from crashing into Savage's meat locker. My father said she was the worst driver in Sagadahoc County. Nobody was quite sure just how she had obtained her license, although her son-in-law, Orville, said she got it from Sears Roebuck.

She didn't start up her car like ordinary folks. She turned over the motor with the accelerator pedal floored. I listened while she revved the engine to full throttle. Suddenly, her Chevy burst backward out of the garage, crossed the road, continued across an open field and came to rest teetering on the edge of a steep embankment above Dave's Cove.

I feared she'd been hurt and was on my way down, when she opened the door and crawled out. She didn't seem at all fazed. She went straight to the next-door neighbor's house. "Looks like I've run aground," she told the woman. "Think you can drive it out for me?" The neighbor sized up the situation and declined. There wasn't much more than thin air for the rear wheels to grab ahold of, and she was afraid the car would topple over the brink to the beach, a good twenty-five feet below. Eventually, a tow truck from Bath pulled the Chevy out. It would be another day before the manure arrived.

In the days to come, the tools Ida dragged out for me were larger and harder to manage: a reel-type mower for her lawn and a bush scythe to hack away at the alder swale just beyond her cottage. With the harder work, Ida said I'd tire sooner and wouldn't get as much done. She allowed me no more than three hours of work in the morning, three days a week, a schedule I didn't mind. I earned seventy-five cents a day and I had the afternoons to pick blueberries; three or four quarts at twenty-five cents a quart, if somebody didn't beat me to my customers. Otherwise, we had stewed blueberries and bread for supper.

In August, it was time for my mother to deliver baby number six, this time at Cornish's Maternity Home in Bath. Mrs. Cornish was Iva's good friend and neighbor. She knew of our poverty and offered to take my mother in without charge. My father paid only Dr. Joe Smith for the delivery. And there was more good news. A kindly neighbor who had had her fill of childbearing donated a crib for the new baby and Ma decided to keep both Clayton and the new baby in her bedroom.

While my mother was away giving birth to my brother Richard—he was born August 17, 1937—Cora took over the bungalow. She cooked, cleaned house, ordered all the groceries and generally kept everything in order while our father was at work with CMP. Quite a chore for a twelve-year-old. She felt quite grown-up, and she looked it, as well. Merton Pinkham took a shine to her and came calling in the evening. Merton was eighteen and we called him Mert. Mert played a guitar and he sometimes brought it along. He and my father played and sang together. Mert, who played better than my father, showed him some new chords

One evening Mert brought along a songbook. Under the words, they showed the frets of a guitar and just where to place your fingers for the proper chord. I thumbed through the pages. It looked easy. Mert assured me it was easy and thought I ought to begin right away. My father took to the idea of another musician in the family and offered to let me use his guitar if Mert would show me a few chords to strum.

Mert was all for it. He said if I liked it, there was another guitar up to his house and I could have it for maybe four or five dollars. It was small but held a tune. He handed me my first pick and left his chord book so I could practice.

I was determined that one day I would pick out a tune on my own guitar. The next morning after my father had gone to work, I took his guitar out of its case. I carefully placed my fingers for the key of C and made my first, PLUNK-PLUNK-PLUNK. Even with the pick, the tone was muted. Then, I labored over a muffled tonic chord, PLINK-PLINK-PLINK. And finally I fingered the seventh chord, PLONK-PLONK-PLONK. I was hooked. After that it was practice, morning and evening, until my fingertips were callused and the chords rang clear and true, except when the old guitar slipped out of tune. Mert came over often. He showed me how to tune up the cranky old "gitfiddle" and offered constant encouragement.

By the time my mother brought Richard home in early September, I could plunk out all the chords for "You Are My Sunshine." Clayton loved to hear me strum, but Richard squalled at the harsh new sounds. My mother made me go out onto the back step to practice.

I wasn't as thrilled about Richard's arrival as I had been with Clayton's, but I was somewhat relieved to know that I could stay in my bedroom—at least until my mother brought home number seven, I thought. But shortly after she brought Richard home from Cornish's Maternity Home, my mother told me she had been deathly ill with his delivery.

"The doctor said if I have any more babies, I might die."

I had no idea why she had told me. I just hoped God wouldn't give her any more babies; I didn't want her to die. Later I concluded that it may have been a cry for help, one she hoped would reach my father's ear.

After her return from Cornish's, my mother was troubled with constant toothaches. Six pregnancies with scant prenatal care had reduced her mouth to a dental disaster area. Her few snaggled teeth sometimes ulcerated and gave her constant pain.

Over the next few months it got so bad my father called Dr. Barrows over from Boothbay to ease her jumping toothaches. The doctor took one look into that decaying mouth and announced he'd have to kill a couple of nerves. He reached into his bag and took out a slow-burning punk stick, the kind you use to light firecrackers and Roman candles. He lit it, shoved it into my mother's mouth and killed those nerves slick as a whistle. And Mama only screamed twice.

The punk did the trick. Once she was pain-free, Mama was anxious to get back into the church. She asked me if I'd like to go with her one evening. I suppose she'd singled me out because she felt my soul needed a little more saving than the others. Evangelists were coming, she said, Miss Jackson and Miss Spivey from somewhere out west. Miss Jackson played the piano and they both sang.

I hadn't darkened the church door for evening services since my reluctant testimony, and I didn't really care for revivals. There was usually too much preaching and praying and not enough singing. When I squinched up my face in distaste, she quickly reassured me. "These women are different. I hear they're going to tell a lot of Bible stories."

That got my ear. I loved the Old Testament stories. I'd already heard most of them in Sunday School and Vacation Bible School, but I wouldn't mind hearing them again. I agreed to go.

That evening, and for the next three, Miss Jackson held my rapt attention as she told of Daniel in the Lion's Den, David and Goliath, Samson and Delilah, and Joshua and the Battle of Jericho. She and Miss Spivey sang beautifully and the whole congregation joined in.

Among the goodly crowd in attendance on the final night of the revival, sitting with the deacons, was Chancey, a lonely bachelor and intermittent parishioner. Chancey was an oft-repentant backslider who had been born again, and again, and again. For months at a time he'd stay away from the church, doing all those wayward, unholy things that a sinner does. Then, unexpectedly, he'd show up at the church services oozing penitence, as he did that final night.

At the closing of each service Miss Jackson would extend the usual invitation for all remorseful sinners to come forward and be saved. On this night, Chancey heard the call. He leaped up onto his seat, reached his arms heavenward and shouted, "Oh Lord, come down and get me. Take me up to heaven. I'm coming up! I'm coming up!"

His outburst broke the solemn silence. The deacons eased Chancey back onto his seat to a smattering of hesitant hallelujahs from a congregation not ready to believe that this would be Chancey's last need for repentance.

Muttered one faithful churchgoer under his breath, "I'll be right here to catch you when you fall back down."

19

BOWLING ALLEY HILL

On the clear cold days and crisp starry nights of winter, skating and sledding took us away from the oppressive air of the bungalow.

I had taken some of my summer's blueberry money and bought a pair of hockey skates from Herbie Campbell for fifty cents. I spent my Saturdays and some of my evenings with the younger children at Hite's Pond until the ice was thick enough to be harvested as it was every winter, until after 1937 when refrigerators replaced iceboxes.

Then the older kids moved to Charles's Pond, about a mile down the road. My father feared its deeper waters and was reluctant to let us skate there until deep winter weather had set in. Charles's Pond was more fun because the older skaters built a fire beside the icehouse and burned old automobile tires. The heavy smoke left our faces blackened, but the warmth was welcome.

When heavy snows blanketed the ponds we turned to sledding. Someone had given me an ancient low-slung sled. Although the years had weathered its wooden frame a tired gray, its steel runners still gleamed and could speed me downhill as fast as any of the new Flexible Flyer sleds. It was one of those sleds where you grabbed the handles on each side, took a running start, threw the sled down and belly-flopped onto it. I steered by shifting my body weight from side to side.

On nights when the stars seemed so close you could touch them and the snow was so frosty it squeaked when you walked, I'd take my sled to the top of Bowling Alley Hill. The slope cut through the heart of the village, past the ice cream parlor, lodge, icehouse and dance hall and ended up at the general store beside the wharf.

There were sleds of every size and description on that hill, but the biggest and most beautiful was the Rittall family's bobsled. Built by Horace Rittall, a local woodscraftsman, it was a marvel of oak and ornate brass fittings. Whenever they brought it to the hill, a crowd always waited to ride on it. I wanted to put aside my sled just once and ride the bobsled downhill, but there never was enough room.

One evening, after the big sled had taken off with another full load, an idea for my own sled began to take shape. Dennis Moore, another Five Islander, and I were sitting on our sleds, resting before the next slide. He couldn't find room on the big sled either. I suspected that it might have been laid to his seasonal affliction, a runny nose. From November to April, he seldom knew a dry day. In the cold air it ran down and down until it was about to roll over his upper lip; then he'd give a mighty sniff and retract the whole thing. On a downhill run, you wanted to be upwind of him.

Dennis's sled, a hand-me-down from his brother, was almost a replica of mine, except that it was longer. His was a pointer; mine was a shooter. If we could pool our resources, we could make our own bobsled.

I was deciding how best to persuade Dennis to sacrifice his sled for our common good, when he said to me, "I wish we had a bobsled."

I suggested we build one of our own.

"What'll we build it out of?"

"We'll use our sleds, yours and mine. Yours up front and mine on behind."

"It'll take more'n sleds," Dennis argued. "We'll need somethin' to connect them together."

That's when Chet Mack got into the act. He'd been pushing the Rittall sled. He'd tried to jump on, but missed and landed in the road. He'd been sitting on a snowbank, taking in our talk. "There's a plank on the ledges over to Dave's Cove."

"Whereabouts at Dave's Cove?"

"Just above high-water mark."

"Well, what are we waitin' for?" Dennis shouted. He threw down his sled. "Give me a push and climb on my back," he told Chet. They took off. I was just a few steps behind.

After school the following day, work began in earnest. Under the house I found some four-by-fours and a steel rod. Dennis contributed some bolts and nuts from his brother's boat engine. Chet brought a baby carriage wheel for steering.

After a couple of afternoons with my father's hammer, saw and drills, our masterpiece was finished. I asked Dennis what he thought of it.

He stepped back and gave it a thoughtful once-over.

"I dunno," he said, "that plank looks like its awkw'd to me."

Chet didn't take kindly to Dennis's criticism of his share of the sled, and he let Dennis know it.

"Dennis, you couldn't tell awk wood from pine."

Dennis didn't get it.

"It'll work," I said.

It was a monstrosity, but it was our monstrosity, the product of our own boyish ingenuity and resourcefulness, held together by a genuine awk wood plank. I set about getting it ready to run that night.

Just after dark, we moved up Bowling Alley Hill like ants pushing dung up a hill. Rittall's bobsled was there at the hilltop, looking magnificent in the moon-washed snow. We jockeyed our sled into position not four feet from it. The big sled took off a split second ahead of us. I expected it would soon be way out front, but we were neck and neck as we passed the ice cream parlor. We approached the dance hall in a dead heat, and I began to think that we just might beat them downhill. Then disaster struck.

The road surface on my side had been plowed down to the bare gravel. The sled hit the bare spot and stopped short—I didn't. I was catapulted over the steering wheel and into a monstrous snowbank. I pulled myself out just in time to see the Rittall's sled racing toward the store. Dennis and Chet picked themselves up off the roadway, bruised but undaunted. As we trudged back up the hill, we said nothing. We didn't feel defeated. Except for a bad piece of luck, we might have won. And that win would have been all the sweeter, because the sled was truly ours.

Both sleds would slide down that hill again and again that evening and evenings to come, but never as a contest. Rittall's sled could have beaten ours downhill most every time. I'd wait until they were on their way down, then I'd load up with stragglers who wanted a ride. I had to do something about Dennis's affliction, though. I persuaded him to get behind and help Chet push, so he'd be downwind of the rest of us.

At the foot of Bowling Alley Hill, across the road from the ice cream parlor, was an open field. It stretched from Five Islands Road all the way to Hite's Pond. It was our Five Islands ball field. It was small, as ball fields go, squeezed in, actually. Along the first base line, there was a high ledge, where the girls usually sat to watch the boys play. The dance hall—Liberty Theater—ran along the third base line.

Grandpa Rowe's house was just the other side of the dance hall. Pop-fly balls sometimes bounced off the dance hall roof and crashed through Grandpa's upstairs bedroom window. That slowed the game just a tad, especially when that ball in Grandpa's bedroom was the only one we had. The outfield had a permanent downward slope. A missed grounder could cross Five Islands Road and roll all the way to the ice cream parlor steps.

After the spring rains had washed the hill bare and the field had lost its sponginess, the bigger boys gathered for baseball. At first, because of my pint size, I came only to watch. By far the shortest among the kids my age, I sat on the ledges with the girls and looked forward to the day I'd be out there on the field. The spring I turned eleven, I brought the battered fielder's glove Vinnie Davis had given me and, with all the other boys, fell in around Vinnie and another boy who were choosing up sides. I sidled in closer to Vinnie, hoping he'd spot me and choose me for his team.

Vinnie was always helping us younger boys learn how to play sports. He'd already shown me how to throw and catch and how to swing the bat. Once, he tried to show me a thing or two about basketball, a disaster if ever there was one. The minister, who doubled as a Boy Scout leader—had brought a bunch of us boys and a basketball over to the Grange Hall, where he had set up a basket in the upstairs room. Vinnie, just out of high school, came over to help. Right away he named me a guard, stationed me under the basket, and told me to stand there and guard it—but he didn't say against what, and I didn't ask. Guard duty was going just fine until, for some reason, the reverend threw me a pass. I was so busy guarding the basket, I didn't see the ball coming until it hit me in the face. There were stars, tears and blood. The game was halted while the reverend practiced some of his Boy Scout first aid on my nose. By that time I'd had enough of basketball. I sat on the sideline and watched.

But this day it was baseball, and I was going to play. Vinnie picked me. He had to, I was the last one left. He told me I could play shortstop and bat first in his lineup, a tough place to be when it's your first "major league" at-bat. I grabbed the smallest bat I could find, stepped up to the plate and swung at the first pitch. I was way out in front of it. It popped up and curved over toward the dance hall, glanced off the roof and crashed through Grandpa's dining room window. There was groaning and bitching from the sidelines, but Vinnie knew just what to do. He gathered the players 'round him, took off his New York Yankees hat and passed it around.

"You guys know the routine. We've got a window to pay for here."

He allowed it oughta take a couple of bucks for materials. He'd set in the new pane of glass himself. Money and hat in hand, he went over to ask Grandpa's wife, Geneva, who just happened to be Vinnie's aunt, if we could please get the ball back so the game could go on.

If the at-bat was bad, shortstop was horrible. In spite of Vinnie's encouragement from over second-base way, I played the infield matador style. When a hot ground ball came at me, I'd step nimbly aside and wave my glove at it as it bounced on into the outfield. But by the fourth inning, I'd screwed up enough courage to stick my glove in front of a grounder and knock it down; then I'd pick it up and throw to first.

The next game, Vinnie told me I'd probably be more at home in the outfield. He was wrong. When I thought I was camped under the ball with my glove in place to catch it, it sailed over my head. If the ball got past me and crossed the road into the tall grass, the game was delayed while the outfielders searched for it. It was easier to spot than most balls, though, because of the black electrician's tape Vinnie had wrapped around it after the cover had been knocked off.

Because I didn't have much luck chasing after flies, I'd sometimes play deep and stand there and wait for the ball to come to me on the first bounce or the second. That brought on some snide remarks about the statue in the outfield. They hinted that I was in the field only because Five Islands was hard up for left fielders. But I knew better; I was there because I had a special talent for finding lost balls in the tall grass. They stuck me out there for the next couple of summers, until it finally occurred to me that just maybe athleticism wasn't one of the traits my father had passed along to me.

20

GIRLS' SHOES

Overall, 1937 was a bad year at the bungalow. After Richard came, Central Maine Power left, and my father and most of the other villagers were laid off. Fortunately, eight years after the Depression began, things were looking up, and many of the other laid-off CMP workers got other jobs out of town—but not my father. His health worsened and his trips to the veterans hospital in Togus were more frequent. His ulcers refused to heal, chronic bronchial problems plagued his gas-damaged lungs, cataracts formed on both of his eyes, and his few teeth abscessed and caused him constant pain.

He was only forty-three years old.

By this time the town had taken his bungalow and the swampland along with it for nonpayment of taxes. I had expected he'd muster up a special cussword or two for the occasion, but he was too numbed by the crushing weight of poor health and privation to manage even a "cripple-toed" or a "moss-backed." Let 'em have it, he'd said. If they turned us out, they'd have to find some place to put us up. They'd never find anyone to buy it anyway, he said, run-down like it was. He was right. To add insult to injury, he also lost his means of making his voice heard. Because of nonpayment of his poll tax, they'd taken away his right to vote.

In spite of his physical problems, he hounded Bath Iron Works
for a job. The shipyard was expanding, preparing to build warships.
He held high hopes of finding a job in the carpenter shop, the tin
shop, or in any one of the building trades. Almost daily he stood with
other hopefuls outside the Bath Iron Works gate. Occasionally, someone would come out of the company employment office and call out
their need for a shipfitter, a welder or a burner. Each day, a few men
would find work; the rest would straggle home.

Someone told my father that the best way to get a BIW job was
to have someone who already worked there put in a good word for
him. So he buttonholed acquaintances who worked at the yard, some
of them our Five Islands neighbors, and asked them to vouch for
him. If any recommendations were made, they didn't help.

He took to calling on BIW foremen at their homes from time
to time to plead for a job. He told them of his abilities with tools and
explained about his large family and his willingness to work. He was
never hired.

He told my mother one day, "I don't know why, but everyone
seems to be against me. It's a sad state of affairs when not a one of
them will turn a hand to help a disabled veteran find a decent job."

It seemed that almost every week, someone we knew helped a
relative or friend find employment. We were now the poorest family
in Five Islands by far. My father even sent an application to the
Portsmouth Naval Shipyard at Kittery, nearly one hundred miles away.
The extra points a war veteran could get on his civil service exam
should give him the edge he needed to be hired, he said. It didn't.

The growing war effort strengthened the economy and the
darkest days of the Depression were over for many, but not for my
father or for us. He couldn't spend his days outside Bath Iron Works,
waiting for a job that might never come. He took out his sample cases
and once again hit the dusty roads. Because of the higher employment,

more people were buying. Sales were brisk, but not brisk enough to feed six children. There was little else for work except occasional part-time jobs as a carpenter's helper.

There never seemed to be enough for us to eat. My father ran up his grocery bill at the store until his credit reached its limit. Unfortunately, my grandparents were in no position to help us out financially. But for periodic town support—free groceries from the general store at the town's expense—government-surplus foods, hand-me-down clothing from caring neighbors, and help now and then from Iva and a few other of my mother's kind relatives—who, while not wealthy, were surely better off than we were—we would not have survived.

As conditions deteriorated, the tension between my parents worsened.

"Why can't you get home and set down to supper like the other men do?"

He'd fire back, "Look at this floor—it hasn't been swept in two days."

Then she'd take her turn. "I got a houseful of kids to see to. You never turn a hand to help."

And on it would go.

Their clashes were depressing. And worse, their wrangling spilled over to us children. We snapped at one another until my father lost his patience, jammed his hat onto his head and stomped out the door, while my mother scolded, "Now, look what you've done. You've drove your father out of the house."

On those dark days, I wished my real father would come back, but he never did.

Our survival during those lean times may have been due to my mother's ability to make do with the raw materials at hand. The low cost of canned foods and the small garden my father kept made vegetables more readily available to my mother's talents than meats. There was a turnip and potato smother—turnip smothered in potato or potato smothered in turnip, depending on which vegetable was more plentiful at the time—a tomato and potato casserole bake, and sometimes creamed peas on crackers or biscuits. It always amazed me how far she could stretch a can of green peas. For the rare occasions when we had meat, there was a concoction of fatty hamburger mixed with water and flour. She called it a fricassee and served it on potatoes.

It was at the dinner table that I learned some of my best survival techniques. Sometimes, in spite of my mother's considerable stretching abilities, there just wasn't enough for my hearty eleven-year-old appetite. That's when Irving's finicky eating habits kept me from going hungry. After a few bites of something he didn't like, he'd say he couldn't eat that junk and push his plate aside. I'd keep my eye on him until he left the table; then I'd pounce like a bony stray cur and finish his plate, a meal that could have helped to fill my mama's belly. I didn't know that her meal was often mostly what, if anything, we kids left behind on our plates.

Sometimes my father worked a shift as head chef at the bungalow. He'd clip a recipe from *The Boston Post* and try it out. At first there were simple, tasty little meals like Aunt Jane's Dinner, a canned corned beef and potato casserole. He might have been just fine if he'd stuck with the recipes and not tried to create his own fancy foods with French-sounding names. I remember one dish—Hi de Floi De-oo, he called it—a concoction of canned pineapple chunks and chipped beef fried in lard, if you didn't have any Crisco handy. It didn't even look appetizing. I forced it down. To this day the mere thought of pineapple and chipped beef on the same plate turns my innards downside up.

We drank evaporated milk because with the two babies drinking fresh milk, we couldn't afford more. My mother could add enough water to a seven-cent can to squeeze out a full quart of milk, but it really wasn't fit for drinking. I took to watching Clayton suck hungrily on his bottle, and wished I could get just a taste. Once I snatched his bottle up, pulled the nipple off, took a big swig, and set it down again before anyone noticed.

Not even whole milk could satisfy Richard. He was a fussy baby, especially in the wee hours of the morning. He'd start off with a whimper, which Mama usually ignored, until he let loose with a hunger cry. She'd crawl out of bed, light the lamp, warm his milk on her Sterno stove, feed him, change his diaper and put him back into his crib. I can still see her standing there, barefoot while the Sterno did its work, her frail frame showing through her raggedy nightgown.

Sometimes, even after he was fed, Richard would set up a howl fit to wake up the whole house. It really didn't take all that much, though, what with the thin walls and all. With the night-feeding of five little ones behind her, my mama had a let-him-cry-it-out attitude. She'd go back to sleep, but I still hadn't gotten used to hearing a baby cry at night. I'd take my little brother from his bed and rock him in my mama's oaken rocker, all the while humming "You Are My Sunshine" under my breath. When he finally slept, I'd tuck him back into his crib.

Just humming a song wasn't enough for me, though. I wanted to play it on a guitar. Mert's guitar, the one he said I could buy. But where could an eleven-year-old boy get five dollars in a hurry? Bottles were the only thing I could think of. If I could find enough milk or soda bottles to return for a couple of dollars of deposit money, I could give Mert a down payment and he might let me have it. I knew just where to start. A whole boxful of empty milk bottles was just sitting there on the back step, worth a nickel each. My father waited until he had a dozen or more before he returned them to Savage's store. He'd never miss a couple now and then.

After several returns I realized that the milk bottle scheme was taking too long. And I couldn't keep taking them from my father because he needed that money to put toward what he owed on his grocery bill. I needed another source. The summer people sometimes stored empty soda bottles under their porches, by their boat landings or in their sheds, and left them there when they closed up in September. The big ones were worth a nickel, the small ones, two cents. The first few cottages turned up a whole dollar's worth of loot, and I managed to do it without breaking a single lock or window. When I had two dollars, I gave it to Mert, and he let me have the guitar. I could pay the rest in the spring, he said.

With my new instrument, I was on my way. By spring of 1938, I could play the old favorites like "You Are My Sunshine" and "Home On The Range." When the radio was working, I'd tune in the Nashville station and listen to the Grand Ole Opry. I knew most of the Roy Acuff and Ernest Tubbs songs by heart, and accompanied myself on the guitar.

The squabbling between my parents carried through the spring of 1938. And we children couldn't understand why. I knew it must have had something to do with our being poor, because they hadn't done that when we were younger, when the family was smaller and we'd had enough to eat.

My father was hired to build a home for a local fisherman, and he was late for supper on many a day. One evening long past mealtime, my mother went out to Schoolhouse Road and waylaid the fisherman's brother. He told her my father was at the unfinished house, all right, but he was inside shooting craps with the fisherman and a few other men. When he finally did arrive home, she was ready for him.

"Just where have you been?"

He was taken aback by her shrill tone. "Me and some of the boys stayed around after I quit work—just talking."

She got right up into his face, screaming, "Don't you lie to me, Tommy Hanna. You been shooting craps."

That got his temper up. Only this time it wasn't "cross-eyed, knock-kneed, double-jointed." He came right back at her. "I don't need your say-so to spend my own money. If I want to shoot craps, I'll do it."

Now she was near hysterical. "A poor excuse for a father, you are!" she shrieked. "A houseful of kids going hungry and you gamble away the few pennies we have."

He pulled a handful of crumpled dollar bills out of his pocket and tossed them onto the table "I won. Five dollars."

She brushed them onto the floor. "I won't take a penny of your tainted money."

He bent to retrieve his winnings while she railed. "I try so hard to put enough food together to feed these kids. And you scarcely turn a hand to help." She dabbed with her hankie at a fresh flow of tears. "I'm tired of living like this. One of these days I'm just goin' to end it all."

That scared me. I believed she meant every word of it. My father only aggravated her all the more. "If you want to do it, don't let me stand in your way," he yelled.

"You think I won't? I got a shelf full of pills up there. I been saving up for it. There's enough there, if I take 'em all at once."

My father stuffed the bills into his pocket and jammed his hat back onto his head. "Go ahead. See if I care."

Then he went out and slammed the door.

My mother sat at the table and continued to sob. She didn't make a move for the medicine shelf, but I stood by it just in case she tried. I guessed she had just wanted my father's sympathy. After a while she dried her eyes and got up to do the supper dishes.

A half-hour or so later my father walked through the door carrying a brown paper sack. He set it on the table and took out a pint of ice cream and a few pieces of chocolate candy.

"For you," he said to my mother.

She brushed it aside. "I won't eat anything that's bought with tainted money." I noticed she didn't throw it away, though. If the ice cream was going to sit there and melt, I felt she ought to let me have it. I wasn't sure if tainted ice cream could hurt me, but I was willing to take my chances.

Nothing more was said about the gambling. We all sat around in silence until finally, with hope for a taste of her treat fading, I went to bed. I hadn't yet heard anyone say they were sorry, so I worried that my Mama still might do something crazy. When I got up the next morning, I found the empty ice cream box and a few candy wrappers on the kitchen table.

My parents' set-tos were no big secret to our neighbors, some of whom lived so close they likely heard every word. And neither were the times my father was forced to go before the Overseers of the Poor and ask for food for his family. Everyone on the island knew when the Hannas were "on the town." Even our schoolmates knew, and would find ways to let us know they knew.

I'm not really sure when their attitude first exploded into pure meanness against us. I think it might have surfaced with the shoes when I was about eleven. A neighbor had given my mother a pair that her daughter had outgrown. One look and I knew they were girls' shoes. They had a flap on the front. Boys' shoes would never have a flap.

My mother had Irving try them on. They were too big. They fit me perfectly and were in good shape, far more presentable than my oxfords, which were embarrassing in their own right with their soles glued in place and held by a band of heavy cloth tape. Still, they were girls' shoes, and I wanted nothing to do with them.

"You'll wear them to school tomorrow," my mother declared. "No one will know the difference."

I grumbled all the way to school in my girls' shoes with the front flap flapping. No one had noticed by recess time and I was beginning to think I'd get away with it. Then, one girl exclaimed loud enough for everyone in the schoolyard to hear, "Hey, those used to be my shoes. My mother gave them to your mother."

"He's wearin' girls' shoes," a boy taunted.

Other boys took up the chant. "He's wearin' girls' shoes."

My shame and anger exploded and I swung at my tormentor. Down on the ground we went, a tangle of arms and legs. It was over before either of us could do the other serious harm. The teacher separated us and sent us into the schoolhouse.

When we went home for lunch, I discarded the shoes and put on my taped-up ones. I left for school with Cora, thinking I'd have no more trouble. I was wrong. Trouble came from school to meet me.

As we approached the schoolyard, we were confronted by a group of a half-dozen or more taunting and jeering schoolmates. The boy from the morning's squabble said he owed me something, and he meant to pay me back right then and there. We grappled and tumbled to the ground. He was stronger than I. Soon I was pinned flat on my back, encircled by the jeering group. I had never in my life felt so alone and friendless, and I haven't since. I was determined not to cry, but I had lost the heart to fight. Meekly, I said, "I give."

The boy rolled off me and the group dispersed. When I left for home at the end of the day, I'd decided to quit school altogether.

My mama had other plans. The following morning she sent me off to what could have been another long day if not for Herbie Campbell. Herbie, fast and strong, and who could heave a baseball like the great Johnny Vander Meer himself, was two years older than I and had just begun to fuss with his grooming, especially his hair. He liked to comb his long hair straight back—no part—and slick it down with a pomade. When he came into the schoolroom that morning and took his seat just across the aisle from me, his hair was slicked back and pasted down, every last hair in place. It gleamed so, it almost hurt your eyes to look at it. Right away, I could tell he wasn't wearing his usual hairdressing.

Nothing was said about Herbie's hairdo until his class went down front to the recitation seat and the teacher began sniffing the air. She left her desk and came 'round to sniff at each of them. When she got to Herbie, she stopped and sniffed again.

"Herbie," she said, "what's that on your hair? It smells like bacon."

Herbie sheepishly admitted he'd used the leftover fat from that morning's bacon and eggs to slick down his hair. By this time, the warmth of the classroom had dissolved the fat and it was dribbling down the back of his neck and onto his collar. Mrs. McMahan suggested he get on home for a shampoo.

We all had a good chuckle over Herbie's bacon-head, and by the time he returned bacon-free, with his mother's promise that she'd get him some Brilliantine hairdressing, I'd decided to stay in school, until the end of the school year, at least.

I took Herbie aside—he hadn't been one of yesterday's hecklers—and told him how spiffy I thought he'd looked, even with his bacon-fat hair. It seemed to please him, so much so that he felt obliged to protect me from any further schoolyard set-tos.

21

RICE AND RAISINS

The winter of 1938–1939 was even more devastating for the Hannas. It began when the CS 1, the old Studebaker, died and was sold for junk. It worsened when my father's health took another downward turn. I first noticed it when he and I were walking up to Grampa Hanna's one Sunday afternoon. Halfway up Bars Hill he stopped, gasping for air. Just a little pain in his chest, he said. He'd be okay after a short rest. He stood there for several minutes with his hand against his chest before we could continue. We finished the walk at a slower pace.

The following week, a thoughtful neighbor took him to Togus. The doctors there told him he had angina and warned him against strenuous activity, bad news for a common laborer. At the suggestion of the doctor who diagnosed him, he applied for a veteran's disability pension. While he waited to hear, his only source of income was his door-to-door sales. Without a car, access to his customers was limited and sales dropped. Occasionally, a neighbor drove him on his rounds, but more often he was reduced to delivery on foot.

Early that winter Percy was again forced to cut off our credit at the general store until we could put a little something toward our growing bill. Our remaining supply of surplus food until the next delivery consisted of rice and raisins. Every day, for nearly a week, that was our diet: rice with raisins, raisins with rice. Through it all, my mother still managed to find a little humor.

"Tonight, for a change," she said, as she filled my plate, "we'll have raisins on rice."

Who could laugh, or even crack a smile, with a plate of raisins and rice in front of him for the third straight day? Sometimes she'd say things like, "Children in China would love to have this food" and I'd be thankful, thankful that I didn't live in China.

In my father's desperation, nothing was sacred to him—not even the money from my Cloverine and stamps sales. One day I found him at the kitchen table, the money from my cans in front of him. He was counting it.

"I'm going to borrow this for a few days," he said.

"You can't," I said. "It's not my money. It belongs to Cloverine Salve and the stamp people."

The last thing I wanted to do was cheat the Cloverine people, who sent boys like me all those nice gifts.

He gathered up the money—three dollars or more—and shoved it into his pocket. "Your little brothers need milk; we all need bread."

"When will you pay it back?"

"As soon as I get a little money ahead."

I knew I'd never see that money again.

"But they'll come after me if I don't send it in."

"If they trouble you, you let me handle them. They had no business sending that stuff to a kid, anyway, not without his father's consent. And I didn't give any consent."

After he'd left with a pocketful of change, I checked on my stamps. The heat from the kitchen stove had softened the glue. Most of the stamps were stuck together. Now I was in serious trouble. I could already hear the sheriff knocking on my door. You're under arrest for destroying stamps and stealing from Cloverine Salve. I'd

surely wind up in jail. When the threatening letters from Cloverine
Salve and the stamp merchants did come, my father tossed them out.
Eventually, the letters stopped.

One morning as we were preparing for school our father told us
there was no more food in the house. He planned to see the Overseers
of the Poor that morning to ask the town for more credit at the store.
But if they turned him down, he warned us, there wouldn't be anything to eat when we came home for lunch. I fretted through the
morning classes and came home at noon with the others. There was a
kettle of corn chowder on the stove, but my father wasn't there.

Ma was worried.

"They've taken your father to Bath to see Dr. Smith. The
Overseers want another doctor to check him over for heart trouble.
They want him to cut bushes along the town roads to pay for the
help we're getting. And you know what the doctors at Togus said
about hard work."

When we came home from school in the afternoon, my mother
was in tears in the kitchen. Dr. Smith had pronounced my father
healthy, with no sign of heart trouble. He had told the Overseers my
father was just lazy. The Overseers had my father arrested for nonsupport and had taken him before a judge. He'd tried to plead not guilty,
but the judge said if he did that, he'd have to post bail or go to jail
until his case came up. If my father pleaded guilty, he would be
allowed to come home, as long as he promised to cut the bushes. I
didn't know a whole lot about the nonsupport law, but I didn't see
how my father could have supported his family if they'd kept him
in jail.

"He's down cellar sharpening his scythe right now," Ma said. "He'll start cutting in the morning."

When my father came up from the cellar, I expected fire in his eyes and a string of choice cusswords on his lips. I was wrong; his chin hung down almost to his chest. All he said was, "Tommy, why don't you run to the store and get me a can of Velvet."

I couldn't wait to get away. At the store, Percy Savage wanted to know if I intended to pay cash for the tobacco. When I told him I didn't have any money, he said to me, "You tell your father the town won't pay for his smokes."

I flushed with shame and fled out the door.

When I told my father, his face took on the most awful expression. He was about as close to breaking down as a man dared come. Regardless of any differences, at that moment I felt deeply sorry for a defeated man.

The next day, he took his scythe in hand and went out to join the road crew. He stayed on with them until his door-to-door sales picked up and he found work helping build a couple of houses, employment that would carry him over until the spring of 1939, when he'd go to work at the Ledgemere boathouse readying boats for the summer vacationers. The government provided its share to his welfare when the Veterans Administration finally conceded that his illnesses were service-connected. He began to receive a small monthly disability check.

Neighbors took disapproving note of our lean times. Around the village there were whispers that, just maybe, some of Tommy Hanna's problems could be laid at his own doorstep. Then the Cushman's Bakery deliveryman said it out loud. Down at Percy's store they were discussing the Depression, which was starting to wind down, when my father allowed how hard it was to raise a family these days. That Cushman feller came right out and told my father he wouldn't have near as much trouble if he didn't have so damned many kids.

He came home, wound up like a two-dollar watch. "Who is he to tell me how many kids I should have, I ask you?" he fumed to my mother.

My mother agreed that he had no right to say such a thing.

22

CHASING BUTTERFLIES

Our troubles with the town were scarcely behind us when
Grandma Hanna's health failed. Aunt Ruth came to take care
of her. She wouldn't allow any of us children to visit Grandma. And
that was just fine with me. I was afraid my father would take me
with him when he visited, but he usually saw her alone.

By the spring of 1939, she was gone. I felt no inconsolable grief
at her passing, and though my mother said little, she must have been
relieved. I wasn't told to attend her funeral, and I didn't ask. My
father and Cora were the only ones in my family who cared enough
to go. My father's sister, my Aunt Ruth, came to keep house for
Grampa Hanna.

In late spring that year, my mother suffered a more damaging
loss; her washing machine washed its last load. The gear that drove
the agitator quit after swishing countless loads of laundry. It needed
a whole new set of gears, something we couldn't afford. My father
set the washer outside.

Aunt May had passed on by then. No more help would be coming from her. My mother went back to the washtub and hand-washed
all our clothes on a washboard. The wringer spared her from wring-
ing them out by hand. It was slow work and our dirty, smelly laundry piled up in a corner of one bedroom. Sometimes, when I was in

a hurry for clean clothes, I'd take mine from the pile and wash them in a bucket.

The Five Islands Improvement Society, mostly summer women, usually shifted into their annual benevolent mode just after Memorial Day. The society's goal, among others, was to give assistance to the needier families. That spring, they chose to improve us. They offered to buy my mother a new washing machine, a gasoline-powered one, this time. My mother had a fear of gasoline around the house and she declined. They offered a hand-cranked machine. She accepted.

When she told my father the good news, he was furious. "Who do they think they are?" he fumed. "These money people, always letting it be known what they can do for the poor. It's all for show. Now they can pat each other on the back and say, 'Look what we did for the poor Hanna family.'"

Obviously, my father was not that averse to taking help; we'd gotten plenty of handouts up to that point. But he still hadn't gotten over being let go as a caretaker on Malden Island, and this time got his back up against rich people wanting to give his family aid.

My mother held out her cracked and bleeding hands.

My father was adamant.

"We don't need their washer. You just tell your highfalutin' society friends just what they can do with their machine."

My mother must have told them exactly that, because a few days later they delivered a new washer to the house. She had a load of wash in it and was cranking it up before my father even knew it was there. Nothing more was said about it.

Not long after, my father hit upon a scheme that he was sure would raise his family out of poverty. He'd show those Five Islands improvers that he could stand on his own two feet. A magazine article he had read provided the spark.

"It says here that certain kinds of butterflies are worth a lot of money," he told my mother one evening. Collectors were willing to pay fabulous sums for rare monarchs. He showed us the pictures. On warm summer days, the fields around the village swarmed with butterflies. Any one of them could be that rare monarch, he reasoned. If he could just find two or three of those beauties, he'd be set for a whole year. My mother wasn't so sure. She reminded him that he didn't even have a net and that he couldn't go chasing through the fields in his condition.

He wasn't to be swayed. "I still have my fish net needle and some twine. I can knit a net. And I won't have to chase too far if I make the handle long enough."

In spite of my mother's skepticism, he spent his evenings knitting until he had himself a fine-meshed net. He laced it onto a makeshift wire hoop and attached the whole thing to a six-foot pole. Before taking to the open countryside, he tested it out on the winged insects in our yard. Through the living room window, I watched him take long, futile swipes at his flittering prey. It took considerable practice to net his first prize, a common moth.

After a day in an open field he managed to net three butterflies. He took out the Bible and carefully pressed them between its pages. When they were sufficiently flattened, he took them to a Bowdoin College professor who had some knowledge of insects. He confirmed that indeed there were rare and valuable butterflies out there, but said my father's specimens were quite common. One was no more than a colorful moth.

The professor he talked to must have been a geologist. He convinced my father that the real money was in rocks—meteorites, actually. They were constantly blazing down from the heavens and landing in the fields and along the shore. He showed my father a sample meteorite and showed him what he should look for. He even broke out his rock hammer and showed him how to look inside a promising specimen.

My father came home believing that there were people out there just waiting to hand him large sums of money for a few small chunks of the heavens. He shared with us his vision of finding a goodly chunk of the untold wealth that was just lying around waiting to be picked up by the knowledgeable rock hound. And for a while, I was excited, too.

In his spare time away from the boathouse, he continued his forays into the fields and along the shore. Now he carried a ball-peen hammer along with his net. One day he came home bursting with excitement. He had been scouting a rock pile at Sandy Cove Beach when he found a fist-sized specimen that looked like the meteorite he had seen in the professor's office. Then he cracked open another one of the rocks and found the inside filled with the imprint of seashells.

"Fossils," he told my mother. "These seashells are old. They could be worth something."

The Bowdoin professor evaluated his find as a very probable meteorite. He chipped off a piece to send to a geologist. He paid my father a few dollars for the fossil rock. My father brought the good news home to us, and we waited anxiously for word on the meteorite.

When word of my father's field trips spread around the village, some snickered, some laughed out loud. Their ridicule reached my father's ear, and he was hurt by it.

"What do they want from me, anyway?" he said to my mother. "They complain if I'm on the town. They won't help me find work, but when I try the best way I know to earn the money to pay my own way, they laugh."

"Don't pay any attention to those fools," my mother fumed, "they'd laugh at their own mother."

Though he continued his forays in the field, most Five Islanders figured that the odds of his finding anything worthwhile were about the same as finding a pot of gold at rainbow's end.

They were right.

The meteorite sample was never authenticated.

And my father never, never did catch that elusive butterfly.

23

A SQUARE PEG

In June of 1939, with my mother keeping her washer cranked up and oiled and my father spending his free time in the field with a butterfly net and a hammer, I graduated from Five Islands Grammar School. I was just shy of thirteen. Mrs. Pinfold, our teacher, named Olive Williams valedictorian. She named me salutatorian.

I hadn't the slightest idea what a salutatorian was supposed to do, and I said as much to Mrs. Pinfold. She said I'd have to make a speech on graduation night. When I told her I knew even less about speeches than I did saluting, she offered to help if I'd stay after school. She broke out a book on Maine history and geography. Together, we composed what amounted to a salute to the great State of Maine. She handed it to me and said I should memorize it before graduation day. If there was one thing I could do well, it was memorize.

Back in sixth grade, the teacher announced shortly before Lincoln's Birthday that the fifth and sixth grades would memorize the Gettysburg Address and recite it. I got right to it, and by the designated Friday I had it down pat. That afternoon I sat and listened as one after another of my schoolmates stood and faltered. Then it was my turn. I breezed through my oration in a manner that would have brought a smile to the face of Abe himself.

That was a proud moment for me, and I felt even better about it when the teacher informed the group that I was dismissed from classes for the rest of the day. The others would remain and work on their assignment. My schoolmates were probably too busy memorizing to notice, but there was a decided strut in my step as I left the classroom.

Of course, all that memorizing doesn't help a whole lot when you're on the business end of a clam hoe, but on graduation night in 1939, before a goodly crowd and my four classmates in the Town Hall, I breezed through all sixteen counties and every major river and town from Fort Kent to Kittery, without a single prompt from Mrs. Pinfold. I must have done my parents proud, though I can't help but wonder if there may have been a few heads nodding off before I finished.

I wanted to go on to Morse High School, which was twelve long miles up the road in Bath. I had no idea how I'd get there. Some of the others had already decided not to go on. Only Herbie Campbell was going for sure. His mother had already found a ride to Bath for him.

"Don't count too much on going to high school this fall, because it may not happen," my father said.

I couldn't believe he'd say that.

"Why not? You always said you wanted me to have a high school diploma so I can get a decent job."

"I don't have two dollars a week to spare for your fare to Bath," he said.

Georgetown paid tuition to Bath, but the parents had to provide transportation to the school. Local workers headed to Bath Iron Works were usually willing to squeeze in one more passenger for two dollars a week, but my father had eight mouths to feed. Those two dollars seemed like two hundred to him.

My mother told me not to worry, she'd find a way. She'd found a relative in Bath to put Cora up for the school year; maybe she could find someone for me. First off, though, I'd need a summer job to earn some money to buy school clothes.

By Memorial Day, she had me working for Jody Stevens— strong as a bull—on his one-acre farm that grew vegetables for the summer people. For a dollar a day, six days a week, I picked strawberries and pulled weeds.

At the same time, my mother was gaining weight, and it wasn't from overeating. Gift number seven was on the way. No cash this time either. I recalled Dr. Smith's warning, but neither she nor my father seemed to share my concern. Still, I fretted through the weeks that followed. This time, too, I was sure I'd be displaced when the new sleeping arrangements were handed out.

There just wasn't room for a third baby in the master bedroom.

I continued to hope for high school, and for a time in early July, I thought a solution had been found. I came home from work one afternoon and was surprised to find an unusual guest, Annie Folsom, sitting in our living room with my parents. Miss Folsom, a schoolteacher from Massachusetts, spent her summers in a tiny cottage in Five Islands overlooking the Sheepscot Bay, and she was one of my regular blueberry customers. My mother called me in and I sat down with them.

"Tommy," Miss Folsom said, "your parents and I have been talking about your high school education." She glanced at my father, then she turned to me. "How would you like to come to Massachusetts and live with me this winter so you can go to high school?"

Visions of Iva's clean, airy room, white sheets and a room of my own flashed in my head, and I knew there could be only one answer. "I'd like that," I said, trying hard, but not too successfully, to hide my excitement.

My father had a look on his face that worried me. "Your mother and I will have to talk it over. Why don't you run over to the store and see if there's any mail, while we discuss it?"

I walked slowly to the post office, my head awhirl. My father just had to say yes. I took my time getting the mail and dawdled all along the way home. I wanted to give them time to work out the details. I couldn't think of even one reason why either of them would want to interfere with my future, a future that didn't look too promising from inside our bungalow.

Miss Folsom was gone when I dropped the mail on the kitchen table and went into the living room. Before my father spoke, I knew what his answer would be. "We decided it would be better if you stayed here with us."

Better for who, I wondered. I couldn't hide my disappointment. My father refused to explain his decision, other than to say Massachusetts was too far away.

"It's early," he consoled. "Something will turn up before fall."

How could he be so mean? He says he wants me to go to high school and when I get the chance, he kills it. I wondered why he wanted me around, anyway. About the only time he talked to me was to point out something I'd done wrong.

Ever since my father learned of his heart trouble, he was afraid to go into the woods or on the water alone. He sometimes designated me as his companion when he went wooding or selling on one of the islands. I didn't mind rowing or pulling the handsled, but I never could do anything to his satisfaction. I resented his put-downs. I continued to work every bit as hard as he expected me to, confident that he'd eventually recognize it. But the harder I tried, the worse things got. One time, I rammed the boat into the ledges near McMahan Island, losing an oar overboard in the bargain. He had to paddle with the one oar until he overtook the other, already drifting down Sheepscot Bay. All the while he ticked off half a dozen or more reasons why I was of little use to him.

So it was hard to understand why he didn't want me to go to Massachusetts. Besides, with me gone, there'd be one less hungry mouth to feed—probably the hungriest one of the lot, at that. And with the new baby coming, they could use the space.

I didn't have long to fret. My mother's cousin, Minnie Paisley, came down from Bath. The first thing she said was, "Have you found a place for Tommy to stay yet?"

When my mother said she hadn't, Minnie explained that was why she had come. "He can stay with Bill and me if he wants to. There's only Isabelle. There'll be plenty of room."

Bill was her husband, a Scotsman from the Old Country, with a heavy burr and a fierce countenance. I was somewhat intimidated by him and worried that I might not fit in at his house. Isabelle was Minnie's widowed daughter.

Cora and I as teenagers outside the bungalow.

My mother accepted and set about preparing me for Morse High School. She broke out the Sears catalog and together we made out an order for slacks, shirts, socks and shoes, a mackinaw, and winter hat. It took every penny of my sixty dollars in savings but, as Ma said, I would "look presentable" when I went to school.

I was given a list of courses I could take my freshman year, including physics and science, neither of which I dared tackle. My father advised me to take something practical. I settled on the shop and mechanical drawing. A square peg was about to try on a round hole for fit.

The thought of leaving little old Five Islands Grammar School for big new Morse High School was scary—and with good reason. The confusion began even before classes started in the fall of 1939. I walked up to the south door and found it locked. A dozen or more girls were standing around waiting to get in. They told me this was the girls' entrance, and to go around to the boys' entrance at the north door, which would be open in a few minutes.

When the door opened and I entered that cavernous building, I was lost. There were three floors of classroom space, with corridors running in all directions. Someone led me to my homeroom where I would start each school day. There were as many seats in that one room as we had in all of Five Islands Grammar School. My home-room teacher gave us a schedule so we'd know when and where to go for different subjects.

I looked around at all those strange faces, none of which I would ever tie a name to, and wished I were back in Five Islands.

That feeling of not belonging would never change. The teachers didn't help. They saw me as just another hick from "downriver."

Mr. Pomeroy, my mechanical drawing teacher, especially didn't like me. It wasn't anything he said; it was just that he looked at me like he thought I'd just done something I ought to be ashamed of.

After the theft, he was sure of it.

He kept a box of loose change—no more than two or three dollars—in his desk drawer. He used it to buy drafting paper, pencils, and erasers, that sort of thing, for poor students like me. One day it was stolen.

Grim-faced, he announced to the class, "Someone in this room is a thief." He was looking directly at me. My face flushed, my ears burned. He thought I did it! I dropped my eyes and stared at the drafting table. Mr. Pomeroy went on. "If the person who stole it will come forward, nothing will be said."

He waited in silence. I didn't look up, but I was sure he was looking at me. When no one moved, he told us to go back to our drawing.

"But if anyone wants to talk with me after class," he said, "the offer still goes."

Later, I had a question that needed Mr. Pomeroy's advice. I fidgeted while he reviewed my work and showed me how to correct it. When he handed my work back to me, he looked me in the eye. "I hope the young man who took the money had a good use for it, don't you?"

Red-faced, I snatched my drawing from him and hurried back to my seat. I promised myself that I'd never again ask Mr. Pomeroy for advice. After that, whenever I needed help I asked the boy at the next table, until Mr. Pomeroy caught me and told me to quit bothering the other students.

My work suffered. My drawings were a mass of smudges, erasures and marked-over lines. They deserved the failing grade Mr. Pomeroy eventually gave me.

Except for Herbie and Cora, I didn't know any of the five hundred Morse students. Because of my shyness, I would never become fast friends with any of them. Mostly Herbie and I hung together. During lunch hour we'd walk downtown. Herbie went home to Five Islands each night. And that left only Cora, who'd be busy after school minding children; besides at thirteen, I didn't want to spend all my free time with my sister.

My father didn't mind me chumming with Herbie. Even my mother approved of him. She had a talent for sorting out boys and, after a careful evaluation of his character, she pronounced him "a good boy" even though he was a Catholic. Since he hadn't seen much of the inside of the Catholic Church in Bath, she reasoned, he probably wouldn't contaminate the few Protestant principles she hoped I still had.

In November, my mother's birthing time was near and my father wanted Cora home to take care of the little ones until our mother had recuperated. Cora enjoyed school and didn't want to quit, but she did.

Shortly after she came home she met Harlan Pinkham—in the romantic sense, that is. She'd known him most of her life because he was guitar player Merton's older brother and our cousin, to boot. Cora had hung around with his sisters, Audrey and Helen. He outscored her in years, twenty-seven to fourteen, but they seemed to hit it off right from the start.

I doubted that Harlan was taking a fourteen-year-old seriously on a man-to-woman basis, and I believed that my father would put a stop to it shortly. I was wrong; he did nothing. But when you come right down to it, how could he forbid Harlan to do just what he had done fifteen years earlier? Besides, he liked the Pinkham brothers, all seven of them. He often visited with them, true Down Easters all, who liked their occasional game of craps.

But soon Harlan began standing Cora up. Rumor had it that he was visiting an old girlfriend on the far side of town. It was apparent to my father that Harlan wasn't taking the whole affair as seriously as Cora was. On one such evening, my father found Cora in tears. He was incensed that the gallivanting Harlan would toy with his daughter's affections and decided it was time that Harlan declare his honorable intentions toward Cora, if he had any. I don't know what passed between them, but Harlan came back. The couple kissed and made up and my father seemed satisfied that his teenage daughter's honor had been preserved.

In late November, my thirty-three-year-old Mama, about to bear her seventh child, packed up and moved to Southport to stay with Aunt Ruth until her time came; then she'd go to Packard's Maternity Home for the delivery. Once again Cora took over the care of the house and the younger ones. On the third of December, my mother gave birth to Blaine. The delivery was difficult, and she hemorrhaged badly. She was slow to recover.

After Christmas break Herbie didn't return to high school. Way back in November he'd confided that he had lost interest in it. He hadn't been doing well and wanted to quit. His older brother had been a straight-A student in the college prep course, and Herbie was tired of the comparison. I guessed he'd finally convinced his mother that he'd be better off digging clams.

With Cora and Herbie back in Five Islands, I felt more alone than ever. My only close friend was Charlie, an eighth-grader who lived next door to the Paisleys. He wasn't the outdoorsy type. Except for an occasional skate at a nearby pond, we generally stayed inside. He taught me to play cribbage.

Living with the Paisleys wasn't all I had hoped it would be, either. Oh, I had all the privacy I lacked at home. I slept in my own bright airy room in my own bed between clean white sheets. There was a bathtub where I could take a bath whenever I wished, and all the good wholesome food I could eat. And Minnie was sweet and tried her best to make me feel welcome, but I never really felt at ease there. Bill's sour disposition didn't make it any easier. When they coined the term "Dour Scotsman," they surely had him in mind. He constantly complained about one thing or another. Whenever we were both in the house, I stayed in my room on the third floor. I seldom saw him except at mealtime.

I took to staying inside after school and listening to radio soap operas. Stella Dallas and Lorenzo Jones became two of my closest friends. The whole year might have been a total loss if it hadn't been for one great act of kindness from Minnie's daughter, Isabelle—bless her thoughtful heart. We were just finishing supper one evening; the discussion was the movies.

"Tommy," she said, "you don't get out of the house often enough. You ought to go see a movie once in a while."

I explained to her about my parents' objection to children in movie houses, adding that I didn't have the money anyway.

She was incredulous. "Thirteen, and you've never seen a movie! Well, it's high time we did something about that. As soon as there's a suitable show for children, you'll go and I'll pay for it."

I couldn't contain my excitement. Maybe I could go tonight, I told her. Never mind that I just might be shaking hands with the Devil.

She broke out *The Bath Times* and checked the movie schedule. The only show available was *Goodbye, Mr. Chips*. "That's a grown-up movie," she said. "You may not find it very interesting."

She suggested I wait until something better came along.

I was afraid she might change her mind or forget. I said I wanted to see *Mr. Chips*. She dug into her purse and came up with a quarter, enough for a ticket and a box of popcorn.

Isabelle was right; it wasn't a movie for a thirteen-year-old, but I was so awed by people moving across the screen and talking to each other, that I stayed through the newsreel, the short, and on into the second showing of the movie.

That movie and a couple of others would prove to be the highlight of my stay in Bath. I was one miserable teenager. I didn't feel as though I was wanted in the Paisley household and I didn't really want to stay there, but neither did I want to return to the squalor of the bungalow.

As my unhappiness grew, my grades, never more than passable, tumbled. My teachers didn't seem to understand the shyness of a backwoods country boy, and this prevented me from taking an active part in classroom activities and discussions. I was failing mechanical drawing altogether. I began to believe that my father was right: I was nothing more than a dumb kid.

It didn't surprise me when Minnie took me aside one Friday afternoon shortly after the 1940 new year and gave me the bad news. She and Bill were too old to handle a teenager in the house full-time, she said. We both knew it was my grades that troubled her, but I didn't let on. I just stood numbly while she went on. She'd get in touch with my mother right away. Isabelle would drive me home on Sunday afternoon. She patted me on the shoulder. Maybe my father could find me another Bath family to stay with.

I hurried upstairs and began to pack, feeling more like a failure than I ever had. Minnie was just being kind. There was no other family I could stay with. My father wouldn't even try. And surely he still couldn't afford the two bucks a week for carfare.

I became a high school dropout.

24

FATHER AND SON

Once I was back under my father's roof, he took to putting me down like it was my fault I'd dropped out of school. He seldom spoke to me unless it was to criticize. Still, I was reluctant to snap back at him. He continued to criticize, and my resentment grew.

Everything came to a head on the way home from one of our wooding trips. His health was in such decline that he was scared to go alone into the woods. I was recruited to go with him. On this day, I was pulling the sled while he pushed it from behind. The sled was an awkward ark of a thing that looked more like a sledge. It was about five feet long, a foot high and two feet across, with oaken runners a good two inches wide. Each of the four corners held a removable stake that kept the load from rolling off. Empty, it was easy to control. Loaded, as it was now, it sometimes went every which way.

We were on a downward slope in ankle-deep snow when I stubbed my toe on a hidden tree stump and fell, face-first, onto the ground. The sled continued on until it fetched up against the stump. The load slid forward, pinning my leg to the frozen snow.

My father rushed over and began working the logs back onto the sled.

"You bollixed it again," he said. "You could have ruined my sled."

His eldest son was lying in the snow with a pile of wood on his leg, which may have been broken, and he was worried about the sled.

"Can't do anything right, can you," he fumed as he shoved aside the logs.

I wanted to get his attention.

"I suppose you want me to grow up to be more like you, have a houseful of kids."

I knew he wouldn't put up with a smart-aleck son, but his reaction was more than I had expected.

"You watch your mouth, young man. Just because you're too big to spank, don't think I won't hit you. I'll take you out behind the house, and we'll duke it out, man-to-man."

I didn't want to fight him. I told him so, but I needed to respond in kind, let him know I wasn't a little kid he could just push around. "But you'd better watch your step," I said. "One of these days I'll be bigger than you; then I'll beat the shit out of you."

My defiance must have taken him aback. All he said was, "Let's get this wood out of here."

I said nothing, and together we righted and reloaded the sled. Neither of us ever mentioned the incident again. We lived under an uneasy truce. I was relieved for that, but to my way of thinking, the damage was done.

In the late spring of 1940, my father found full-time work that would take him into the winter. Warner Eustis, a Boston business-man, had bought the Ledgemere property from the Boyntons and brought in his own architect to design and build an elaborate cot-tage. He hired local people to help. He paid fifty cents an hour for a six-day week, more money than my father had ever earned.

He broke out his saws and hammers, hoping to sign on as a car-penter. Instead he was given work cutting trees and burning slash. Later, he helped the other laborers blast a cellar out of the ledges beside Sheepscot Bay. He must have been disappointed, but I didn't hear him complain. Things were looking better than they had in some time. He even bought a cord of wood from Jody Stevens because his full-time job left no time for wooding. While he worked, I sawed and split it.

With our last go-round still in my mind, I set out to prove to my father that I could do a few things right, maybe even a few things better than he could—and gain some respect in the bargain. For years he had messed around with *The Boston Post* crossword puzzle, and he never did well with it. He could finish about half, if you didn't count the spelling mistakes and the erasing. I already knew some of the words he'd missed. Still, if I wanted to make a serious effort to show him up, I'd have to do better. Our little dictionary just wouldn't do it. Vesta let me bring the puzzle over to her house and use her dictionary and encyclopedia. They were old, but still better than anything we had. Even with all that help, I couldn't finish the puzzle. I saved it and, when the answers came out in the next day's paper, I filled in the blanks. I figured if I ever saw those words again, I'd know them. And it worked.

After weeks with the encyclopedia and the copying, I was close to success. And I had learned a few things, too—important things: a three-toed sloth is an ai, a whirlwind is an oe, a household god is a lar, and a salamander is a newt; or, if he's a little feller, an eft.

Then came a day when I filled in every blank all by myself. I took it home and set it down in the living room where he'd be sure to see it. If he did, he never let on. If I wanted to show him up, I'd have to be more direct.

I took to tossing offhand questions into my conversation. "Are there any newts around here?" I asked him at supper one evening.

I could see he was stumped. "What's a newt?"

"A salamander," I said. "You know, one of those little lizards."

"Can't say that I've heard tell of such a thing around here. Where'd you see that, anyway?"

"In your crosswords—the part you didn't finish," I said, just to let him know I was a step ahead of him.

He shrugged and let the conversation drop. I wasn't easily discouraged, though. I was sure I was getting to him and continued to find ways to let him know that I didn't think he was so smart.

"What's a three-letter word for newt?" I asked him one day when I was finishing his puzzle. When he didn't reply, I said, "Oh, I see it now. It's an E-F-T, a little newt, like we talked about. It fits right in. Sorry I asked. I should have known that one, anyway."

If he got the hint, he didn't let on.

I found still another way to make him look dumb, and I wasn't at all backward about using it. When he played his guitar, he plunk-plunked the chords. Mert showed me how to mix runs of melody with the chords so that I was playing both at the same time. I picked it up right away and added a few touches of my own. When I had it down pat, I waited until he was within earshot, then I played. First, I plunked out a tune the way he did, then I swung into my own way of playing it. He had to know that my playing was far ahead of his, but he never mentioned it. No matter how well I did—the guitar, the crossword, or anything else—he wouldn't praise me. It just wasn't in him.

25

MONKEY BUSINESS

That spring the boys in my age group—Russ Harford, Leon
Williams and Johnny MacGillivary—broke out their bikes and
rode out of the village, leaving me to hoof it all alone. I didn't own a
bike. I'd never owned one, and probably never would unless I could
find a way to earn extra money. What Ida Hinckley would pay me for
gardening, along with some of my blueberry money, I'd have to
spend on clothes. And the berries wouldn't be ripe until later in the
summer. I could only wait and hope warm weather would bring a
choice job opportunity or two for a bikeless teenager. My hope was
rewarded with choices that only a teenager would make.

In May, Vesta's husband, Orville, offered me a dollar a week to
mow his lawn. And a good-sized lawn it was. Orville's lawn and his
hand-pushed reel-type mower were never meant for each other. I'd
have keeled over from the heat if it hadn't been for Vesta. Every half-
hour, she'd bring me a cold glass of lemonade, and make me rest on
the ledge in front of her house while I drank it. There were times
when I almost quit. Each week I put aside a half-dollar toward my
bike. My only expense was an occasional French vanilla ice cream
cup and a bottle of cream soda.

In June, the Cunningham family offered fifty cents to anyone
who would empty the slop bucket at their cottage once a week.

Under their outhouse, they kept a five-gallon pail. When it was near full, it had to be toted down a steep, rocky path and dumped into the Sheepscot. It was a job no self-respecting boy wanted, but I was desperate. I agreed to their terms, all the while planning to add the whole half-buck to my bike fund.

Right off the bat, I discovered just how mean this task would be. Even though they had sprinkled lime all around, the stench would gag a maggot. I started down the treacherous trail, fearful that I might trip and spill the slop all over myself. When the odor threatened to stifle me, I tried holding my breath until I was forced to gulp in air. When I dumped the bucket, I could almost see the germs floating away on the tide, and worried what awful diseases I was sucking into my lungs.

The bicycle fund was well on its way when I realized I had an even greater need. During those few short months I'd spent with the Paisleys, I had changed. I'd added inches to my height. I was almost as tall as my father. My voice had cracked, then dropped a few octaves. There were other changes I didn't understand. I had sprouted hair on parts of my body where I didn't think hair grew. And lately, I'd developed an uncontrollable urge to get next to a girl. But whenever I did, I'd light up like a Christmas tree and get this warm glow all the way down to my privates. I was in bad need of a girl, but I had no idea what for, or how to go about getting one. Up until then, the most daring thing I'd ever done was join a bunch of boys and hike over to the LeChaise place in Georgetown Center to take a gander at the statue of a naked lady in his backyard. Folks around Five Islands claimed it was a statue of Mrs. LeChaise, but that was probably no more than a rumor; no one in all of Georgetown had ever seen Mrs. LeChaise in the altogether.

My father must have known what was happening to me, because he sat down his teenaged son to have a talk. It didn't help. All he said was that my privates were my "manhood."

Then he warned, "You monkey with your manhood and you'll
grow up to be foolish."

He said it as though I should already know what monkeying
was. I didn't know whether or not to believe him. But there was a
grown man in the village who talked and acted foolish. A few clams
short of a peck was the way some put it. He must have monkeyed
with his manhood. I had no idea how to monkey with my manhood,
but I was so scared I'd grow up to be like that man, that I was very
careful when I used the chamber mug.

In spite of my caution, I'd wake up some mornings and the heat
would already be there—I feared that I'd monkeyed in my sleep. I
asked Irving if that had ever happened to him and he said he didn't
think so. I was so concerned about going lame in the brain that I began
to do the multiplication tables in my head, sometimes all the way up
to the table of tens. Certainly, a foolish person couldn't do that.

Finally, I did what any bright young boy of my time did: I went
to an older boy for answers. I figured that during those two extra
years Herbie had been around, he'd learned some things I needed to
know. I was right. Not only did he know, but also he was more than
willing to share his knowledge with me. Right then and there he gave
me an Introduction 101 to a subject that had never appeared in any of
my textbooks. Those little personal hygiene books they'd given us,
which showed a picture of a girl and a boy with no clothes on who
looked just alike, except that the girl's hair was longer, hadn't been
any help. You just can't take a whole lot of needful information from a
book like that. Herbie explained the whole thing in terms I could
understand and tied all that in with how babies were born.

Suddenly, it all made sense. And now that I knew all I needed
to know about girls, I'd have to go out and find one. I didn't have far
to look. She had been there all along, just across the road. Charlotte
Gray was going on thirteen and blossoming into a pretty young

woman. Her brown hair hung down her back in pigtails, there was a smattering of freckles on her nose and she was gaining weight in all the right places. I was smitten.

I took to hanging out in her yard just hoping for a chance to speak to her. Herbie made me fearful about making a baby, but he said just fooling around could be a lot of fun, too. I planned to get to that as soon as I found out what fooling around was. Herbie hadn't bothered to explain it, and I hadn't asked. I didn't want to show too much ignorance. And I couldn't just up and ask Charlotte if she'd like to fool around. I tried to charm her with small talk, but I was mostly tongue-tied. Once, I got close enough to kiss her, but lost my courage. She must have guessed what I had in mind; she turned her head away and ran inside.

Maybe it was the triple whammy I'd been handed by nature that caused problems. Besides my runty build, I also freckled. I had a face full of them, some as big as a dime. And under the freckles was the baby face. I had the kind of face that made little old grandmotherly types want to pinch my cheek and say, "What a cute little boy"— downright embarrassing for a teenager. Puberty eventually chased away the freckles, but my baby face would be around a while longer. Maybe, I decided, if I knew a little more about this fooling around, I could beat my curse.

So it was back to Herbie.

This time I came right out and asked. He wasn't sure himself, but thought it was somewhere between kissing and making love. If I wanted to find out, he said, I'd have to hook up with a forward girl. In his book a forward girl was one who didn't wait to be asked— she'd make the first move. And from what I'd told him, he decided, Charlotte just wasn't a forward girl. Unfortunately, first-movers among Five Islanders were in short supply and were snapped up right away. Herbie doubted I'd find one anytime soon.

He was wrong.

I was hanging around the wharf late one July morning, leaning against a piling, waiting for the steamer *Virginia* to drop off the mail and freight from Bath. Leon and a few of the other boys were there, off to one side whispering among themselves. I could tell by the way they looked in my direction every now and then, they were up to something that concerned me. Finally Leon came over and said, "That girl over there wants to meet you."

I looked around.

"What girl? Where?"

"Glennis. She's sitting right there on the edge of the wharf."

Glennis was a slim young redhead from Massachusetts. She was about my age and attractive, although not as pretty as Charlotte. Her parents had a cottage on Harmon's Harbor and were down for the summer. She was just what I needed—a girl who had made the first move. Then, I panicked. What would I do? What would I say? I was excited and at the same time fearful. I thought it over for thirty seconds or so before I said I didn't think so.

Leon grabbed my arm.

"You're coming with us; Glennis is waiting."

I wrapped my arms around the piling and hung on for dear life. "No."

Leon began to pull. The other boys joined in and latched onto my legs, trying to break my death grip on the piling. A part of me hoped they'd succeed. Together, they heaved and pulled me free, nearly separating me from my pants in the process. They marched me, still kicking, across the wharf toward Glennis, who was pretending mightily not to notice the scuffling going on behind her.

"Glennis, this is Tommy," Leon said; then they turned and ran, leaving me red-faced and alone with who I was hoping would be my first girlfriend.

She looked up at me and smiled. "Hi, Tommy." She had a nice smile.

I shuffled my feet on the weathered planking and said "hi" back. I managed a smile that felt more like a grimace. She slid over and made a place for me next to her.

"Why don't you sit down?"

I had just dumped Cunninghams' slop bucket and was worried the smell was still on my clothes. I eased down beside her, keeping a respectable distance between us. Thankfully, she took the lead and asked me all about myself; then she told me about herself. Gradually, I relaxed.

When she got up and suggested that we go for a walk over to the beach at Sandy Cove, I fell in beside her. She reached out, grabbed my hand and held on. The heat began to spread; I tingled all over and felt red in the face. I didn't dare look down, but I knew my excited condition must be visible to anyone who cared to look. We were coming abreast of the ice cream parlor. Leon and the boys were sitting out front, not saying anything, just grinning at us.

I dropped her hand, and herded her onto a narrow path that led down to the shore. We walked in silence, single file. The tiny beach at Sandy Cove was crowded with bathers.

"Let's walk along the ledges," I said.

She didn't object.

I led her past the beach and didn't stop to sit until we were hidden from the crowd by a stand of trees that came all the way down to the ledges. She sat so close to me that our thighs touched. I tried desperately to think of something witty to say, but I could only manage my concern that the seagulls might drop something on our heads.

Glennis wasn't interested in talking right then, anyway. She brought her face close to mine and she had this funny kind of smile. Then, without so much as a how-do-you-do, she kissed me. It wasn't

My good friend Herbie Campbell.

a grown-up kind of kiss, just a gentle brush of her lips against mine.

She smiled that smile again.

"Was that the first time you've been kissed by a girl?"

When I nodded yes, she said I shouldn't worry about it. She didn't know a lot about it either, and we could learn together. I thought that was about the best idea I'd ever heard, and I told her so. We sat and talked small talk, which went well until she asked me where I lived. I was too ashamed of the bungalow to point it out as mine to anyone from away, especially a summer girl.

"Just up the road," I said. I was afraid if she saw my stilted home, sitting on that ledge wrapped in tar paper, she'd drop me. And this might be my only chance all summer to have a girl.

She persisted. "Where up the road?"

"I'll show you someday," I said, never intending to do any such thing.

I changed the subject and steered clear of the bungalow until she said it was time for her to go home. Still holding her hand, I walked her all the way to her driveway. I watched as she walked down the drive and said to myself, Yessir, she's gonna be my girl. I'd take a lot of ribbing from the guys, but I didn't care.

When I passed the ice cream parlor, all the boys but Aubrey Steen had gone home to lunch. He had some encouraging news. "You still interested in buying a bike?"

I told him yes, but I still didn't have enough money.

"How much you got?"

"Around ten dollars. It takes at least seventeen."

"I know where you can get a secondhand one for less'n ten."

I hadn't considered a secondhand bike, but suddenly it seemed the only way to go. "Where?"

"My brother knows this guy in Bath. He says the guy wants to sell. C'mon over to my house and we'll talk to him about it."

Aubrey's brother Dick said the guy would let me have the bike for seven dollars, but it would need a new tire and tube that would cost another three bucks or so at the hardware store. "If you want to go see it, I'll drive you to Bath, but you'll have to ride the bike home, 'cause I'm not coming back until late."

I had a five-dollar bill, five ones and about a dollar in change stashed away in a jar in my cubbyhole. I dashed home, took out my money and told my mother what I was going to do. She was afraid I'd be wasting my money on a piece of junk, but I was determined.

The bike looked to be in pretty good shape, except for the tire. Dick took me down to Rogers' Hardware. Then he helped me put on the tire and adjust the brakes. His friend tossed a spare section of chain into the basket. It would come in handy for mending chains, he said.

I paid him, hopped on my bicycle and headed for Five Islands. I was on top of the world. I had gotten a bike and a girl, all in the same day. So what if she was forward? I didn't care, so long as she didn't try to go too far. After what Herbie had told me about making babies, I didn't want to be a father at my age, no matter how much fun it was getting there. I'd have to go on the town, and then they'd say, "Just like his father."

The trip home took a lot longer than the trip up. I got off the bike and pushed it up all the long, sloping hills. When I reached Five Islands, I had intended to stop by Glennis's house and ask her to go for a ride on my bike, but I was too tired. I went straight home and was in bed early.

The next morning I hopped on my bike and was at Glennis's driveway when she came out. She was on her way for a swim at Charles's Pond at the foot of the hill. I rode alongside her and sat on the ledge beside the pond while she swam. I didn't join her in the water because, like many Five Islands kids, I didn't know how to swim. So I just watched. She was tiny for a thirteen-year-old—not yet developed—and she didn't fill out her one-piece suit the way Charlotte did. Afterward, we sat together on the ledge while she dried off. She asked me if I danced. I said no, so she offered to teach me to jitterbug. I said no to that, too.

I wasn't sure, but I thought I must be in love with Glennis. Whenever I wasn't gardening for socks and shorts money during the day, we were together. Sometimes we'd hold hands, sometimes we'd kiss, but mostly we just sat and talked. In the evenings when we played baseball at the field, she came by to watch and, if I had a nickel, I'd buy her a Coke.

On Labor Day weekend, Glennis and her family packed up and drove back to Massachusetts. She gave me her address and asked me to write, and she promised to do the same. She wrote a couple of times and I answered; then her letters stopped and I heard no more.

Labor Day marked the end of a perfect summer—first girl, first kiss, first bike. If I hadn't been so busy enjoying myself, I might have seen what was coming that fall. Blaine finally brought it to my attention. He cut loose with a first-rate hungry baby cry around two A.M.

one October morning. I awakened from a sound sleep and roused myself out of bed. Walking into the kitchen to see if I could quiet him, I came upon an all-too-familiar scene, right down to the same raggedy nightie with a tattered hem. My mother was standing barefoot beside the flaming Sterno. Even in the flickering lamplight, there was no mistaking the protruding belly that couldn't be hidden by the flimsy gown. Number eight was on the way.

I pretended I hadn't noticed. I just turned, ran to my cot and and crawled into it. For a long time I lay there, wondering, puzzling. I just couldn't forget the sight of my beaten-down Mama standing there, toil-worn and threadbare. I couldn't help but feel sorry for her, but this time I knew they couldn't blame it on God. Hadn't my father stopped to figure out how he could provide for us all? I made up my mind, right then and there: I'd be out of this place as soon as I was old enough to earn my own keep.

26

THE DOMINO KID

Herbie and I were a couple of lovesick puppies. With Glennis out of sight and soon out of mind, I continued to burn an economy-size torch for Charlotte. Herbie had an undying and unrequited passion for my cousin, Gracie Pierce. So we sat, Herbie and I, and we commiserated.

And while we commiserated, he'd light up and drag on his cigarette. I thought he looked real grown-up with that butt hanging from the corner of his mouth and the blue smoke drifting up past his nose and his eyes. It made me want to smoke, too. Herbie would have given me a cigarette right then, but I said no. If I lit up in front of him and started to cough, sneeze and tear up, I'd be embarrassed.

I went home to find a place where I could practice smoking in privacy. But in a bungalow crammed to its doorjamb with little ones, the only place where I could find even a pinch of privacy was the outhouse. I took a couple of brimstone matches from the matchbox in the cupboard and headed for the outhouse. I was ready to start smoking.

My father's roll-your-own technique had always fascinated me. Before I tried it with tobacco and papers, though, I thought I ought to practice making up a cigarette with something not quite as strong as tobacco. Beside the outhouse door I picked a dead weed. I slipped inside and crumbled the weed into a fine brown powder. I tore a

Courtesy of Thomas Hanna

Me and my guitar. "You are My Sunshine" was a favorite.

page out of the Sears Roebuck catalog right there beside the seat, trimmed it to size, made a gutter as I had seen my father do, dropped in the weed powder, and rolled it carefully. I put one end into my mouth and lit the other. The whole thing flared when I dragged on it, singeing my eyebrows. My lungs, eyes, and nose filled with acrid smoke. I gasped for air, tossed the still-flaming paper down the hole and ran outside, coughing and struggling for breath.

I sat on the sawhorse beside the woodpile taking in great gulps of fresh air. My lungs cleared, but it seemed I could still smell something burning. I was sniffing the air when my father rolled into the yard. He, too, sniffed. "What's that smoke—Good Lord, the outhouse is on fire!"

Smoke poured out the open door. He dashed to the well, pulled up a bucket of water and ran to the fire scene. I followed him in. He tossed the water into the hole. The blaze sputtered, crackled and died. The outhouse was saved, but the hole was charred all the way around.

I thought my father might take a switch to me, but he merely warned me. "Smoking's a man's business and you're too young. Don't let me catch you doing such a darnfool thing like this again."

I nodded my head. That seemed to satisfy him. He took out his drawshave and carved away the burnt portion of the hole. When he had finished, the seat was serviceable but too large for the under-sized Hannas. That's where the two-seater came in handy.

There'd be no more practice sessions for me. I went straight to Herbie and told him I was ready to smoke and asked him what I should do.

He smoked Camels at thirteen cents a pack. I wasn't sure I wanted to spend that kind of money until I knew I could handle this smoking thing. My father's smoke had sometimes made me cough and my eyes burn. I chose Dominos; they were only a dime, but even that was hard for me to come by. I'd need another source of income.

It was back to the used-bottle business for me, and I did quite well at it. Seems I always had a pack of Dominos sticking out of my shirt pocket. Now and again I'd take one out in public and light up, so that every one would know Tom Hanna was smoking Dominos. It got so that Herbie and some of the others dubbed me The Domino Kid.

Herbie needed extra money for his smokes, too. He was a hunter and a sometime trapper in the island's woods. Furs were hard to come by on Georgetown Island, though. That's when I learned just how far Herbie was willing to go to get a hide.

I was at the store when Herbie came in and asked me if I'd help him skin a pelt that day. He'd pay me a buck. Ten packs of Dominos! I said I'd do it. I should have asked what kind of pelt first.

The evening before, Herbie and a friend had been walking down Oak Road. A skunk blocked the road ahead and refused to move. They'd thrown rocks at it. One of them must have hit it. It crawled off into the bushes. This morning he'd found it dead in the grass. That was the pelt he planned to skin, with my help.

Who'd pay for a smelly old skunk hide, anyway? I wanted to know.

Some guy at Bay Point would give two dollars for one, he assured me.

I wondered how I'd stand the smell until we got it skinned. I was still wondering as I held open the bag while Herbie dropped in the carcass. The stench was still with us when we opened his mother's cellar door, which was where he planned to skin it. I told Herbie his mother would skin *him* when she got a whiff of our prize.

Herbie didn't think the smell was all that bad, and to prove it he pulled the skunk out of the sack by its tail and laid it across his father's chopping block. He hadn't yet asked me to help and I wasn't about to volunteer. He owed me a buck just for standing next to the skunk and breathing, I figured.

Herbie pulled out his knife and began to cut. In the process, he must have hit the sac where the skunk perfume was stowed. He could have used his knife to cut the air that escaped the carcass.

His mother's scream meant that she smelled it right away. "Herbie! What are you doing down there? Is that a skunk I smell?"

He yelled up that he was skinning it, and he'd be through in a few minutes.

"Get that skunk out of my cellar, NOW! And clean up your mess."

Herbie hustled the skunk outside. I suddenly remembered that my mother wanted me to lug wash water for her. I didn't need his dollar, anyway. Picking up returnable bottles was a whole lot easier. Herbie must have thought so, too; he never mentioned the skunk again.

Herbie and I spent the next couple of months periwinkling by day and, in the evenings, playing cards around his mother's kitchen table.

27

DEATH OF A LABORER

In early December of 1940 the grates in the old Glenwood B stove collapsed into the ash box. My father gerry-rigged the old ones; then, flush with a full paycheck from his fifty-cent-an-hour job for Warren Eustis, broke out the Sears Roebuck catalog and ordered a new kitchen range, using the Easy Payment plan. My mother picked out a white one with a hot-water tank on the back and a warming oven on top to keep your food warm in case you were late for supper. The mail carrier's truck brought the huge packing crate from Bath and set it on our back step.

That evening my father and I uncrated it. Piece by piece we set it up. My father wheezed as we wrestled with the heavier parts, slick with packing grease. We were hefting the stove onto its base when it slipped out of my grasp and mashed the back of his grease-covered hand. He looked as if he wanted to jump all over me. Instead, he reeled off his customary cross-eyed cussing routine.

"You oughta let me get the grease out of that and put something over it before you get hydrophobia or something worse," my mother said. Hydrophobia was still my mother's greatest fear. To her, any bloody wound was an open invitation to the dreaded rabies bug.

My father shrugged it off and wrapped his bloody hand in a handkerchief. Only when we had completed the setup and he had laid a fire on the new grates did he let my mother soak and clean his wound in hot water.

He returned to work at Ledgemere the next day. By that evening, a discolored open sore covered the back of his hand. It worsened until he could barely move his fingers. Ugly red squiggles spread up his arm. My mother was worried, but he refused to see a doctor or even to talk with the nurse in town. The next morning he awoke with a bad chest cold and a burning fever, too sick to get out of bed.

"I guess I'll have to go to Togus," he told my mother.

My mother collared me and had me run up to George Gray's to ask him if he'd take my father to Togus. The deacon had taken him once or twice before, and he didn't hesitate to help again. My father had barely gotten out of bed and dressed before George's car pulled up out front. He looked old and feeble as the deacon practically carried him to the car and he struggled to climb in. To me it was just another in a long list of such trips, but my mother was in tears.

He'd been gone for a few days when his sister, Ruth, stopped by the bungalow one night after I'd gone to bed. She talked to my mother in hushed tones. I heard "blood poisoning" and "pneumonia." Aunt Ruth asked my mother if she'd like to go to Togus to see him. When my mother said no, Aunt Ruth left, and I drifted off to sleep.

Early the next morning, I went out to the woodpile and cut some firewood for the stoves. When I came back into the kitchen with an armload of kindling, I found Aunt Ruth sobbing. My mother and my sister Cora were with her. They were crying, too.

I stopped, glancing from one to the other. Aunt Ruth looked up at me teary-eyed and said, "Tommy, your father's dead."

I wanted to shout, "No, he isn't!" But no words came. I dropped the wood into the box, not fully understanding the impact of what she had said, even though death seemed a fitting visitor on that bleak

December day in that barren room, stark as the poverty that suffocated us. I collapsed onto the woodbox and stared at my aunt.

I knew I was expected to join them in sorrow, but tears refused to flow. I felt no overwhelming grief; only a disturbing sense of relief. I had mourned the loss of my father a long time ago—a father who read to us, told us stories, took us on picnics and for rides in the Model A. I had lost him when his family grew beyond his limited means to provide for it, and he no longer had the strength, the resources or the will to give them the loving attention and support they needed. I wanted to make my mother and my aunt understand, but I couldn't without making it sound as though I wished my brothers had never been born. Guilt kept me silent. I could only stand with my mouth open and stare at my aunt.

She, possibly mistaking my silence for unspeakable grief, attempted to console me.

Courtesy of Cora M. Owen

My father. He died in 1940. He was only forty-seven years old.

Courtesy of Thomas Hanna

My Auth Ruth, my father's sister, as she looked around 1960.

"Tommy," she said, "your father's in heaven. He's with the Lord."

Her soothing words rang hollow. I held my silence. Then she said something else—words that I would hear over and over and would grow to hate: "You're the man of the family now."

Her tone was heavy with implication. There was no Aid to Dependent Children or similar assistance in that era. At fourteen, as the oldest son in a family of seven—soon to be eight—children, I would be expected to find a job and help support my brothers and sisters. I heartily resented the imposition.

Sensing my discomfort, my mother suggested that I run to the store and get a quart of milk and put it on her bill. I dashed out without a word, and I heard her say to Aunt Ruth, "He needs to be alone for a while."

The air inside that kitchen had been oppressive, but the outside world proved every bit as foreboding. I was fearful that I might not appear the proper grieving son. Sonny Stevens, a boy about my age, was at the store. "Heard about your father," he said, which was about as close as a teenaged boy could come to a condolence.

"Yeah," I said, "happened last night, I guess."

He looked at me as though he expected tears. When he didn't find any, he shrugged sheepishly and turned away.

Grandpa Rowe's wife, Geneva, was behind the counter. She sometimes minded the store in the early morning while Grandpa readied the outgoing mail in the post office at the rear of the store. I mumbled my order for the milk without looking up. She was her usual dour self and gave no show of compassion.

"Guess you'll have your hands full now, young man," she said, as she handed me the bottle. While she wrote it down on my mother's account, I slipped out and headed for home, wondering how long Percy Savage would continue to extend credit to a widow with no means of support.

Aunt Ruth had left when I returned. The first of the sympathizers had begun to drop in. They would continue to come throughout that day and the next. Many of the visitors, due in part to a lack of a coordinated effort, and in part to a surplus of government flour and raisins, brought pies. Mince pies, to be exact. Our countertop was full of mince pies. Vesta's was last. Mother saw her coming from next door. The telltale package she carried spelled P-I-E.

"Oh, Lord, not another mince pie," my mother groaned.

Vesta came through the door. "I brought you a nice mince pie," she said. Then she glanced at the countertop and everyone burst out laughing. The merriment was a welcome relief.

Late that afternoon, Grampa Hanna stopped by. Because of his gentle quiet way, I didn't know what to expect. He didn't say a whole lot. In his view, there probably wasn't a whole lot that needed to be said. He took off his hat, sat in a kitchen chair and placed Richard and Blaine in his lap, one on each knee, and gently rocked them. Tears streamed down his weathered face and he wept as hard as I have ever seen a man sob. He gently put the children down, put on his hat and went out the door. I was ashamed, not for Grampa, but for me. I couldn't squeeze out a tear.

Services were held at the Second Baptist Church in Five Islands on December 24. I had made up my mind early on that I didn't want to attend. Perhaps if my father could have found some way, in his last years, to be closer to me, I would have gone and wept with the others. Some of the younger family members were just recovering from being sick, and I pleaded with my mother that I was also too sick to attend the funeral. Calling on some sixth sense that gives a mother of seven a special understanding, she hit upon the perfect solution. She was nearly eight months pregnant and feared that her attendance at the funeral might put her in labor. I could stay home and look after her, she said. She must have realized that I wasn't all that ill, but she never insisted on knowing the real reason I didn't want to go. I was grateful for that.

When Cora came home from the burial service—they had somehow managed to carve a grave out of the frozen Maine sod—I was ready to put death behind me. That evening, I was listening to radio station WWVA from Wheeling, West Virginia, on our battery-powered set. A country singer was wailing the spiritual song, "Will The Circle Be Unbroken?"

"Shut it off, shut it off!" my mother cried, her grief rekindled.

I switched to another station. Tuning out the song punctuated the end of my boyhood and thrust me, resisting mightily, into premature young manhood.

28

THE MAN OF THE FAMILY

M y mother was awarded a small pension as the widow of a disabled veteran, and an equally small amount for each of her
children. But that just wasn't enough. She needed additional help.
Mary and Irving were the only ones in school. The four youngest
were not yet ready for school, while Cora and I had already quit.

Neither Cora nor I were working full-time jobs. Cora wouldn't
find work until summer, when she earned a few dollars a week at a
board-and-breakfast place, scarcely enough to buy her clothing. That
left only me.

My mother quickly showed me just how seriously she had
taken Aunt Ruth's "man of the family" proclamation. In January, she
found a job for me clerking at a First National store in Bath. Her
cousin's husband managed the store, and he took me on to replace a
boy who was out sick. I'd work six days for a weekly wage of eighteen dollars. I'd board with Iva for three dollars a week, and the rest
would go home to my mother to help feed the family. I was ready to
argue about the skimpy pay and the fact that there'd been no mention of any spending money for me, but the thought of Iva's clean
sheets and a bathtub appealed to me. I agreed to go.

Most of First National's regular customers delivered shopping
lists to the store in the morning, and then we clerks filled the orders

Courtesy of Thomas Hanna

The Hannas in the early 1940s. (l to r): Clayton, me, Mary, Cora, Richard, and Irving. At just fourteen, I suddenly became the man of the family when my father died in 1940, and I was expected to work to support my mom and my seven siblings.

and bagged or boxed them for pickup later in the day. Some days I filled orders; some days I manned the cash register. I liked the work and quickly learned the prices and location of most items.

Life with Iva and Charlie was pleasant. The food was good. I had plenty of privacy. No one entered my room except Iva, and her boys left my things alone. She did insist that I go to church on Sunday.

One of Iva's boys, Norman, owned a violin and was taking lessons. Occasionally, I'd break out the guitar and we'd play "You Are My Sunshine" or "Home on the Range." Sometimes I'd sing. It wasn't an artistic success. I wasn't sure whether I accompanied him or he accompanied me, but we did manage to stay together most of the time.

When I wasn't working or playing the guitar, I found time to dream of Charlotte and her freckled nose and pigtails. I missed seeing her. I was tempted to write her but I couldn't work up the courage. Besides, I wouldn't know what to say.

The job lasted only until late spring. The boy I had replaced was ready to come back. Besides, the manager told me, I didn't have a Social Security card. He could get into trouble hiring a fourteen-year-old for full-time work.

I packed my suitcase, tucked my guitar under my arm and moved back to Five Islands. I hadn't been back or heard anything from or about my family since I'd left. I walked through the door and right away I noticed that the woodbox was gone. The old woodstove was now an oil stove. My mother had run out of firewood, and even if there'd been more to cut and split, there was no one there to do it. Irving was too frail, my mother said.

There was a change in my mother, too. I hardly recognized her. She had gotten a beauty parlor permanent. No more curling irons for her. Her old snaggle teeth were gone, replaced by a new set of dentures. She'd suffered complications after having her teeth extracted, and nearly died, according to Cora, but no one had told me about that at the time.

My mother looked a full ten years younger than she did before I had left, and now looked like a thirty-five-year-old woman should. She assured me right off that the money for these improvements had come from donations at the time of my father's death, and was not from the money I had been sending home.

Still, I was surprised.

"You looking for a man?" I asked.

"I could be," she said.

She not only could be, she was. She was keeping company with Ivan Pinkham, a likeable, gentle soul, a shy, retiring bachelor about my mother's age. He lived at home with his father and a half-dozen brothers and drove a 1930s car. He was a nice-enough guy, but ambition wasn't his strong suit. Around the stove at Savage's store, they allowed that he was probably the most shiftless man on God's green earth. I figured that had to be some kind of compliment, coming from his chief competition for that title.

Ivan laid his lackadaisical ways to poor health. He let it be known that his doctor had told him he had an ulcer, and that a working man's labor was a no-no for him. This didn't seem to trouble him a whole lot. He was content to work an occasional tide gathering sea urchins. He'd row the skiff while his brother took aboard the urchins. His father gave him just enough money to buy his cigarettes and gas for his car, with change left over for a crap game with his brothers.

When the tides were wrong, he left his sea egging and taxied people to Bath to do their shopping at the A&P or the First National. He usually took my mother to Bath with him and she did her shopping, or they just sat in his car parked on Front Street and watched the shoppers come and go.

He spent most of his evenings at the bungalow listening to the radio and playing Parcheesi with my mother. If his car was on the fritz, as it sometimes was, he'd stay home; the mile walk from his house to ours was just too much for him. I didn't mind having him around. I figured my mother had spent seventeen years of drudgery with my father, so she deserved a little fun. But if she wanted someone with enough gumption to help care for her children, she was working on the wrong man.

With the prospect of any support from Irving anytime soon almost nil, I was still hoping for someone else to help with family expenses. Irving, twelve, was still in grammar school—two years behind because of early health problems. He'd still be in grammar school until he was fifteen. My mother wouldn't have allowed him to work anyway, because of his health.

My relationship with Irving was about to take a turn for the worse. Over the years, we'd mostly kept to ourselves with our own friends, but during my stay in Bath, Irving had been hanging around with some of my crowd: Johnny MacGillivary, Russ Harford, Aubrey Steen, and Carl Rowe. When I rejoined the group, I wanted Irving out of it. No self-respecting teenager, especially one who was the man of the family, wanted his kid brother around, especially not a brother who'd run home and tell Mother whenever Big Brother did something Mother shouldn't find out about. Irving didn't see it that way. He had a mind to hang around.

I couldn't very well smack him because my mother would be all over me, but I had developed a sharp tongue and I used it unmercifully to heap ridicule on my younger brother in front of my friends. That usually drove him home in a rage so terrible that he looked for ways to hurt me. He hadn't quite gotten up the courage to attack me, so his payback was limited to messing with my personal gear.

I came home one evening after one of our more vocal set-tos. Irving was not at home. My mother was in the living room, worry on her face. My collection of movie star and fighter plane pictures that I'd kept under my mattress had been ripped to shreds and tossed onto my cot.

My mother shrugged helplessly. "He shouldn't have done that, but don't you two go to fighting over it."

I sat down on my bed. "You just wait until he gets home. I'll beat his friggin' head in."

I didn't have long to wait. I leaped off my cot in the living room and charged into him, screaming. I slammed a vicious blow to his middle. He collapsed to the floor in a heap and went into his wounded quail act. Whenever I hit him, he used it to gain sympathy.

Courtesy of Thomas Hanna

My mom. She was just thirty-four in December of 1940 when she found herself a pregnant widow with seven children and no real means of support.

He groaned, he moaned. He clutched at his chest. I wasn't impressed, but my mother was taken in by it.

She knelt beside her groaning offspring.

"Look what you've done to your brother," she said, near to tears. "He's probably dying."

"Ma," I said, "can't you see he's faking it?"

She couldn't. He stopped moaning after a while and she helped him to his feet. He struggled to look every bit the abused child. She sat him in a chair, all the while glaring at me, her bullying son. Proud of myself, I took my guitar and slipped outside. I sat on the back step, strummed my guitar and sang, not minding the sibling suffering going on inside.

One afternoon in early June when I came home from the base-ball field, my mother announced she'd found me a job. Roland Peterson was looking for someone to deliver groceries on McMahan Island. She'd told him I'd take it. Peterson and his wife owned the general store at Robinhood village on the north end of Georgetown Island. They provided groceries and ferry service to the summer residents of McMahan, which was just off the east shore of Georgetown Island, midway between Five Islands and Robinhood.

On the north end of the mile-long island was a boys' camp. My father had occasionally worked for its owner back in the 1930s. On the south end were a dozen or so summer cottages, most on the east shore, overlooking Sheepscot Bay. The summer colony also included a lodge and a small seasonal post office. There were barracks-like buildings, too, to house the teen workers.

"McMahan Island?" I said. "How am I gonna get there—swim?"

She'd covered all bases.

"Harlan said he'd sell you his skiff for three dollars."

Harlan was a sometime clam digger. He had planned to use the skiff to ferry his clams ashore, but he never seemed to find the time for clamming that summer, what with his lobstering and loving the daylights out of my sister Cora.

"But I don't have the job yet," I protested. "How can I buy a boat?"

She was still that step and a half ahead.

"You can pay Harlan out of your first week's wages." She pointed toward the door. "Now you march yourself right down to the store and make that call."

I rang up Mr. Peterson, he explained the job, then hired me before I could change my mind. He wanted me at the McMahan Island boat landing by seven each morning, Monday through Saturday. I'd help Aubrey Fullerton deliver milk and groceries, then

I'd take the *Viking*, his little lapstrake boat, over to Robinhood and have lunch with the Petersons. After lunch I was to do odd jobs until four o'clock. They'd ferry me back to McMahan Island and I'd row home. The pay was twelve dollars for the week. Then, in what he seemed to think was a charitable afterthought, he added, "On Saturday you deliver only milk and then have the afternoon off."

I thanked him for his generosity and hung up.

On the very first morning I discovered just how difficult this job was. To reach the McMahan boat landing, my boat had to pass through the narrows that separate McMahan from Georgetown Island, a fifty-yard-wide stretch of sometimes turbulent water. On a flood tide, the flat-bottomed boat could skim the water and coast to the landing, but that first morning the tide was at full ebb. One day I would learn to take advantage of the eddies and backflows, but that day the greenest of greenhorns rowed full into the teeth of the outrushing tide. Twenty minutes later I was a good fifty feet behind where I had started and fearful that I might pull my arms out of their sockets.

But for a lobsterman on his way out to haul his traps, I might have missed my first morning on the job altogether. Noticing my predicament, he idled his boat alongside me and asked where I was headed. "Toss me your painter, and I'll give you a tow." He secured my skiff to the stern of his boat, took me through the narrows and cast me loose just off the McMahan landing.

The *Viking* had already tied up at the float and Aubrey Fullerton was offloading the milk onto a pair of wheelbarrows in the roadway above the landing. While I secured my skiff, he sized me up.

"You can't weigh over one-ten soaking wet. You sure you can handle this job?"

When I said I could, he motioned toward the one remaining wooden case holding several quart bottles of milk.

"Take this up and put it on the wheelbarrow."

It was about mid-tide and the ramp leading up to the roadway stood at a good thirty-degree angle. I was in for a major tussle, but I wasn't about to let Aubrey think I couldn't handle one little old case of milk, thirty-degree list and all. I wrestled it up and eased it into the wheelbarrow. Then I turned real quick and swaggered away, hoping he couldn't see me gasping for air. I didn't even want to think of doing this at dead low water.

Aubrey grabbed the handles of one wheelbarrow. "Okay, you take the other one and follow me."

We followed the wagon road up to the center of the island a couple hundred yards away. Aubrey stopped and transferred the bottles into smaller containers. With each of us taking a cottage at a time, we delivered our cargo, picked up their empties and brought the wheelbarrows back to the landing for seconds.

Around nine-thirty, the *Viking* arrived at the landing and we unloaded a dozen or more baskets of groceries. The island caretaker

Courtesy of Gene Reynolds

In the foreground middle is Malden Island off Five Islands harbor. The island at the top is McMahan Island, where I delivered groceries during the summer of 1941.

had brought his horse and cart to the landing to pick up incoming freight. "Put your groceries on the back and I'll drop them off at the top of the hill," he told Aubrey. From the hilltop, delivery was a snap.

Shortly after noon, we pulled up to the landing beside Peterson's store back at Robinhood. Once inside the white frame building, I could see that Peterson's, with its shelves and shelves of S.S. Pierce, the Cadillac of canned goods, was special. Savage's at Five Islands didn't carry S.S. Pierce. His regular customers couldn't afford it. They considered it food for Summer Complaints.

The Petersons' cook asked me, "Would you like to wash your hands in the bathroom before you eat?"

A bathroom! It had a gleaming white wash basin, sparkling chrome faucets, all beside a flush toilet. "They're money people," my mother had told me. Now I believed it. Few people in Georgetown could afford a bathroom. At fourteen, I was totally awed by all that high-class living.

Lunch was served around a massive oak table in a dining room that in my mother's house would have slept six. Mr. Peterson brought the discussion around to me. "How did Tom do this morning, Aubrey?"

"A tad small," Aubrey said, "but he can carry his share of the load."

I stared at my plate and tried to conceal my pleasure.

Mr. Peterson turned to me and said, "Good, but the day's only half over. Mrs. Peterson will find something for you to do around the store this afternoon."

Mrs. Peterson introduced me to a wheelbarrow and a shovel and set me to work clearing away what looked to be a minor mountain of gravel and rocks beside their spanking-new gasoline pump in front of the store. I filled barrow after barrow and carted them to a dumping area down by the shore. The thought occurred to me that if I had a choice of hauling gravel or milk, the milk would win hands down.

I'd been shoveling for what seemed like an hour, but was probably no more than twenty minutes, when I got a thirst for one of those cream sodas from the cooler just inside the door. I didn't think Mrs. Peterson would mind because she had been so nice at dinner.

I threw down my shovel and went inside like I owned the place, took out my soda, popped the cap on the opener on the side of the cooler and took a swig. Mrs. Peterson watched me, but she didn't say anything until I sat down on one of the customer's chairs beside the door. "Young man, we don't pay you to hang around the store drinking soda. There's work to do out there."

I fished a nickel out of my pocket, but she said, "That one's on me, but from now on you pay a nickel like everyone else."

I guzzled my drink and hurried outside, mentally adding Mrs. Peterson to my list of people I could learn to dislike.

Around 4:30 I was on my way back to McMahan. Once there, I cast off my skiff and rode the ebbing tide all the way to Five Islands.

On my second week of work Mr. Peterson approached me. "I've been thinking—perhaps you could come to McMahan on Sunday morning and deliver the Sunday papers."

This was an unwelcome turn of events.

"I don't work on Sundays," I said. This was not out of any deep and abiding faith in the Almighty; it was merely a teenager shying away from working seven days a week.

For a few seconds, he stared at me as though I were an ungrateful child. And then he said, "Well, if you don't come in on Sunday, I can only pay you eleven dollars a week."

I didn't want to believe what I had heard. I wanted to tell him what he could do with his job, but I needed the money, and steady work for fourteen-year-olds in 1941 was hard to find. I bit my tongue and said, "I'll take the eleven dollars." And then with an air of defiance, "I won't work on Sunday."

I stayed on at eleven a week. Sunday work was never mentioned again. Mr. Peterson joined his wife at the top of my list. But,
as my father used to be fond of reminding us, "Every dog has its day."
When outside work was scarce, Mrs. Peterson shipped me off to the
warehouse to "spruce up the place." I found myself amid cases and
cases of bottled soda—warm but wet—and shelves of boxed cookies
and crackers. I divided my time between sweeping, stacking and
munching. For every twinge of conscience that clogged my throat, I
took a swig of soda and thought about the eleven dollars. Then I discarded my guilt as easily as I had the empty cookie boxes. If the
Petersons noticed an open carton or an empty bottle, they didn't
mention it.

The summer moved on. I turned fifteen. On Labor Day weekend, I made my final run to McMahan. At the end of the day, Mr.
Peterson met me at McMahan landing and handed me my final
pay—along with a couple of surprises.

"You've been a hard worker this summer, Tom. Most young
men would have quit, but you stayed with it. So I've decided to pay
you the twelve a week. You'll find an extra ten in there."

Before I could express my thanks, he reached into his pocket,
pulled out another twenty and handed it to me. "And a little bonus
from Mrs. Peterson and me for all your hard work."

I was so excited, I almost forgot to thank him, and I almost
confessed to him about the cookies and crackers. As I rowed through
the narrows on the outgoing tide, I moved the Petersons to my list of
people I liked.

I sold the skiff back to Harlan for two dollars—used skiff, he
said—and vowed that under no terms would I return to Peterson's
the next year. But the summer hadn't been a total loss; I had dared
take on a man's job and had done well. I was primed for the challenge of full-time work. And a naive teenager had learned a couple

of lessons he'd never forget: A man is only as good as his word, and don't be too quick to judge your elders.

After the long, hard summer at McMahan's, I wanted a small vacation, but my mother had other plans.

"We have to find you a new job," she said.

I told her I wasn't ready for that, but her mind was made up. Now that I was fifteen she'd send to the state for my Social Security card. I'd get hired quicker that way.

I took to sleeping late. My mother couldn't abide a slugabed. One morning after her second call, I still wasn't up. She was not to be denied. She brought a glass of cold water and dumped it on my head. The bedding was soaked. I crawled out protesting and slipped into my trousers.

I was the man of the family, she said. I had a responsibility here and it was high time I tended to it.

"Why do I have to do it?" I shot back. "They're not my kids."

"Because you're the oldest," her voice was rising, "and there's no one else."

I got right up into her face. Weeks of pent-up bitterness spewed out with as much meanness as I could muster.

"Someday I'm going to see that man in Hell, and I'm gonna ask him why he had so damned many kids."

The anger drained out of her. Her face blanched. That shot had hurt her. She was ready to cry. I finished dressing, jammed my hat onto my head and stormed out of the house. Before I had gotten halfway to the store, I had cooled down and regretted what I'd said. It was just that at fifteen, I didn't want to be the man of the family. I wanted to be a teenager, doing teenage things, like messing around with a car.

And there just happened to be a beat-up car parked right out front of the store, a Model A Ford coupe. It belonged to Mansfield, the boy who used to tend the fires at the school. Now eighteen, Mansfield had quit school two years earlier and bought a lobster boat. He had just come in from tending his lobster traps. Herbie was with him, waiting for the tide to change so he could go dig clams. A couple of other boys were hanging around the Ford. I joined them and climbed on to the running boards to check out the inside of Mansfield's car.

Without warning, Mansfield started the engine, shoved it in gear and moved up Bowling Alley Hill. I clung to the door and screamed for him to let me off. Mansfield cut loose with one of his idiotic giggles. "I'm goin' to take you all the way to Bath," he yelled.

I believed Mansfield was just far enough off-center to do it, and I was terrified. "Let me off," I begged. "I can't hold on." All Mansfield did was giggle some more and step on the gas.

By the time we passed Charles's Pond and began the long climb up Chase Hill, I was sure Mansfield was headed for Bath. I had to jump off or fall off. As we neared the crest, the overloaded Model A slowed to a creep. I leaped off and hit the ground running, trying to stay on my feet, but the car had been moving too fast. I lost my balance and skidded along the blacktop.

Mansfield stopped the car and backed up.

"You goddamned fool! You goddamned fool!" He pulled abreast of me. "Are you hurt?"

"I don't think so," I said, still trying to catch the wind that had been knocked out of me.

"Get inside," he ordered.

Herbie opened the door and I crawled in. I hadn't broken any bones, but the pavement had scraped my knee and skinned all the meat off my left elbow. Blood oozed out of the nasty wound and stained my shirt. Herbie gave me his handkerchief.

All the way home Mansfield railed at me. "Don't you tell anyone about this and let them know what a goddamned idiot you are."

Herbie agreed with him. By the time Mansfield stopped to let me out at the store, I was ready to apologize to Mansfield for being so stupid.

I stopped in at the store and bought a dime's worth of chocolate candy and went home. My mother was sitting at the kitchen table. She wasn't crying, but her eyes were red. She didn't speak. I dropped the bag of candy on the table and rummaged through the cupboard for the Cloverine. I found some gauze and tape and was fixing myself a bandage, when she noticed the blood on my sleeve. She wanted to know how it happened.

"Me and some of the guys were scufflin'. Somebody threw me down onto the road and I skun my elbow on the tar."

She was suddenly all mother, and one of her little boys was hurting. She gave it a practiced once-over. "That's a nasty-lookin' mess. It'll take more'n Cloverine Salve to fix that."

She opened the cupboard and brought out the Epsom salts. She heated a pan of water until it was about as hot as I could stand; then she dumped in the salts and ordered me to stick my elbow into it.

I cringed at the thought of putting my raw meat into those hot salts. She grabbed my arm. She thrust my elbow into the pan and held it there as I moaned and squirmed.

"Don't be so spleeny," she chided. "You'd think I was killin' you."

She left me to soak on my own while she took out some tape and a bandage and smeared it with Cloverine Salve. She dried the elbow and bandaged it. "There; let's see what that will do. Should be better by morning."

By morning, it was worse. Over the next couple of days, red streamers were moving up my arm toward my shoulder. Aunt Ruth got together some money to pay for gas and I got a ride to the doctor, who confirmed I had blood poisoning and gave me some Ichthammol that worked almost overnight.

It was back to looking for work, but in spite of my best efforts—and my mother's—it was not forthcoming. Finally, Mert Pinkham offered to take me periwinkling with him. His father bought periwinkles and sea urchins and shipped them to Boston and New York. He allowed it would take two to carry a bushel of periwinkles over the slippery seaweed.

Mert showed me how to maneuver over the treacherous, weed-covered rocks. He taught me to find the shallow tidal pools where great clusters of periwinkles, some as big as your thumb, could be scooped out by the double handful. I spent my time gathering periwinkles for a buck and a half a bushel. The best I could do on a twelve-foot tide was two bushels.

Mert and I periwinkled on into the fall. As the days shortened and the cold deepened, there were times when my hands dipped in icy water turned white and numb within seconds.

29

WARTIME WORK

I t was along about this time, nearly a year after my father's death, that Johnny MacGillivary, my second cousin, and I began a long and close friendship that lasted past our teen years. Both of us had our eyes on Charlotte Gray, but neither one of us were able to get to first base with her. I suspected she was playing one of us against the other. Together, we joined the ranks of rejected suitors. The following year Charlotte would be off to North Yarmouth Academy, and we would see her only during school vacations. I considered NYA girls out of my league, anyway.

Johnny, still in seventh grade, earned his spending money janitoring at Five Islands Baptist Church. Each Sunday morning he built fires in the two large woodstoves at the rear of the church, and all day he stoked them so that the faithful could worship in relative comfort through evening services. Sometimes I accompanied him on his rounds.

One Sunday evening in early December, as he brought a new supply of wood into the church, he casually mentioned, "The Japs bombed Pearl Harbor today."

"Where's Pearl Harbor?"

He shrugged. "Some place in Hawaii."

I remembered Hawaii as a place way out in the middle of the Pacific Ocean. His remark meant little to me.

When I came home that evening, my mother was listening to the radio. Reports were coming in from the Pacific, and over the next couple of days we gradually learned the extent of this sneak attack on our Hawaiian naval base. President Roosevelt told us we were at war with Japan—although war was a word that still had little meaning for a fifteen-year-old in Five Islands, Maine.

Roosevelt's declaration brought an immediate increase in the number of young men drafted into the service. Thousands more enlisted monthly, including Herbie Campbell. Suddenly, there was a shortage of laborers to work in defense industries. Younger and younger men were being hired to fill the jobs of men now gone into the service. That shortage would speed me, with my new Social Security card in hand, to my next employment.

In March of 1942, Iva called on my mother again—no presen-t'ment this time—to say she'd found a job for me at the Bath Box Company. She said that as long as I sent most of my money home to my mother, I could stay with her for $5 a week, up from the previous $3 per week board now that I'd be making more money. Once again, I packed my suitcase, grabbed my guitar, and moved in with Iva. The following morning I checked in with the manager at the box factory. He told me they were making wooden ammunition boxes for the U.S. Army's thirty- and fifty-caliber machine-gun shells. My full-time job paid fifty cents an hour—just this summer I had been making only $11 a week. I was assigned to a man with a table saw. It was my job to keep the area around his saw clear of wood scraps. I bundled and tied them, then brought them to a man on the gang saw. His saws cut them into kindling.

As the months went by, life at Iva's was uneventful, sometimes boring. I made few friends, none female. Occasionally I attended evening church services with Iva to show my appreciation for what she was doing for me. I had very little contact with my mother or my siblings. They didn't make the effort and neither did I. Every Saturday I sent home a money order for fifteen dollars, except for those weeks I needed clothing.

I was satisfied with my job—until I got to know Stubby Warner. Stubby was my age, but had been working at the box factory for several months. He was doing the same job as I, at a different saw. He made the mistake of telling me one day that he was getting fifty-five cents an hour.

I immediately barged in on Mr. Knight and asked him why I wasn't getting the same.

"Seniority," he said. "Warner's been here longer than you."

When I protested, he offered me the fifty-five. I took it, but intended to leave as soon as something better came up.

Late that summer of 1942, I spotted a newspaper ad in *The Bath Times*. Volpe Construction was looking for help constructing houses at the north end of Bath. Volpe had won a government contract to build Lambert Park, a housing development for shipyard workers. The pay was seventy-five cents an hour, with overtime, too. With that kind of money, I could give more to my mother and still have enough left over for an occasional movie, something I hadn't done since I'd moved back in with Iva.

I told Mr. Knight I was leaving. "What's the matter," he said, "you want more pay? Okay, I'll up it to sixty."

"Volpe's paying seventy-five," I said.

"Yeah, but that's only temporary. It'll be over in less than a year. Box factory will still be here. Besides, here you'll be working inside where it's warm and dry. That Lambert Park is a swamp. Gonna be cold in the winter, too."

I'd heard that the land for Lambert Park was wet and boggy. The government had purchased it from one of Bath's leading families, and, rumor had it, the government had been taken.

In spite of his persuasive arguments, the lure of higher wages won. I quit, packed my bags and moved back to the bungalow. Because of the jobs, two buses were now running daily trips from Georgetown to Bath for a few dollars a week fare. I gave my mother Iva's five plus a few more and rode the bus to work, along with the rest of the dropout gang who hired on with Volpe as carpenter's helpers.

The first workday a straw boss showed us around the site. Single and double ranch-style houses and duplexes were in various stages of construction. The walls were prefabricated in Woolwich, trucked in on a flatbed, and then hoisted into place and nailed.

Mr. Knight was right. The entire area was muck up over our ankles. Every step I took, I risked leaving my gum rubber boots in the mud. I was working with a man who was shingling the sides of the houses, so I was lucky enough to spend most of my time up on staging. Down below, the general helpers slogged through the muck carrying heavy loads.

I helped my carpenter rig the staging; then we laid the cedar shingles along chalk lines and nailed them. We started in the middle. He went in one direction, I went in the other. Hoping to impress my mentor, I fitted and nailed, fitted and nailed, with hardly a moment for a deep breath. I reached my end before he did and sat back to wait for him to compliment me. He frowned as he checked my work. He picked up the shingles I had left in my stack "You see these? They're all narrow. That's because you used all the wide ones to get to this point. If you kept that up, one half your wall would be all wide shingles and the other half all narrow. And that looks like hell."

I was afraid he'd make me take mine off and do them over. All he said was, "From now on, just mix them up as you go."

I thought he might tell my boss, but he didn't, and shortly I was as quick and sure a shingler as he was. He sometimes let me lay out the chalk line for the next tier.

A good paying job, reasonable hours, and spending change in my pocket; I had everything except a girl. I was still pining for Charlotte, but not so much that I couldn't be had if a girl were forward enough.

My cousin, Mary Lou Pinkham, brought the bold one I'd been looking for into my life. And she hadn't really set out to do it. Mary Lou attended North Yarmouth Academy, some twenty-five miles away, and occasionally brought a school friend home with her on weekends. One Friday evening in late October, I had gone down to the store looking for Johnny. There I met Mary Lou and a couple of her friends. She had an NYA girl with her. Another redhead, tiny, but attractive. I took to her right away. Mary Lou introduced me to Helen, and for a few seconds I dared to entertain the thought of making it with a high-class girl from NYA.

Then, before I had time to savor the prospect, Mary Lou said, "You haven't seen Johnny, have you?"

Here we go, I thought. I'm finishing second to Johnny again.

And that's when Helen, bless her red-headed heart, said something for which she would forever hold a warm spot inside me. She rolled her big blue eyes in my direction and told Mary Lou, "I'd rather stay right here."

I couldn't believe it. An NYA girl wanted to keep me company. And she wasn't interested in meeting Johnny, someone Mary Lou had probably praised to high heaven.

"Let's go out and take a walk around town," Helen said, looking at me.

I was halfway out the door before anyone had a chance to suggest otherwise. Outside, a bright autumn moon had risen over the

Sheepscot and I could see Helen's features as she walked close to me. She was even more attractive in the soft moonlight.

As we came abreast of the ice cream parlor, I managed to say, "Why don't we sit here for a while?"

That's when Mary Lou showed good grace and tact.

"Why don't we just leave you two alone?"

Bless you, I said to myself.

The other girls left and the old fears returned. Here was my big chance to practice what I had learned from Glennis, and I was afraid that I'd be tongue-tied again. I needn't have worried. Helen led the conversation and everything else for the evening. After we'd chatted through the get-acquainted stage, she moved in, stuck her face close to mine, wrapped her arm around my neck and showed me what a real kiss was like. I couldn't get enough of it. After she had put me through a series of tongue-twisting exercises, I was panting and not caring if the whole world checked out my manhood.

We carried on that way until she looked at her watch. "It's almost ten. I have to go in now. Mary Lou's folks said ten o'clock."

We slowly made our way to Mary Lou's house, our arms wrapped around each other. I kissed her good-night and she went inside. But not before she promised to see me the next evening. I floated home. I was in love again.

Saturday night was more of the same, and when it was over, she promised to write. Now my life was complete. I had it all.

The joy of a decent job with good hours didn't last long. My boss at Volpe told me that I might be expected to work overtime. All of us had signed up knowing this, even though, riding the bus, we couldn't get to the site until seven-fifteen and had to leave no later than four to have time to walk downtown to catch the Bath Iron Works bus, which left promptly at four-fifteen.

After about the third week, my boss said he wanted his crew to work from six to six. I explained about the bus.

He listened patiently, then he said, "Stay up here in our barracks. There's plenty of room."

Volpe had constructed a long, low building just across the street from the worksite and filled it with cots and lockers. Workers could stay there for a few dollars a week. Of course there was no provision to feed the tenants. If I stayed, I'd have to take my meals in a diner downtown. I mentally counted the cost for room and meals. It would take quite a chunk out of my paycheck and I'd still have to give my mother my "Man of the Family" share. I declined his offer.

"You'd better think it over," he said as I walked away.

He had given the other Five Islanders the same spiel. As one we agreed that we wouldn't or couldn't stay in Bath. We told him so the next morning. He studied us for a while, then he said, "I'll need you boys in another job today." He brought us to an area where crews were laying foundations. All the underpinnings were made of cinder blocks. Our job was to carry the blocks from a flatbed truck to the site. The added weight of cinder blocks forced our feet deeper into the muck. We were slogged through the mire without a breather until the ten o'clock coffee break. When I went to get my coffee, I noticed another boy up on the staging with my carpenter, looking down at me.

At lunch I asked my boss when I was going back to carpentering. "I have to put you where you're needed most," he said, and walked away.

It turned out that what he needed most from those who wouldn't work overtime was full-time general helper types to bring blocks to masons, pipe to the plumbers and heavy timbers and roofing materials to the carpenters. We all held our ground about overtime and worked our butts off for seventy-five cents an hour while the carpenters did the shingling and the roofing.

30

BIW

F all chilled down toward winter. The ground froze and walking at the construction site was easier, but the building materials got no lighter. Fed up with construction work, we Five Islanders kept our eyes and ears peeled for jobs more suitable for bright young teenagers.

In early December of 1942, a year after the attack on Pearl Harbor, we heard the news that Bath Iron Works planned to start hiring sixteen-year-olds after the first of the year. We'd heard rumors of good jobs before, but we decided to check this one out. We left work a few minutes early and stopped by the BIW employment office. They couldn't promise us anything definite but took our names and addresses and said they'd notify us.

Every day when I came home from work I checked the mail. Finally, the week before Christmas, it came; a notice from BIW saying they would begin hiring sixteen-year-olds the first Monday after the New Year.

My elation at the prospect of a BIW job was dampened by a setback in my love life. Helen had been hit by an attack of homesickness and had left North Yarmouth Academy to return to Connecticut. We continued to write. She was confident that we would see each other soon and talked of my coming to visit her. I secretly made plans to do just that as soon as my BIW job allowed me to put away a few dollars.

I gave my notice to Volpe and, on the appointed Monday morning in January, I and about a hundred other sixteen-year-olds from as far away as Lewiston, descended on BIW. First, we sat down and filled out an application. When asked what I wanted to do, I put down carpenter. My experience with Volpe ought to count for something.

After that came the physical. A doctor poked, prodded and peeked at both ends until I was declared fit to be a BIW helper. Then, without regard for talent, aptitude or experience, we were parceled out to various departments. I was tapped for the Outside Machinist Department. A machinist! That was even better than a carpenter. I pictured myself at a high-priced lathe of some sort, turning out the special kind of ship parts that only a machinist could make.

A dozen or more of us were taken to the outside machine shop to see Joe, the wizened foreman. To my juvenile eyes, he didn't look like he'd make it through the war. He gave us all a lecture on the virtues of hard work and the evils of absenteeism. I was assigned to a machinist in the gun director crew. I had no idea what a gun director was. My machinist, Rollins, was old, too, sixty if he was a day. He was a close-mouthed man from somewhere Down East, and he was standing at the office door beside a god-awful big toolbox.

He studied my five-foot-four undersized frame, shook his head, and sighed. "I guess we'll just have to make the best of it."

He pointed to the toolbox. "Now, if you'll just pick up that box, we'll go on up to the director."

When I hesitated, he informed me, "Helper always carries the mechanic's tools."

The box was every bit as heavy as it looked. With a little assistance from him, I hoisted it to my shoulder and followed him out the door.

"Where's the gun director?" I wanted to get this load off my back.

He pointed to a spot at the very top of the ship. "Right up there."

I followed him up the gangway and up a few inclined ladders. When I struggled under the load, he helped me wrestle it up to the next level. Finally, we came to a round, turret-like structure about five feet across and five feet high with a boxy compartment atop it. There was an open hinged door in the side of the turret.

While we rested and I caught my breath, he explained that that box up there was the gun director. It had a telescope inside and turned 360 degrees to locate the Jap ships we'd sink.

There was no high-priced machinery in sight. "Where's the lathe?"

"What lathe?"

"If I'm going to be a machinist, there ought to be a lathe around here somewhere."

He must have thought I was joking, because he had himself a hearty laugh before he set me straight.

"There ain't any lathes up here, son. There was a milling machine here when they smoothed out the foundation, but it's long since gone."

"What am I supposed to do up here, anyway?"

"You see all those bolts and bolt holes up there around the base of the director? Well, you and me are goin'ta sit on that stagin' and drill some more of them bolt holes with the biggest damned air drill you ever saw. Then we're gonna bolt that contraption to the foundation. Now, let's go back to the tool crib and check out the tools we'll need."

The tool crib was in a corner of the outside machine shop. The mechanic called out to the tool clerk his required tools. "Air drill, air hose, drill bits, drill board and hook, carbon tetrachloride, strong back, old man . . ."

Strong back? Old man? I had a lot to learn. The first being that the strong back and old man were two heavy pieces of steel that I had to wrestle to the top of the ship every morning, along with the equally heavy air drill.

My dream of machining my way to shipyard glory shattered, I settled in to the boring routine of drilling and bolting at the top of the ship. My mechanic showed me how to set up the strong back and old man to hold the air drill in place and align it so that the holes were bored straight and true. Then, the drill board and hook were rigged to give leverage against the drill and force the drill bit into the steel plate. Finally the plate was doused with carbon tet to soften it and speed the drilling time.

The drilling wasn't too difficult to master once Rollins had marked out the spots for the holes, but bolting was another matter. I could never remember which way to turn the wrench for tightening the bolt. Whenever we started bolting, I'd hold my hand in front of me and turn my wrist in a clockwise direction; then I'd say to myself, "RON—right on." Rollins would give me a funny look, but he never asked me why I was making strange hand signals in thin air, and I was afraid to explain; I'd never get a raise.

I couldn't have chosen a worse time to sign on for an outside machinist's job, because the arrival of 1943 ushered in one of the most intense cold waves in memory. For days on end, I woke up to ten- to twenty-below temperatures. On the coldest of those workday morns, I returned to my childhood ways. I stood on a kitchen chair beside the stove to grab some of the warmth that hovered in the air just above. There I was, my feet in the chair and my head inside the warming oven to take a little frost off my ears, trying to tell my mother what to cook me for breakfast. It came out in a hollow voice that reminded me somewhat of Mr. District Attorney, my favorite radio character. In a measured stentorian voice that was like hollering down an empty rain barrel, the DA came on the air and promised to maintain law and order. I remembered his words, and while my mother cooked my oatmeal, the oven and I entertained her with our own booming DA soundalike:

"And it shall be my duty as District Attorney not only to prose-
cute to the limit of the law, all persons accused of crime perpetrated
within this county, but to defend with equal vigor the rights and
privileges of all its citizens."

My mother laughed. But then, she was always one of my
biggest fans; she always laughed when I clowned around like that.

I'd leave home before the fires in the stove had taken the chill
from the house and climb into an equally chilly bus. Early boarders
grabbed the seats closest to the heater in the front; the rest shivered
in the rear. The air outside was so chilled that the low spots along the
road to Bath were fogged in with sea smoke, or what we Down
Easters called vapor.

On those frigid mornings, the moisture in the air drills froze
solid within seconds. We could do nothing but crawl into the turret
and huddle next to an electric heater. The moisture from our breath
and the heat from our bodies condensed and clung to the turret
walls in a heavy white frost.

Most days during that cold snap, the temperature rarely got
above single digits. Work on the directors and in many of the other
trades was at a standstill. By midmorning the turret was crowded
with workers looking for an inside shelter and a place to pass the
time with idle conversation. And the talk, the way it can in a group
of men with nothing better to do, eventually got around to women.

"We oughta have a woman up here to keep us company," one
young man suggested.

When there was general agreement, he slipped out, and shortly
brought back a woman acquaintance from the cleanup gang. I
thought she'd come for some friendly conversation, until I noticed
that her coveralls were split open at the crotch. He took her up into
the director; then, one by one the men paid her a visit.

When it came my turn, I refused. "Go ahead," they coaxed, "it's only a buck a throw."

One fellow offered, "If you don't have the money, I'll pay for it."

I couldn't admit that this would be my first time. It was almost embarrassing that a full-time shipyard worker and man of the family to boot had never known a woman. I just didn't want my first time to be like that, though, and I stuck to my guns. Mostly the men accepted my refusal, though there were a few suggestive remarks that I might not have what it took to do the job.

The weather finally broke and we escaped our icy prison. With the spring of 1943 came an added change to the gun director job. The shipfitters built a framework of bars and bolted it to the top of the director. I asked my mechanic what it was for. He didn't want to discuss it at first. "It's all kind of hush-hush," he said, "some kind of gadget that tells where a ship is. May even take the place of the telescope."

If it was some kind of secret, I didn't think they'd want me talking about it, so I said no more. Later in the day, though, he said to me just above a whisper, "I think they call it a radar. They're going to put it on the ship down in Boston."

I just nodded my head and vowed never to repeat that secret word again for as long as I worked. It did give me a thrill, though, to think I was working on a secret project.

Outdoor work in the brisk air was invigorating. As we worked, I tried to engage my taciturn mechanic in conversation. Rollins seemed not to mind that I did most of the talking, mainly about my family and the tough times. He was sympathetic about my father's passing and arranged for me to get as much overtime as I wanted. Actually I wanted very little of it, but I couldn't let him think his helper was a common ingrate. And the pay was good. A full seven days with double-time for Sunday earned me fifty-eight dollars, less my social security and union dues. I still couldn't believe that one man could earn that much money in one week. In my book that was good living. The previous summer I was only earning $11 per week.

I was so flush that I decided it was high time I went to work on replacing Sadie's living room ceiling at the bungalow. I was able to pay Bath Lumber on time for a half-dozen four-by-eight Celotex panels, more than enough to cover up Clark Gable and the 1935 Ford advertisement as well.

Right away I discovered that putting up Celotex was a two-man job; you can't hold and nail at the same time. The only available help at the time was my four-eleven mother. Even when she stood on her tiptoes and reached as high as she could, she was still a couple of feet away from being of any help. Sister Cora wasn't a whole lot better. Irving wasn't strong enough to help, my mother said. So I made my mother a stick, a T-square kind of rig from a couple of pieces of strapping. She'd go to the far end of the panel and hold the T end of the stick flat against the ceiling while I stood on a step stool and nailed my end. The work was slow going, mainly because of all the BIW overtime. I could only work evenings and Sundays, at most.

In mid-spring, the good life and the work on the ceiling was interrupted. One Friday afternoon, I came home with a sore throat. I bought a box of cough drops and ignored it. Sore throats were common in the harsh Maine climate. The next morning, my throat was on fire.

My mother looked inside. "Tonsillitis," she pronounced. "Should be okay by Monday."

She wanted to give me an aspirin, but I couldn't swallow it. She was forced to admit that she'd never seen a case of tonsillitis this severe. What I really had was strep throat, an infection that could lead to more serious illness. The infection hung on for three days before I rolled out of bed, weak and shaky, but happy to return to BIW. Winter's back was broken and the early spring sunshine warmed us as we worked.

I had been back for just a week or two when my feet and ankle joints swelled so painfully I was forced to leave work on Friday afternoon. That evening I soaked my feet in hot water. It seemed to help, but by Saturday morning I could barely walk, and the stiffness had spread to my knees. My mother rummaged through the medicines in the cupboard and brought out some kind of minty-smelling ointment to apply to the joints. It provided only temporary relief. Still, she seemed confident that it would clear up in a few days.

She completely missed the mark on that one. I came down with a severe fever. The pain and swelling spread to my hands, shoulders, and neck until my joints popped out. I couldn't roll over in bed or turn my head. My mother gave me a milk-bottle urinal and a borrowed bedpan.

By week's end it was all over Five Islands that Lulu's boy Tommy was severely under the weather. That brought Lloyd Pinkham, who was now a town selectman, to the bungalow. He had been a schoolmate of my mother's, and since my father's death he had come 'round to help whenever he could.

He came into the living room where I was laid out on my sister Cora's brown metal bed, and checked me over. He told my mother that I should be in the hospital. When she complained that she had no money and no way to get me there, he said he'd see about it and not to worry about the cost. He left. By late afternoon an ambulance had delivered me to a Bath Hospital bed. Lloyd had gone down to the store and told Grandpa Rowe. Between them and a few others, they had collected enough money to hire the ambulance. Lloyd had arranged for the state to foot the hospital bill. Even though I was working, there was no money for extras or an emergency like this.

I was in the hospital's one large ward, which had fifteen or so beds, each with a curtain for privacy. A single bathroom, which wouldn't do me any good until I could get up to use it, was beside my bed. The man in the next bed must have just come in from the operating room, because he was breathing out ether fumes. The whole place reeked of it, fit to put us all to sleep.

Dr. Grant was a white-haired man with a Down East country-doctor air that gave me confidence in him. He asked me a lot of questions about my symptoms and when he had finished, he told me I had rheumatic fever. It was serious, he said, but he could cure it.

Aubrey Steen, father of one of my Five Islands buddies, was in a bed just across the aisle from me. He had fallen down some stairs and fractured a bone in his neck. Though he was in traction, he remained in high spirits. The way he cracked bad jokes about his illness made the rest of us less apprehensive about our own.

After supper I told the nurse I needed a urinal, but when I tried, I couldn't go. I tried throughout the evening without success. By morning, I still hadn't gone and I was getting anxious. The harder I strained, the less it seemed I was able to accomplish. Miss Downing, the head nurse and terror of the hospital, came 'round and glared at me as though I were deliberately holding my water. She threatened, "If you don't go on your own within the next fifteen minutes, we'll put a catheter in and drain you."

I had never seen a catheter, but I didn't think it was something I'd like. Aubrey, who had been taking in the whole scene along with the other patients, had a suggestion: Get me up into a chair beside the bathroom and turn on the water in the tub. The sound of running water would make me want to go, he said. Miss Downing was skeptical, but other older patients vouched for its effectiveness. Finally she said to one of the nurses, "Call Dr. Grant. If he'll give permission for the patient to get out of bed, we'll try it."

Within minutes, the nurse was back with permission for me to sit up. She helped me into a chair beside the bathroom door and handed me a urinal. I held it ready while she turned on the water.

Aubrey and the others had been watching the proceedings with interest. Now they became my cheering section.

"C'mon, Tom."

"You can do it!"

"Let her go!"

I tried to relax and listen only to the sound of water splashing into the tub. Suddenly, uncontrolled, it began to flow. "It's coming!" I yelled, "It's coming!" A cheer went up from my audience. I filled the urinal and called for another. It, too, was nearly full when the nurse carried it away to another cheer.

Aubrey was ecstatic.

"I declare you Champion Pisser of Five Islands—make that Sagadahoc County."

After the first urinal episode, Miss Downing allowed me to sit in a chair whenever I had to go, but without benefit of running water.

Over the next few days, the swelling in my joints subsided. I was still unable to walk without discomfort, and at night, my knee joints sometimes swelled and popped out, causing excruciating pain. Even so, Dr. Grant sent me home, on the condition that I take his prescribed medicine, carried exclusively by McFadden's Drugstore.

"Something I concocted myself," he confided. "Guaranteed to work."

My mother sent someone to Bath to pick me up. I said goodbye to Aubrey and thanked him for his help. He handed me the logo cut from an Old Gold cigarette pack.

"Your Champion Pisser's medal, sir."

I hobbled into McFadden's to pick up the prescription. Mr. McFadden took it down from a shelf at the back of the room. It was in a plain brown bottle, pint size, with a handwritten label. He wiped away the dust and read the instructions aloud. "Three tablespoons in a half glass of water twice a day. Shake well before using."

I held it up to the light. There were things floating around in the bottom of the bottle. I didn't think I should rile up that sediment before I drank it, and I told McFadden as much.

"This stuff is made of roots, herbs and barks," he explained. "That's what you see at the bottom. Medicine may not do you much good if you just take it off the top."

At home, my mother said, "We'll get some of this into you right away." She read the instructions, shook the bottle vigorously, measured the dose into a jelly glass, added the required water, and handed it to me.

I stared at the brownish liquid with that gunk swimming around at the bottom. It looked like vinegar from Grandpa's barrel at the store that had the slimy glob of bacteria and yeast floating on the top—and probably tasted worse. I took a sip and nearly gagged. I'd never tasted anything so bitter. There was a very good reason for the added water. Not even the Almighty himself could have downed it straight.

I pushed it aside. "I can't drink this crap."

"You have to," my mother said, "if you want to get well."

She continued to insist, but I wouldn't put any more of that foul-tasting liquid into me. My mother could only scowl at me, not knowing how to force four ounces of bitter medicine down a sixteen-year-old's throat.

That night my knee joints swelled, popped out again and locked. I yelled for my mother. She propped up my knees with a pillow, bathed them in wintergreen and applied a hot iron to the joints until I could straighten out my legs.

The next morning, Aunt Ruth came by to check on my progress. My mother blabbed about the medication. Dr. Grant's remedy still sat on the table, untouched. My stern-faced aunt took a no-nonsense approach. She picked up the glass. "Tommy," she said, "you're going to drink this whether you like it or not."

When I shook my head no, she turned to my mother.

"Lu, mix me up a drink exactly like his. And then I'm going to drink it right down, just to prove how easy it is."

She turned to me, "When I finish, you're going to drink yours the same way. And remember, if you drink it right down, you only get one bad taste. If you sip it, you'll get a dozen. If the taste is too bad, take a teaspoon of sugar."

Her idea appealed to me because I wanted to see the look on her face when she had a mouthful of that gunk. My mother measured out the medicine, added water and handed it to her. Without hesitation, she raised it to her lips and chugalugged. She set the glass down and wiped her lips with her handkerchief. She shuddered, and I thought I detected a grimace behind that hankie.

I picked up my glass. I hated what I was about to do, but I couldn't let an old woman show me up. I downed it just as she had done. She was right; one horrible but brief aftertaste and it was gone. The sugar my mother gave me might have helped. Each day from then on, my mother mixed and I drank that foul potion, floating glob and all, just like it said on the bottle. And I began to improve. Even so, there were days when my swollen feet refused to let me stand. I'd crawl out and ease into my mother's rocker. Then in my makeshift wheelchair, I'd hitch myself from the living room to the kitchen to take my meals at the table.

Within a couple of weeks the swelling in my joints subsided until I could squeeze into my shoes. By the time I was into my second pint of Dr. Grant's miracle potion, I was out of doors and ready to return to work. I needed to. All the while I'd been out of work, I'd been paid just twenty a week in workman's compensation. I'd given the whole thing to my mother to buy groceries.

BIW was not as ready to take me back as I had thought. First, they said, the company doctor must examine me and give his permission. He agreed to my return, but said I must do light, inside work. I was assigned to the outside machine shop tool crib. The cramped space was populated by two elderly men—sixty, or so— also considered unfit for outside yard work. They were a couple of old mother hens during my recuperation days. They wouldn't let me heft the heavier air drills and strong backs.

Once I was on my feet again, I spent little time around the house and my ceiling project suffered for it. The 1935 Ford was long gone, but Clark Gable was still looking down on us. Cora must have had something against Clark, because she took to needling me about finishing what I'd started. That upset me mightily. Here I was, "Man of the Family," and the only one contributing. Cora had been hired by Bath Iron Works, too, but my mother told me she wasn't asking anything from Cora because she was saving up to get married. I wondered how much Harlan was saving. And on top of all that, Cora saw fit to criticize me. That rankled me.

One day, after she'd yelled at me one time too many—"You're never goin' to get this ceiling done"—I lost it. I grabbed the T-stick, and took a few mighty swings at the ceiling, all the while screaming, "If that's the way you feel, I'll take it all down. It's my ceiling; I put it up there, and I can tear it down if I want."

Before I could inflict further damage, my mother came in and persuaded me to quit my foolishness. I put away the T-stick and never again touched that ceiling. Eventually, Cora and my mother paneled over where Clark had been, and did a pretty fair job of it. They smoothed out most of my damage, but one or two deep gouges stayed there for years, reminding me of one of my dumber days.

31

TIME TO GO

In April of 1944, I decided to join the U.S. Navy.
I'd been mulling it over since my seventeenth birthday, but Dr.
Grant had advised against it. My heart wasn't yet strong enough
from the rheumatic fever, he said. He doubted they'd take me anyway, once they learned about it.

I'd already visited the Navy Recruiting Office in Bath, careful not
to mention the fever. When the recruiter learned of all my depend-
ents, he said that when I enlisted, the navy would pay me $60 a
month. They would send half of that to my mother to care for her, sister Mary and my little brothers. And I'd need my mother's permission.

It seemed my seagoing ancestors were calling me to my new
home on the ocean. I sat down and listed all the reasons why I
should join the navy.

First on the list was my age. I'd soon be eighteen and Uncle
Sam would point his bony finger at me for duty in the army, where
I'd crawl around in the mud and wear olive drabs, which are not as
attractive as navy blue. And I was terrified of marine boot camp.

Then there was my deteriorating relationship with Irving.
Irving and I recently had what proved to be our last major set-to. I
had bought myself a three-cell flashlight. One day Irving tried to
sneak past me with my light in his hand. I waylaid him and we had at

it right in the middle of the kitchen. My mother tried to get between us, and I had to take care not to hit her. Finally, Irving raised the flashlight in the air and brought it crashing down on my thumb. The lens and bulb flew in one direction, the batteries in another. Irving fled out the door. My mother made me promise not to hit him again. It was the hardest promise I ever kept, but the incident turned me ever nearer to the navy.

Next was my job at BIW. It had a pink-slip warning attached to it because of a strawberry milk incident. I had sneaked out to the lunch wagon five minutes earlier than my official break to get some strawberry milk. And I got caught. I didn't want to be a career tool clerk—helper—anyway.

And finally, there was Franny.

The previous summer, Johnny MacGillavary and I took to rowing across the Sheepscot to Cozy Harbor on Southport Island because we had heard that the girls were prettier and friendlier there. We met up with Louise, Tillie, and Frances. Louise and Tillie remained my good friends, but I fell madly in teenage love with Franny's dark-haired beauty. Johnny and I visited Cozy Harbor often from summer on into the fall, but Franny was usually unavailable for some reason or another. With the coming of April, after a hard, cold winter, we could again row across the bay. What better way to make my reappearance than in navy blues? I'd knock the bobby sox off her. I could slip in four weeks of boot camp and be ready to romance by summer.

Armed with my fistful of arguments, I broached the navy subject with my mother. She had her concerns. What about my health? Did I remember what Dr. Grant had said about my heart? I'd already checked with him and he'd said okay, I lied.

What about her and the boys, she asked. What would they do for money?

I explained to her about her share of the Navy allotment and the thirty dollars I'd get to keep. She seemed relieved. I mentioned that Irving would soon be sixteen and he could quit school and go to work at BIW, same as I did.

We jawed about it for a while until I convinced her the navy was the smart way to go. She even promised to set aside my thirty dollars so I'd have a little something when I got home. Meanwhile, I'd belong to the Naval Reserve (V6) for the duration of the war, plus six months.

I left Five Islands unceremoniously and was sent to the Sampson Naval Training Center on the east shore of Lake Seneca in New York State. It was boot camp, really. And before I could graduate from it, I had to learn to swim. For a boy who'd never been more than knee-deep in water, this would prove a mighty task.

There must have been a dozen or more of us non-swimmers. To qualify, we had to swim one length of the pool, and jump off the abandon-ship platform with a life preserver. "Those who can't complete the required swim and jump will come to the pool every evening for one hour until they can," the instructor said.

When it was time for the abandon-ship drill, I knew that even with a life jacket I'd never be able to jump into that deep water from twenty feet up. By twos and threes, the men climbed up rope ladders to the platform. As each group took its turn, I edged farther back in the ranks, until finally there were only two of us left to jump. Together, we stood on the platform, neither wanting to take the plunge. What seemed like a thousand feet below us, a half-dozen or more shipmates yelled up their encouragement.

Me and Ma in the 1940s. My decision to join the U.S. Navy was one of the best and most important decisions of my life.

"C'mon, Hanna. You can do it. Just cup one hand over your balls, pinch your nose with the other and jump."

I must have stood there a good ten minutes working up my courage. Several times I thought I was ready, but I only managed to inch a little closer to the edge of the platform, where my courage deserted me. Meanwhile, my reluctant shipmate leaped and hit the water with a great splash and disappeared. Seconds later, he surfaced, spitting and coughing.

"It's easy," he called up.

The instructor was getting impatient. He climbed up beside me and nudged me closer to the brink. "Let me show you how to do it."

He leaped, but as he did his arm swung out and I toppled off the platform. I hit the water seconds after he did and went under. The life jacket fetched me up and I surfaced, spewing water. Hands grabbed me and pulled me over to poolside where I could grasp the rope ladder and climb out. Behind me, I could hear my mates cheering me as though I'd accomplished a great feat. When they finally pulled me out of the pool, I had to admit they were right. I believed that I'd be a first-class swimmer before I left boot camp.

After boot camp I was eventually assigned to the USS *Prince William (CVE-31)*, an escort aircraft carrier, where the navy put me to work chipping paint and swabbing decks. The *Prince William* operated out of San Diego for fifteen months, ferrying planes, ammo and aviation gas to the Pacific. After the war ended, we ferried troops home from the Pacific theater.

It was aboard the *Prince William* that I received news in a rare letter from my mother that Herbie Campbell's plane had been shot down over France. Herbie was missing in action. I hadn't cried since I was seven or eight, a record that would have made my father proud. But upon reading about Herbie, I lost the battle to keep my lip from quivering, and the tears welled up.

Then I realized that Ma hadn't said he was dead, just missing. I told myself that the French would rescue him and hide him until the war ended. And I believed it. Later, though, I learned the truth: Herbie had indeed been rescued by the French Underground after his plane crashed. Only, after his rescue, he volunteered to join the group and was killed by the Germans.

This time I couldn't hold back and my lip didn't just quiver. I bawled.

It was Chastine, the leading seaman aboard the escort carrier USS *Prince William*, who had first broached the subject of wild women to me. He was older than me, in his late twenties, and from somewhere in the South.

"As soon as we dock at San Diego, you and me are goin' on a seagoing sailor's liberty," he said. "First off, we'll get something to drink. None of your three-point-two beer."

He was flabbergasted when I told him that at eighteen, I'd never had a drink of anything stronger than lemonade. "I'm not old enough to drink, anyway," I told him. "If they check my ID, I'm done."

"You leave that little matter to me," he said. "Now, what about a woman? Ever had one?"

I told him about Franny.

"That's kid stuff," he said. "I'm talking about getting between the sheets with a real woman."

I didn't want to admit there'd never been what he called a real woman. I mentioned how close I'd come that day at BIW. He reminded me that close only counts in horseshoes. Finally, I conceded that just maybe I hadn't had my first time yet.

"Did you hear that, men?" Chastine yelled, "Hanna's still got his cherry. What are we gonna do about that?"

"Take him out and get him laid," someone yelled back.

"That'll come right after the drinks," he said.

Chastine's intent to rectify the unpardonable state of my chastity made me happy. I could understand why he wouldn't want one of his deck seamen to be tabbed as the only virgin in the whole Second Division. I could hardly wait for San Diego.

The day before we docked, Chastine handed me an ID card with my name on it, one that said I was twenty-one. The next day, after 1600, I ate chow, showered, shaved, slipped on my dress blues and met Chastine at the gangway at 1800. A ferryboat brought us to the Fleet Landing on the mainland.

We went to a bar called the Pirates Cave, one of those places so dark on the inside that you can't see the back of your hand when you first come in from the sunlight. The burly guy at the door barely glanced at our cards before he waved us in. Chastine seemed to know his way around the place, and I thought he must have a couple of women lined up for us in here.

We took seats at the bar. A half-dozen other sailors had already bellied up and were comfortably stooled. Chastine took off his hat, rolled it up and tucked it into the waistband of his blues. Then he rolled up the cuffs of his sleeves so the dragons would show. I followed suit.

"Seagram's Seven and ginger," he told the barkeep. "And one for my buddy here."

I stirred the cubes around with the swizzle stick the way Chastine had done and took my first sip while he watched. It burned all the way down and didn't taste all that hot, either. I held back the urge to choke and gulped down a second swallow. Much smoother this time.

When Chastine was satisfied that I could handle my drink, he went to work on his own. He must have been thirsty; he finished the whole thing in about two gulps. I followed Chastine's example, but it took me four tries to finish.

"Now it's your turn to order," Chastine said.

The first drink was sitting comfortably in my gut and I was feeling easy and relaxed. So, what the heck. I snapped my fingers to get the barkeep's attention, just the way the gunner's mate at the end of the bar had done.

I sipped my second drink and looked around. Toward the back of the room were booths. Some had sailors in them; some had sailors and women together. And in the far booth, there were two women alone, not bad-looking either. One of them could be the one Chastine had in mind to fix me up with. If he had any ideas along that line, he surely was taking his sweet time getting to it. He was more interested in telling war stories.

Chastine was ready to order our third drink. By then, it was getting on into the evening and I was feeling a glow inside. I was ready for him to bring on the women. And I told him so. He agreed.

Outside he hailed a cab and we got in. I settled back, thinking how lucky I was to have a buddy like Chastine. He really knew how to take care of a guy. Chastine leaned forward and poked the cabbie in the back. "Can you find us a woman?" I was afraid he might try to use my cherry to get us preferential treatment, but he didn't.

"I might," the cabbie said. "It'll cost you twenty bucks though."

"How many women you got," I wanted to know.

"Just one," he said. "You'll take turns."

I thought of the thirty bucks in my billfold and the dollar woman at BIW, and I wasn't so sure I wanted to go through with such a high-priced transaction. Besides, I'd been counting on each of us having a girl of our own. I thought of those two girls back in the booth at the Pirates Cave. A couple of good-looking guys like us might have gotten next to them for free.

"Take us," said Chastine before I could offer an opinion. Oh well, Chastine was an old hand at this. If he thought she was worth it, she probably was. She must be high-class to be up in the twenty-buck range.

We pulled up at a motel on the highway. The cabbie collected our money. Chastine said he'd go first because he was senior.

I waited in the cab with the driver and fidgeted. The liquor was wearing off. I fretted that I wouldn't be able to do it right. Maybe if I just explained to her about my cherry, she'd understand and tell me what to do.

It couldn't have been more than fifteen minutes later when Chastine returned. He didn't say anything about his visit. It was my turn and I went and knocked lightly on the door. It opened and a short, shapely blonde woman stood in front of me—stark naked. One crazy thought crossed my mind: She didn't have to spend a whole lot for work clothes.

She hustled me inside and closed the door. "Take off your clothes. I want to check your ba-ba."

When she tried to help with my thirteen trouser buttons, I guessed that my ba-ba was somewhere below my waist.

She looked me over the way you'd check a dog for fleas. When she was satisfied that I didn't have anything she wouldn't want to catch, she brought me to the bed and we crawled in. I didn't mention the cherry, but she must have guessed right away that I wasn't sure what to do. With her giving instructions, and me being a fast learner, we had at it. Five minutes later I was dressed and on my way out the door asking myself,

"Is that all there is to it?"

Back in the cab, Chastine was curious. "How was it?"

"All right," I said.

There wasn't much else I could say, since I didn't have anything to compare it to, but at least I was no longer the lone virgin of the Second Division.

32

HOME AGAIN, GONE AGAIN

M arch 8, 1946, was one of the more memorable days in my
young life. Duration plus six had finally arrived. I was on a
train bound for Portland, my discharge papers in my hand. I'd
arranged for my mother and Ivan to meet me at the station.

I bought a ham salad sandwich and a container of strawberry
milk and settled in for the ride. I had some heavy thinking to do. I
mulled over Chastine's final prediction as I had walked down the
gangway for the last time: You'll be back in a year or two.

Maybe he was right.

At nineteen, I'd just been cut adrift, still the same seaman second class I'd been when I left boot camp two years earlier. And I had
no idea what I could do. I had about a hundred in my pocket and no
prospects. I needed a skilled job or I'd turn out to be a common
laborer like my father. The GI Bill could be my answer. The separa-
tions officer at Boston's Fargo Building had given me a pamphlet
about it, and I broke it out now.

The government would pay a part of a returning serviceman's
salary for any employer who would take him on as a trainee. As soon
as I settled in, I'd go to the employment office in Bath and sign up. If
there were no GI openings right away, I'd have to rely on the twenty
a week unemployment the government would pay me, and that just

wouldn't cut it. I might also have to dip into the money my mother had been putting aside for me, out of my allotment. I did some mental math. There should be seven hundred or more waiting for me. It would sure come in handy.

Through the grimy coach window, I spotted my mother on the Union Station platform. I pulled my sea bag down from the overhead rack and dragged it with me to the end of the car where the conductor helped me down the steps. My mother hugged me and gave me a peck on the cheek. She saw my sea bag and guessed out loud that this meant I wouldn't be staying in the service.

Looks that way, I told her.

Ivan wasn't with her. He was waiting in the parking lot. It figured. The parking lot was a good hundred feet from the platform, much too far for him to walk. I hoisted my sea bag onto my shoulder and followed my mother to the car.

Ivan was standing beside a 1941 Buick, one of the last they'd made before the automakers retooled to make tanks and half-tracks. That surprised me. When I left he had been driving an old thirties Ford, about the best a man of his limited earning power could swing. Monthly payments on this baby must be close to a hundred.

He saw me coming and opened the trunk. I tossed in the sea bag and slammed the lid. He didn't offer his hand, just studied his shoes, shuffled his feet and asked how I'd been. The way his jowls hung down over his jaw, I couldn't help but think how much he looked like a sad-eyed basset hound.

Okay, I said, now that I was out of the freakin' navy.

My mother opened the door and I climbed in back. Nice car, I thought. Sea egging must be good.

"BIW's not hiring," my mother said. "What are you gonna do for work?"

I explained the GI Bill.

"What if there's no GI Bill job openin'?"

"Then I might just take the summer off and draw from my fifty-two-twenty club."

She'd never heard of a 52-20, so I explained it to her. "Uncle Sam will pay me twenty dollars a week for every week I don't work, up to a year."

"You planning to do nothing for a full year?"

I could see she was wondering how I could help the family on twenty a week.

"Clammin's good," Ivan piped up. "They're payin' seventeen a barrel at the flats."

"I may have to use some of my savings to tide me over until something breaks," I said. "How much have I got in the bank, Ma?"

She got this sheepish look on her face and turned all red. "It cost a lot to keep the boys. A lot more than I figured."

Somehow it didn't surprise me when she told me my bank balance was zero. Well, I guess if the boys were being taken care of, it was fine.

We got on home and I settled in. Irving, now eighteen, was leaving for the navy, and just in time; I needed his bed. Cora had moved out. She had saved up her Bath Iron Works pay, bought Baker's camp at the top of Bars Hill, the one with my father's second-story lumber in it. What was supposed to be my bedroom was now hers. She had hustled Harlan into it, after a brief stop at the altar.

Mary, a full-blown teenager in need of some privacy, had taken over the middle bedroom. My four young brothers were crammed into the one remaining bedroom. I took over my old cot in the living room.

I checked out the place. The walls were as bare as they'd been when I left, and my brothers looked a might seedy. We did have partial electricity in the house. A neighbor had installed a half-dozen outlets for lights, a refrigerator and a radio. Central Maine Power had hooked us up. I began to wonder what my mother had been spending the allotment on.

The next day I bummed a ride to Bath with Chet McMahan. Chet was a good four years younger than I, but already bigger and stronger. He boasted that he could carry two hods of clams the length of Sagadahoc Bay without stopping for a breather. I believed him.

I stopped by BIW. They had no jobs available, but said they might have an opening in the cleanup gang in a few weeks. I wouldn't hold my breath. I visited the employment office and filled out the papers for my 52-20, and asked if they had any GI Bill jobs—they did not. On the way home Chet stopped so I could buy a clam hoe.

Clam digging was a whole new experience for me. I'd need some help getting started. And Chet knew a lot more about clamming than I did. He'd be handy to have around the clam flats until I got the hang of it.

He filled me in as we rode to the bay the next day. "We'll be diggin' for the big ones on high ground in the middle of the bay. That's a long walk out from shore. When the tide starts back in, you don't have a whole lot of time to get your hods off the flats. Cuts down on your clammin' time."

I asked him why we had to dig so far out from shore.

"In close, all you get is shit clams. Most are little fellers, too close to the two-inch limit. Wardens catch you with too many small ones, they'll fine you." He fished a small brass ring out of his pocket. "If a clam'll fit inside this ring, it's too small."

We pulled into the field at the head of the bay and unloaded our gear. Sagadahoc was narrow—no more than half a mile across—and shallow. At mean low water, with a twelve-foot tide, nearly a half-mile of flats were exposed. Sometimes it seemed you could walk all the way to Seguin Island.

The tide was about two-thirds down when we arrived. The low-lying flats were still being drained by a twisting channel that was shallow enough to be waded to reach the high ground a half-mile down the bay. Carrying a brace of half-bushel hods of clams to the head of the bay where the buyer's truck awaited would be no small task.

Most of the diggers had already arrived. Some were well on their way down the bay, on foot and in skiffs they kept moored at the head of the bay. Off to one side, a tarp had been spread over the grass and a lively craps game was in progress. Chet led me across the flats, showing me where the channel was shallow enough to wade across. By the time we reached the high flats in mid-bay, diggers had

Courtesy of Cora M. Owen

My last four siblings were significantly younger than us older four Hanna kids and seemed almost like a second family. Here in the late 1940s (l to r) are: Blaine, Clayton, Raymond and Richard. By this time I had made the navy a career.

fanned out in a circle and were digging a trench around the perimeter of the high flats. The object, Chet told me, was to drain the flats so the clam holes would open up. When the flats were dry, the diggers walked around the area, stamping their feet. Wherever they walked, holes the size of my pinkie appeared.

The stomping complete, each digger dug himself a hole about a foot deep, climbed in and began to turn over the flats. Chet picked out a spot and set to work. I watched how easily he set his fork and turned over the flats. His first dig brought in four clams all over three inches long. I dug myself a hole and found four clams on my first hoeful. Two of them were impaled on the tines of my fork. Chet had warned me about broken shells, but I threw them into my hod along with the others. On my second dig I found that clams can be tricky. As I pulled over the flats, I saw two of them heading for Asia—straight down. Two hoefuls later, they were safely in my hod. This clamming business was tougher than I had thought, but I was determined to stick it out.

I dug and dug until I thought my arms would fall off. When Chet finally came by, I had nearly three hodfuls of clams. Thankfully most of them had unbroken shells. "Tide's comin' in," he said. "We'd better think about gettin' our clams ashore."

Before we loaded the clams into the boat, we used his bucket to wash the grit off our clams. According to Chet, the waterlogged clams made the hod look fuller. We slogged back to the clam dealer's truck at the head of the bay, and my clams were measured. I had six pecks, a little over half a barrel, nine dollars at the going rate. Chet had a barrel. Some of the older diggers had over two barrels.

As we piled our gear into Chet's car, I couldn't help but envy him, driving his own car at sixteen. I just had to get a car of my own. My opportunity came in the mail a few days later. It was a long brown envelope that smelled of money—my mustering-out pay. I bummed a ride to Bath, cashed my check and hitched a ride to Portland where I bought a 1935 Ford Roadster with a rumble seat, a fold-down top, side curtains and a horn that could shame the one on Seguin Island Light in a dense fog.

Sitting behind the wheel of that Ford, I felt a whole lot better. And I must have looked better, too. The girls seemed to find me more attractive with a set of wheels under me. What a sight I must have made, pulling into the Sagadahoc Bay parking lot in a cloud of dust, horn blatting, top down, rumble seat up and girls hanging out both sides.

And there was one more bonus: Johnny "Mac," my old friend and sometime competition for the choice of femininity in Five Islands, had enlisted in the army and was charming the girls in Tokyo. I had a clear field; Betty, Joyce, Lois. I was already asking, Franny who?

I had been home about a month when Ivan showed up at our driveway one afternoon. He was driving an older Chevy, about a 1936 vintage. I didn't think he'd ever part with that Buick. He honked the horn and my mother went out. He didn't usually expend the effort to walk up to the house if he didn't have plans to sit for a while. They sat in his car for about five minutes; then she got out and Ivan drove away.

"Where's Ivan's Buick?" I asked her as she came through the door.

She got a sheepish look on her face, the same one she'd had when I'd asked her about my money.

"The payments were a little too steep; he took it back." She explained that he had bought this one from a man from Bay Point for twenty dollars a month.

"It doesn't surprise me," I said. "I thought the Buick was too rich for his blood, anyway."

I mentioned Ivan's new car to Cora. I wondered out loud why Ivan had bought the Buick in the first place when it was clear he couldn't manage the payments. As a member in good standing at the Five Islands Baptist Church, she couldn't lie to me. She confessed that Ma had been making the payments for him. When the allotment checks stopped, Ma couldn't afford it either. When I asked if there was more I should know, she finally told me that Ma sometimes gave him money for cigarettes. I couldn't believe what I was hearing. All that money wasted on Ivan. No wonder the boys looked so seedy. I was hurt and angry and felt betrayed. This was something that had to be straightened out right away

I barged into her kitchen. "What's this I been hearing about you giving some of my allotment money to Ivan?"

"He takes me to Bath to buy my groceries."

"He didn't need a forty-one Buick for that."

She became defensive. "It was my money and I could do whatever I wanted to with it."

"It was not your money," I thundered. "It was to buy food and clothes for the boys. And thirty bucks of it was supposed to be mine. You promised. Instead, you gave it to Ivan—car, craps and cigarettes."

She didn't relent.

"Ivan's not well. I love him and I want to take care of him."

"You got it wrong, Ma. First, you take care of your children; then you look for a man who'll take care of you, not take from your children. I got my own opinion of a man who takes money from a widow woman with small children."

She broke into tears, angry but unrepentant. We sat in stony silence for some minutes. Then I told her, "I'll stay on here for the summer and go clamming. I'll pay you board. Come Labor Day, though, I'm outa here."

I kept my word.

33

My Father in the Mirror

J ust after the 1946 Labor Day weekend, I sold my roadster, stowed my boots and clam hoe under the house, and boarded the bus for Boston. My father's cousin ran a rooming house in the South End. She offered me a room for a few dollars a week, although no meals were included.

After I settled in, I stopped by the employment office and signed up for work and my 52-20, in case nothing turned up right away. The second week they told me of an opportunity to apprentice as a plumber under the GI Bill. The government would kick in seventy dollars a month toward my pay. If I lasted six months, they'd throw in a hundred dollars for tools. I still didn't know a Stillson from a monkey, but I took it, anyway. They handed me a slip of paper with an Allston address and told me to see Owen Donnelley. His shop was on a short side street just off Commonwealth Avenue, a narrow, one-story building next to Downey's Bar.

I opened the door, leaned in, and went nose-to-navel with a giant of a man—Owen Donnelley himself. He was an older, graying man, probably in his sixties, a good six-five. There was enough cloth in his overalls to make a two-man tent. He spoke with a trace of a brogue hard for a Down Easter to understand. He asked me about my background. I told him about BIW and the outside machinists. I didn't mention RON. He hired me on the spot. He agreed to add to the government's seventy enough money to bring my pay up to forty dollars for a forty-hour week.

Mr. Donnelley—he liked for me to call him that—had come over from the old sod at the turn of the century, when he was sixteen. He'd come up the hard way, carrying hodfuls of bricks for a dollar a day. When the Irish had taken over Boston's City Hall, he'd joined the police department, until one of his Irish connections got him a plumber's license for a buck or two.

He was a man with a back-o-me-hand-to-ye attitude, and he made it clear that he'd have no truck with slugabeds. I was his third helper over the last several months, he told me.

"Young people today don't have the moxie to get out there and learn on their own," he told me. "They want everything handed to them on a silver platter."

As we plumbed into the winter, I could tell Mr. Donnelley was unhappy with my progress. He didn't come right out and say it, at first. He'd just hint around.

Since coming to Boston, I'd had scant news from my family. My mother hadn't written. I figured she was sore at me for leaving. In early spring of 1947, both of my grandfathers died—Grampa Rowe of a heart attack and Grandpa Hanna of a stroke. I have always regretted that I couldn't pay my last respects to either grandfather. Cora told me later that my mother had been in the hospital undergoing surgery when Grandpa Rowe died. She had nearly died, herself. I was oblivious to it all.

By spring, I knew I'd never make it with a pipe wrench in my hand. My days were numbered, and it all came to a head one afternoon in late May on Commonwealth Avenue. We were working in an assembly building of a manufacturing company. We were there to replace a valve in the building's water main. The valve was in a pit in

the concrete floor. The three-by-three-foot space was about three feet
deep. Donnelley handed me a wrench and helped me down into the
pit so I could loosen the bolts. I straddled the main and bent over the
valve until I was practically standing on my head. From that angle, I
couldn't remember which way was off. I held up my right hand and
turned my wrist in a clockwise direction and said RON under my
breath. But when you're headfirst down a three-foot pit, RON can't
be a whole lot of help. It didn't look right, but Mr. Donnelley was
waiting impatiently. I adjusted my wrench around the first bolt head
and began to turn. It wouldn't budge. I was on my second try, when
something struck me just above my right ear. The wrench flew out of
my hand, and I fell back off the pipe and into the pit.

I looked up to see the ham-handed Irishman glowering at me.
He had fetched me a clout alongside my head. "You're turning it the
wrong goddamned way, yer dumb arse!"

I wanted to tell him to take his damned wrench and his job
with it, but I held my tongue. He didn't. All the while we worked,
he cussed me in Gaelic. We rode back to the shop in silence. As soon
as we were inside, he gave me the news. "Ye'll never make it as
plumber, son. I'll have to let you go."

He paid me whatever salary I had coming, and I walked out of
his life forever, discouraged, but secretly glad to be free from a job
I'd never liked. Now it was back to the employment office. They had
no work. I signed up for my 52-20 again. I scoured the want ads.
Newspaper in hand, I tramped Boston streets, knocking on doors.
Shoe shops, carpenter shops, electrical contractors were all looking
for people with experience—something I had precious little of,
unless it involved a swab or a paint chipper.

So in the early summer of 1947 when I was nearly twenty-one, I
packed my suitcase and headed back to Five Islands. My mother wasn't
particularly pleased to see me. She made it clear I had walked out on

my Man of the Family responsibilities. I reminded her once more that I would never again send her money as long as Ivan or any other man was bleeding her. I did agree to pay her weekly room and board.

I broke out my boots, hoe and hods and returned to the clam flats, intending to make it my summer's work. I couldn't afford another set of wheels. I bummed a ride to the flats with whoever was going that day. Some days I missed out altogether. This time around, clamming wasn't what it had been, anyway. The war effort was over, meat had become more plentiful and the price of clams had dropped. I hardly made enough to pay my room and board, let alone buy cigarettes. I needed a job.

Mr. Eustis, my father's final employer, needed someone to work at his Ledgemere cottage. The pay was somewhere near a buck an hour. I snapped it up. Over the next couple of months I must have chopped down every dead and dying tree in the woods around his cottage and cut them up for fireplace wood. It took me all the way to Labor Day.

In late August when the Ledgemere job was winding down, Roland Peterson called to offer a job demolishing the lodge on McMahan Island. The owners had told him they'd give him the lumber if he'd cart it away.

Aubrey Fullerton, the Lee brothers, Jack and Horny, and I dismantled the building, saving every salvageable board, beam and window. We kept at it until late in the fall when the weather stopped Peterson cold. He quit until spring. By then, the clam flats were cold and icy. Few diggers braved the colder days and I had no way of getting there. My 52-20 had long since run out. I took to periwinkling at Ledgemere, but that didn't earn more than five dollars, even on a good day, when the tide was right and the seaweed wasn't frozen. I cut my mother's board money to ten a week. She bugged me to go out and find a job.

I began to worry what people around town might be saying behind their hands—He's getting to be just like his father.

Perhaps they'd be right. Like him, I wanted to work. And, like him, I was qualified for only laborers' jobs. He had wanted to be something more than a laborer; so did I.

My future seemed as hopeless as my father's had been.

I didn't want to be my father.

34

Salvation

I awoke one morning in late January, desperate for a smoke. My pack was empty, and I didn't have a dime in my jeans. I scrounged among the stale butts in the ashtray until I found one I could get a drag off. I smoothed out the butted edge and lit up. It tasted of the ashtray. A few puffs and I butted it again. What a life. Maybe my old lead seaman was right; I belonged in the U.S. Navy. At least they'd give me three squares, a place to sleep and a few bucks in my pocket.

I rummaged through my old navy records and broke out my discharge papers. I caught a ride to Bath with Gil Standish, a machinist on the swing shift at BIW. He was an old navy man from World War I. That ride marked a turning point in my life.

I told Gil of my intention to reenlist. He heartily approved, but he had a word of advice: "Don't settle for just any old job. You don't want to spend your life swabbin' decks. You're smart; get into something where you can learn a trade." He grinned at me. "Maybe even a machinist wouldn't be so bad."

I grinned right back, and nodded.

The chief recruiter at Bath City Hall had me fill out an application. He told me the pay was seventy-five dollars a month plus another fifteen for sea pay, which was probably what I'd be getting as soon as they could find me a ship. I could sign up for either three or six years. I chose three. He drove me and three other reenlistees to the Portland recruiting center. They gave us our physicals, pronounced us

fit and swore us in. Then they sent us home to await the navy's call that would send us to Boston for assignment.

While I waited for word to leave, my mother wanted to know if I cared that she wouldn't be able to feed and clothe the boys. She hinted at another allotment, and I nixed that right away. I suggested instead that she apply for the state aid that was now available to women in her position. She said she had previously talked to a woman from the state about getting the aid, but the woman told her that since I was going in the navy, she should go that route.

I mentioned a couple of her neighbors who were getting aid— "And their husbands aren't even dead. They're off shacking up with other women. You get that state woman down here before I leave. Let me talk to her."

The state woman came just before I received my orders. I explained to her that unless she gave my poor widowed mother money for her hungry children, I'd put up one hell of a squawk about the other state-aided families in Five Islands. She left after promising, "I'll see what I can do."

Two days later, my mother received word that her state aid had been granted. I'd board the train for Boston feeling much better about my family's prospects. Now if my mother would only spend it for what it was intended.

By the time I left home, my mother had received more good news. She'd been talking to Lloyd Pinkham, a town selectman, about one day buying back the bungalow for taxes owed. She had been living in there all those years rent-free, but she wanted to own the bungalow outright. Lloyd had checked and found that a disabled war veteran's home could not be taken for nonpayment of taxes. He'd promised her she'd get the deed back. Personally, I didn't think owning the bungalow was such a big deal. It must have had some special meaning for her, though, because she was as happy as a clam.

At the Fargo Building in Boston, about two dozen veterans gathered in a classroom on the fifth floor to retake the General Classification Test. The yeoman first class told us it would be much like the one we had taken the first time around. This time, though, he explained the importance of doing well. They'd use the test grades to decide what we'd do in the navy. The higher we scored, the better our chances of getting into one of the better rates. There were several parts to the test and a time limit on each. As I began each new section, the old fear of failure gnawed at my gut, but this time I was determined to prove myself.

After the test, a young lieutenant sat down with me to discuss my options. He was thumbing through my discharge papers and my test results. He questioned me about my background and seemed interested in my education. He was surprised that I had dropped out of school so young, until I explained about my father.

"Your test scores put you in the top fifteen percent in the navy," he said. "That's pretty good for a ninth-grade education. In fact, few high school graduates do as well."

Then he asked me if I had decided what I wanted to do in the navy.

I said I hadn't.

"These test scores say you can be just about anything you want, if you should decide to make the navy a career."

I flushed and thanked him, trying to hide my elation. I remembered what Gilbert had said and decided right then and there, I'd be someone special on this hitch. I told him I'd wait and decide about the navy career after the first three years.

He closed my folder and ended the interview with a word of advice: Apply for some kind of navy school. He couldn't offer me one right now, but I should ask for one as soon as I got settled aboard ship. I was too bright to be a deckhand for the next three years.

I thanked him and left, feeling better about myself than I had in some time. Twice in the last two weeks I'd been told I was bright and I was beginning to believe it.

That confidence was still with me a week later, the morning I walked down the pier at Philadelphia Naval Shipyard, my sea bag on my shoulder, holding orders to report to the light cruiser USS *Huntington* (CL-107). She was a beautiful ship, long and low, not high and boxy like the *Prince William*. A man could be proud to serve on a man-of-war like this.

The petty officer of the watch logged me in. He introduced himself as Ed Lynch, radarman third class.

"How'd you like to be a radarman? A lot of our guys are being transferred off the ship before we leave for the Med cruise in June," he told me. "We'll be needing some new strikers."

Radar! A twinge of the old fear, but then I said to myself, why not?

"I suppose I'd have to go to some kind of school first," I said.

Not right away, he said. He'd been in the radar gang for three years, and had made third class without any schooling, aside from what he got right there on the ship. I said I'd give it a try.

I couldn't believe this was happening to me. T. L. Hanna, RADARMAN! It sounded great. Lynch said they'd probably make me a first-class seaman and then give me a radarman test some time before my six-month trial period was up. If I passed, they'd give me a designated radarman striker's badge, something they'd never be able to take away from me. And Lynch said he could give me a head start. He'd be aboard until June, and he'd teach me a hell of a lot by then.

He was as good as his word. I learned, and I was amazed at how simple it all seemed. By the time Lynch left the ship, I could turn on and operate the radars, solve basic maneuvering board problems and maintain CIC status boards. I could even get behind the big Plexiglas plotting boards and write backwards.

The morning Lynch left the ship, I stood at the quarterdeck to watch him walk down the gangway for the last time. We shook hands and he handed me his Radarman Third Class Manual. It was to be my Bible, he said. "Study this every chance you get."

Just before he saluted the colors, he turned and yelled at me, "You'll make a damned good radarman if you just stick with it."

Yessir, I said to myself, as I turned in that evening, this could be the start of a great career.

And it was.

For twenty years.

And a new life.

The fog had lifted.

35

THE BUNGALOW, REVISITED

M y mother and I sat alone together in Cora's living room in
Wiscasset on a late-spring afternoon in 1989, the morning of
her eighty-third birthday. I'd come to sit with her while Cora
shopped. Mother had been with her since last June, when Cora
brought her up from Connecticut where she'd been working as a
housekeeper. When she'd complained of feeling poorly, Cora brought
her home for testing and treatment. A series of surgeries over those
next few months had failed to halt the spread of malignancies that
gnawed at the months she had left.

She had accepted her fate with grace and dignity. Yet, even as
her attentive children gathered 'round her to lend their support, she
was, in a sense, lonely, bereft of the male companionship she'd
always craved. Ivan had passed away over twenty years before. A succession of gentlemen friends had followed, none of them financially
prepared for wedlock. A brief marriage to Jim, a retired factory
worker, had ended upon his passing.

Our conversation that spring day got around, as it sometimes
did, to the bungalow. My mother had already said good-bye to it, the
only truly valued possession she had managed to cling to through the
years. Cora had recently driven her down to Five Islands and they'd

ridden past the old place. She looked upon it for what she must have known would be the last time. They didn't go inside.

The bungalow belonged to Richard now. She'd sold it to him, but only after giving me first refusal. I think she thought I'd be more financially able to keep and maintain it. The years had been kind to me, probably kinder than to any of my brothers and sisters. My "great career" had extended to two great careers. I had retired from the navy as a senior chief petty officer in 1965 at the age of thirty-eight, after twenty years' service, and had gone to work as a value engineer at Bath Iron Works. Now sixty-three, I had been totally retired for more than a year with an ample income and a comfortable nest egg.

I wondered why she hadn't just given the house to Richard outright. She wouldn't need the small amount of money it would bring. Then I remembered she had once told me she'd hoped to be able to "leave a little something" to each of her eight children, and the money from the sale would allow her to do just that.

But something else was on her mind. She got up from her chair and was pacing the floor. She asked me if I remembered the portrait of her mother that used to hang on the living room wall in Five Islands. I said I did, and remarked that I'd wished I'd been able to know her.

"So do I," she said wistfully. Then she brightened. "She's in heaven, you know. I'll see her soon, if the Lord will let me."

I asked her why there was any question about the Lord letting her see her mother.

"Well," she said after a painful pause, "I done some things— things that hurt you and your brothers."

The service money.

"I been talking to the Lord about it, lettin' him know I'm sorry, if it ain't too late."

The allotment money was the one thing I'd never completely forgiven her for. Over the years our relationship had been cordial, but never close. We'd visited and shared perfunctory hugs and kisses. She'd seen some lean times, but I'd given her very little money, fearful that she'd spend it on her gentlemen friends. Now she was telling me in her own way that she was sorry.

I was overwhelmed. I wanted to tell her that I forgave her and more, but long-repressed words are hard to come by on short notice. Impulsively, I put my arms around her, hugged her tight and said out loud, "I love this little old lady, right here."

I think she understood. A radiant smile lit up her face and she gave out her little-girl giggle. Then she stepped back in a self-conscious kind of way and changed the subject.

"How you doin' on your chair?"

When she realized she'd never be coming back to the bungalow, my mother passed the word that she wanted each of her children to come down and select an item to keep. I took her oak rocker and promised I'd strip it down to bare wood and refinish it. My father had bought the rocker for her secondhand when they first married, and in it she had rocked each of her eight children. That very same rocker had hitched my rheumatic joints about the bungalow. The broad-grained wood had long since been buried under various coats of paint, but I knew what lay beneath.

I'd barely finished stripping when she asked if I would bring it to Cora's so she could see it. It was outside in my trunk. She came out with me. I lifted the trunk and, when she saw it, she got a sad little smile on her face. She stood there, not saying anything, just smiling. Then she reached out and almost tenderly ran her hand over its unfinished surface. After a minute or so, she finally backed away.

"Richard's planning to fix up my old place," she said, changing the subject. "If you want to remember it like I left it, you better get down there before he starts rippin' out."

I took her up on that suggestion, driving down to Five Islands after leaving Cora's house.

Richard wasn't at the bungalow, but the door was unlocked. I went inside and we were alone together, just the old building, me and the memories. The bungalow no longer looked like it had when I was growing up there. My mother had been able to make some long-term improvements over the years. The walls had been Sheetrocked and decorated with flowery wallpaper. Vinyl siding covered the weathered shingles, and the six-foot drop-off had been fitted with a makeshift set of steps. The outhouse had been replaced by a gas-fired toilet in a tiny room attached to the backside of the house.

I took a turn through the tiny rooms, searching, sensing the memories. The old building was steeped in them. Though many of them railed of hard times brought by the Great Depression, some whispered of good times as well. Right here in the kitchen once stood the Glenwood B where my mother baked our beans and biscuits and heated our bath water and where we warmed our chilblained feet against the oven door. In the middle of the room, on many an evening, we had gathered 'round that oak table with the clawed feet for our reading and storytelling time. In the chimney corner once stood the woodbox I had sat on when Aunt Ruth told me my father had died. In there was my bed where, on a frigid night, I shivered under the covers and huddled close to my brother to steal a little warmth. Back to the living room where the old potbellied stove had belched out its heat in a losing battle with the frosted walls.

I left the bungalow, thinking how it had changed. One day the family that lived there will all be gone, but their memories, the laughter mixed in with the tears, will live on.

You might say to yourself, if, despite everything that happened, despite the bad memories, he can remember the laughter mixed with the tears, then Tommy Hanna has done all right.

I can and I did.

Epilogue

Sometime after my mother's passing, Richard realized the cost to renovate the bungalow would be prohibitive. He sold the house and retired to Florida. He hadn't done much to improve the bungalow, but he had tracked down and acquired Uncle Melvin's lot out front; the L is now a rectangle, as it should have been from the start.

The bungalow, now a summer cottage rental, belongs to a stranger whose tenants know little and care less about the joys and the heartaches those walls have witnessed and whose essence is engrained in its aging timbers.

I made my peace with my mother and I'm glad for it. She may have been neglectful of my younger brothers during those first years after my father's passing while she tested the wings of her newfound freedom, but I'm not so quick to blame her for that anymore. She had spent seventeen years married to a man who believed it was a woman's task to bathe, cook, clean, sew and launder for her children, while the man earned the means to properly feed, clothe and house them. Should she be held totally accountable to her responsibilities when my father had struggled so fruitlessly at his?

Whatever resentment I may have harbored back then against my smart but impractical father has long since been replaced by deep sadness. I regret that in my adolescent years I never knew the kind of closeness a boy wants and needs to have with his father. And I never knew why, but I have come to believe that in his undersized eldest son, he may have seen the possible repetition of his own shortcomings.

Even today, the sadness deepens whenever an Eddie Fisher sings "Oh My Papa," or a John McDermott tells me how he misses "The

Old Man." When I hear a son eulogize his daddy, I wish I could do likewise for my father. But before I could do that I'd have to forgive. And even though I have reached some measure of understanding of why he treated me as he did, to paraphrase one more articulate than I, the road between understanding and forgiveness is indeed a far journey; one I have yet to make. Perhaps I never will.

Sister Cora settled into her tiny home at the top of Bars Hill and found time, between home and church, to raise two sons. Widowed, she lives alone in Wiscasset close to her children and grandchildren. She still devotes her time to church and writes spiritual poetry, the kind you find in church flyers. Her book of inspirational poems will be published soon. A one-time lay preacher, she can still spiel you a right good sermon at the drop of testament because she has a mandate from the Almighty to save all lost souls— a noble, but in my case, futile, undertaking. We are fond of each other, despite that.

My brother Irving, like his older brother, quit school in his teens and went to work. He entered a machinist apprentice program, graduated and spent the most part of his working years as a tool and die maker. Today, he is retired and lives in Woolwich with his wife of over fifty years, with whom he had three children. He is no longer the mean little kid I grew up with, and has turned out to be the kind of brother I can love.

Quiet sister Mary lives today with some of her children down in Baltimore. Mary is the first of only two high school graduates among the eight Hannas. Like her big sister, she married a fisherman, but was widowed when he passed away at the age of thirty-nine. She was left to raise their five children on her husband's social security and military veteran widow's benefits, and she did so heroically. She doesn't often get back to Maine, and I miss her quiet presence, living way down in the South.

The entire Hanna clan in the 1980s: (l to r) Cora, Blaine, Ma, Irving, Mary, Clayton, Me, Richard and Raymond.

There is a great age difference between my four younger brothers and me. My mother once put it best when she allowed that she had raised two families. During the first six years of her marriage she gave birth to us four older ones. Then, after a five-year hiatus, there were four more. I know so little about my younger brothers' early years; they might as well have been the neighbor's kids. When I first left home in 1941, my youngest brother, Raymond, was an infant. So, I can only relate my impressions of the four youngest as I see them today.

Clayton, whose premature death took him from us in 1993 when he was only fifty-eight, was the shiest brother, although he opened up whenever I visited with him over the years. I think of him often. He spent his early working years in a shoe factory, rising to foreman. At the time of his passing he worked for an automobile dealership. His wife, Roslyn, and their four successful daughters have carried on quite well. Roslyn, a retired shoe factory worker, is now Georgetown's assistant postmaster.

Richard, my other high school–educated sibling, is a retired machinist living in Florida with his wife, who he met while serving with the army in Germany after the war. Richard was the most affectionate of the younger ones. He was just seven when I joined the navy in 1944. When I'd come home for weekend visits he'd dash out to meet me and give me a hug and a kiss. I didn't know it then, but he had made me the father he never knew. Maybe if I'd known, I'd have paid him more attention, but at seventeen, I didn't want to be a father—figuratively, or any other way. Shortly after I had finished this book, I wondered out loud whether any of my siblings had appreciated what I had done for the family when I was a teenager. Richard responded with a letter of thanks, just to reassure me that I had indeed been appreciated. Brother Richard is a thoughtful man.

Blaine had started a promising air force career when it was cut short by disabling emphysema. When they cut him loose with a medical disability, he began a second career as a civil servant. Now retired, he and his wife spend six months at their home in Florida and six months here in Maine, where his two daughters and his grandchildren live.

Raymond, the baby of the family, retired from Bath Iron Works in 2005 at the age of sixty-four. He and his wife live in Phippsburg among their children and grandchildren.

As for me, I met the girl who would become my wife when I was home on leave in the summer of 1949. Charmaine Dionne was a seventeen-year-old high school senior; I was a twenty-two-year-old third-class petty officer. Her family had come down from Old Town during World War II so her father could work at Bath Iron Works,

My Wedding Day. Charmaine and I cut the cake on June 25, 1950.

and stayed on. After a brief romance—mostly by correspondence—
we married in June of 1950. We lived in Newport, Rhode Island,
and New Jersey. During my two six-month Mediterranean tours and
a two-month Arctic tour, Charmaine stayed with her parents in
Maine.

Charmaine and I had three children. Thomas was born in 1951,
Lyndon in 1956, Beth in 1959. We lost her to a congenital heart disease in 1965.

Today, both sons work at BIW—Tom as an environmental lab
technician, Lyn as a materials manager. Tom and his wife, Brenda,
live nearby in Bath; Lyn and his wife, Teresa, live in Woolwich. Then
there's Lyn's daughter, my granddaughter, Camellia, thirty, and her
two sons, Taylor and Connor.

Neither of my sons have expressed more than a passing interest
in the bungalow or those early years. Oh, they'll listen politely as I
run on about how tough things were in my day, and they'll shrug
when I recall the kind of hard times they find difficult to imagine,

but they ask few probing questions. Perhaps one day they will turn and look back as I am doing, and try to piece together some of their family history. Hopefully, when that day arrives, what I have written here will give them the insight they need to appreciate the way things were when I was literally shoutin' into the fog.

Lastly, two unarguable truths:

I dipped in my oars and got it done on my own.

And six hens will lay twenty-four eggs in six days.

ABOUT THE AUTHOR

Photo by Dean L. Lunt

Thomas L. Hanna, 2006.

Thomas L. Hanna, seventy-nine, is a long-time resident of Bath, Maine.

Raised in the village of Five Islands on Georgetown Island in mid-coast Maine, he left home at seventeen to join the navy during World War II, and eventually made the navy his career. He retired as a senior chief operations specialist after twenty years' service, and began a second career as a value engineer at Bath Iron Works. He retired in 1988 after twenty-two years.

Then, using writing skills he had honed in the navy and at BIW, he began writing for publication. His articles have appeared in *Down East*, *Reminisce* and *Good Old Days*. He has been married to Charmaine Dionne Hanna for fifty-six years. They have two sons, Thomas Ronald and Lyndon Scott.